Silver Moon

Great Novels
of
Erotic Domination
and Submission

NEW TITLES EVERY MONTH

www.smbooks.co.uk

TO FIND OUT MORE ABOUT OUR
READERS' CLUB WRITE TO;
SILVER MOON READER SERVICES;
Suite 7,
Mayden House,
Long Bennington Business Park,
Newark NG23 5DJ

***

NEW AUTHORS ARE WELCOME
Please send submissions to;
The Editor; Silver Moon books
Suite 7, Long Bennington Business Park
Newark NG23 5DJ

Tel: 01400 283 488

This edition published 2011

ISBN 9781908252081

All characters and events depicted are entirely fictitious; any resemblance to anyone living or dead is entirely coincidental

THIS IS FICTION. IN REAL LIFE ALWAYS PRACTISE SAFE SEX

Slavemaker

by

Sean O'Kane

FOREWORD;

‘The order that became known as “The Guardians” had its origins deep in the dark centuries prior to the Carthaginian invasion of these islands and continued to exist long after Carthage had left. As each new head of the order was elected he took a title that reflected the brethren’s major concerns of the times. So there were “The Loremaker”, “The Spellbinder”, “The Swordmaster” and so on. But with the coming of Owen Daibron and his chosen title of “The Slavemaker”, the order achieved such prominence with Edward 1 and his son, John the Magnificent that for generations, the heads of the order inherited the title of “Slavemaker”’.

Carter’s Concise history of Alba; Volume I

CHAPTER ONE.
Westhorn District. Kingdom of Alba. 1251

The steepness of the gradient and the poor state of the road were attested to by the fact that the carriage had needed two precious horses harnessed in front of the eight toiling slaves to get it up the incline. Magistrate Dunbar scowled out at the rain teeming down from the grey winter sky and listened to the driver's whip hissing in the cold air and then thudding onto slaveflesh. It had better be slaveflesh, he told himself grimly. If any harm came to the horses, he would see to the driver's punishment as personally as he did the women in his district of Westhorn. Slowly the carriage lurched up the incline and presently the welcoming lights of an inn come into view. Urged on by the driver's cries and his ever-present whip the combined slave and horse team steered gratefully into the courtyard.

"My lord, this is an unlooked for pleasure!" The carriage door opened and the bearded, grinning face of the inn keeper peered in.

"Ah, Simon!" Dunbar replied. "Did you not get my message? There is some pestilence abroad north of the river so I thought I would make a sortie over here instead and check all was well on my way to the assize court."

"You're as welcome as always, lord, message or no."

Dunbar climbed down and stretched. Around him the horses were being led away to warm stables and some of Simon Webbley's wives were leading the eight exhausted female slaves into another stall.

"Strip them down and make sure they're warm, then feed them!" Webbley called. Leaving the women to carry out their instructions with the slaves, the men hurried after the horses to make sure they were being tended to properly.

Only once he was certain that no effort had been spared to dry them and feed them well did he look in on the slaves. Now chained and huddled in coarse blankets and squatting in the straw, the tanned and tousled women were tucking greedily into plates of stew and tearing chunks of warm bread off loaves with their sharp white teeth. Some of the inn keeper's wives were leaning over one wall of the stall and taking full advantage of the opportunity to look down on females of an even lower caste than they were.

"Any of your household want to play with these overnight, they're welcome," the magistrate offered.

"A kind offer my lord! These days a man can hardly cope with the number of 'em that need beating and fucking, so a little relief to keep 'em calm wouldn't go amiss at all." He turned to the gathered women and called across, "You can have your fun with these tonight, my lovelies! Fuck 'em with your strap-ons and have 'em do what you want, but make sure they're fit to pull his lordship's carriage in the morning or I'll flay the lot of you at the post, so help me!"

The women scurried away, giggling but with eyes downcast and Simon turned his attention to the magistrate's slaves. "They're an interesting bunch," he said. "Where did you pick them up?"

"Got 'em at an auction up Salop way. Brought in from the mountains up north so they said. They breed 'em small but tough. We made nearly nine miles today and rested the horses until we got to the bottom of your hill."

Simon raised his eyebrows. Nine miles was good going in a slave-pulled carriage. Of course the driver had had to work hard and every slave's shoulders and upper back was criss crossed with pinkish-red weals.

"That's a goodly step," he said. "But it's just as well that Sarum is only a mile or two further on in the morning. I've got a spare team, mind, if you'd rather use fresh and I can have this lot delivered to you once you've finished your business."

"No, I thank you, Master Simon. These'll do fine. They squeal a bit for the first few lashes but then they settle down soon enough."

The two men walked through the kitchens where more wives and slaves were busy, basting, roasting and carving for the men whose voices drifted in from the main bar room. At the far end of the huge range, a wheel some eight feet in diameter was being turned by a naked girl, wearily plodding forever onwards. On the axle turned by the wheel, a spitted deer carcass turned. A woman who was plainly in charge ran a finger along the skin and licked it, then unshipped a riding whip from her waist and began to belabour the unfortunate slave in the wheel.

"Shift your useless arse! You Frankland scum!" she screeched.

The girl yelped but began to step more lively and the carcass turned more rapidly. The woman surveyed it for a moment then turned away, seemingly satisfied.

"It's been a long day, Simon, I look forward to my supper, a good bed and a couple of your best wives or slaves."

"Oh, of course, my lord. This way. You've picked a good night! We're hosting the Province finals of the wifefighting. From bantams to heavyweights! There'll be good sport and some profitable bets for one with as good an eye for a woman as you my lord!"

"Hmm! Well maybe I'll take in a couple of bouts. But I do have to start early tomorrow."

Dunbar settled his large frame at a table in an alcove a little raised above the main floor. Some twenty or so men – a good crowd by the depleted standards of Alba these days were gathered, smiling and drinking around a roped off circle in the centre of the room. This was the wifefighting ring. A wife who could earn money for her husband in the ring was worth money herself and contests were ferocious. A pretty little woman curtsied and laid a plate of meat before him, tucking a stray lock of dark hair back under her mob cap as she made to leave.

"That's a comely one, Simon. I don't recall her from my last visit," Dunbar said.

"No, my lord. I took her in settlement for a bill a few months back, she fucks and works so well I'm thinking of taking her to wife and selling on a couple of the older ones. She was slave to a knight just back from the war. She's Alban stock, he freed her in a raid somewhere. You want her for the night?"

Dunbar studied the woman, she had a pretty, uptilted nose, dark eyes and a full-lipped and well shaped mouth. Beneath the table, he felt his cock unfurl as he surveyed the way her breasts rose and fell with her nervous breathing beneath her thin shift. He could sympathise with Simon wanting to sell on a couple of the older wives out in the kitchen to replace them with this one. There was no limit on how many wives a man could have in law. But there was a limit to how many he could keep clothed and fed, let alone satisfied.

"You know, I think I will, bring me wine girl and then we'll see if that mouth of yours works as well as it looks."

Simon laughed and sent the slave on her way with a smack to her well rounded rump, then he sat down opposite his guest.

"They say the war is going well," he said quietly after a few moments.

Dunbar began to bite into a succulent piece of venison. "They do say so, yes," he replied eventually, eyeing his host carefully.

"Only they took my last horse for the war only three days ago. I'll have to plough with the women again this year and that means I'll be letting two fields go fallow. However hard you whip them, they can't go as fast as horses." Simon shook his head sadly.

"Use oxen then," the magistrate suggested.

"Hah! The price of them! If I sold every woman I own, I couldn't buy a calf!"

"Patience, my friend. His Majesty is a great warrior and he will have the victory."

"He needs to have it quick then, if you ask me. The country's bled dry of men and there's bands of renegade women roaming the country, I hear, with no militiamen left to hunt them down."

The woman returned with a jug of wine and Simon climbed to his feet.

"I'll leave you to it for the present, my lord. But we'll raise a glass or two when the fighting gets under way."

Dunbar waved and then looked at the woman, nervously biting her lower lip. He pushed his chair back from the table a little way.

"Now get under there and don't come up till I tell you," he said. While he tucked into his meal he felt soft little fingers fluttering under his robes and stroking artfully along the insides of his thighs, then there was the tingle of breath across his stirring shaft and finally a hesitant lick from a tongue before the soft caress of female lips engulfed him.

It turned out to be a good night. He won eight sovereigns betting on a woman in the heavyweight division. She was a handsome piece, strong without being fat and was well matched with a woman from Sarum, a large town some miles away. The bout lasted nearly half an hour and provided good entertainment as the women clawed, punched and tore at each other. At any wifefight the contestants all started in their shifts and petticoats and as the contests proceeded, inevitably they stripped each other. The better show they put on the more coins would be tossed into the ring by the men and the more each wife could collect for her husband and perhaps get to keep some. In this case both women were soon fully nude and provided a fine feast of full bodied womanhood. Their breasts shook and shuddered as they struggled, their thighs tensed and their buttocks hollowed. Nails drew deep red lines across pale flesh and punches made the lush flesh ripple. But at last the home grown talent prevailed and she sat astride her victim's face, pulling and twisting her nipples in between raining down blows until the loser's husband threw in the towel.

Magistrate Dunbar was in a good mood as he made his way upstairs with his hand up under the hired slave's skirt.

In the softness of the feather bed in his room much later, he ploughed the pretty little thing's furrow and only finished between her sweetly rounded buttocks, pumping the last of his sperm into her tight rectum when the night was at its darkest.

The following morning was bright and clear and the magistrate and his host took a stroll outside after breakfast. Three of the innkeeper's wives were hanging up washing and two of them had bellies that swelled ripely, promising that soon they would produce the crop whose seeds their master had sown.

"Well done, Simon," the magistrate said, surveying the women. "Let's hope they produce strapping lads to aid the war effort, eh?"

"I already have three serving my lord, and two learning the longbow in the academy at Cwmbran," Simon replied proudly.

The magistrate was about to reply when there was a commotion from the stableyard and Loscar, the grizzled veteran who oversaw the stables limped into sight holding two more of Simon's wives with one strong hand gripping one of each woman's arms. He stumped out into the garden his wooden leg thumping on the grass.

"Found these two up to their wrists in the slaves' cunts. They were supposed to be harnessing 'em, not frigging 'em!" he called.

"Playtime was last night, you wanton bitches!" Simon berated the two who stood with heads bowed, their fingers nervously playing with their skirts now. But their husband stopped suddenly and turned to his guest. "My lord, you recall I mentioned selling a couple of wives to make room for the pretty one you hired last night?"

"I do indeed and I have an auction to hold tomorrow. If you would care to furnish me with the authority to sell on your behalf, I'd be pleased to include these two."

The two women looked resigned rather than horrified as they walked off to collect their belongings. One husband was probably not going to be much worse than another and indeed, Simon Webbley was known to have a heavy hand with a whip. Besides they would get to keep a proportion of their sale price.

In Simon's office the paperwork was swiftly completed and when they returned to the stableyard, the eight bridled slaves, arranged in two ranks of four abreast, pushing two crossbars off the main shaft, were fidgeting and stamping, the driver sat in his raised seat which gave him a clear sight of the eight backs to be lashed to their work and held the reins tight in his hand. The two wives stood behind the coach with their meagre possessions in tough canvas rolls.

They handed these up to the driver to place on the roof and then prepared themselves for the long run to Sarum; it was not for the likes of them to ride with a magistrate, unless he invited them to and he made no move to do so.

The women unlaced their bodices and stepped out of the long skirts to which they were attached, then they undid their petticoats and stepped out of them as well, leaving them dressed only in their shifts which barely covered their crotches. Magistrate Dunbar surveyed them critically as they stowed their clothes under a seat inside the coach.

"A comely enough pair, Simon. You should do well out of the sale," he commented as he noted the long, shapely thighs, Simon had obviously made them work hard for their keep and both women were trim and smooth skinned.

"Aye, and they are a pair too. They make for a good time in bed and can put on a good show for guests as well. Trouble is they can hardly keep their hands to themselves. They're forever feeling up each other or some of the others."

Dunbar climbed in and waved farewell to his host. "I'll have your percentage sent back Simon!" he called as the whip smacked across the backs of the slaves in a rapid tattoo to force out of them the effort needed to get the coach rolling. Then, rumbling and swaying the vehicle swung out onto the road and the two wives trotted behind it, along with the spare horses, while the eight slaves settled down to another day of sweating under the lash.

Inside, Magistrate Dunbar unrolled the latest scroll from the Slavemaker, who the king had charged with overseeing the discipline and good governance of the majority female population, on behalf of the beleaguered male minority. Magistrates were regularly kept abreast of where the state needed condemned females so that they could tailor sentences accordingly. Of course a woman brought before a magistrate was guilty of something – they all were – it was the magistrate's responsibility to make the punishment as instructive and useful as possible. On that morning he read that galley slaves were required and that the salt mines in the north urgently needed fresh blood. It was the Slavemaker's opinion, furthermore, that the minimum punishment flogging should rise to fifty lashes from forty. The weight and gauge of leather for the whips was specified and Dunbar was pleased to note that his favourite implement conformed perfectly. There were some thirty cases awaiting him on the morrow and he flexed his right arm unconsciously. There would be some well-blistered female flesh by the end of the next day.

At mid morning the coach halted to allow for the slaves to be watered and he leaned out of the window to inspect the panting and tousled wives. Both women were mature and handsome enough in any case but their shifts had come unlaced and now their breasts rose and fell invitingly as they gasped for breath. He beckoned to one and helped himself to a handful of soft tit as she stood beside the coach, and when the driver began to ply his whip again and urge his team back onto the road, Dunbar took the girl inside for a while. He had her bend forwards and support herself by her hands on the quilted leather seat while he untied the lacings on his rough woollen trousers and freed his erect cock. The woman's labia were full and plump, the clitoral hood also perfectly defined and already open displaying a sizeable nub of slick flesh. He regretted not being able to whip such an inviting vulva before fucking it but made the best of a bad job by sliding himself into the woman after a cursory exploration with his fingers to ensure she was suitably wet and open. Once inside her to his fullest extent he lifted the woman's shift off her back and leaned forwards to grasp her breasts as they hung beneath her chest. He gripped his fingers harshly into the soft flesh and was pleased that she made no whimper of protest, he was also pleased to note the fading traces of welts across her back. A wife who showed traces of recent discipline usually fetched good money. Dunbar made no move to thrust his way to a climax, instead he allowed the lurch and jolt of the carriage to shift his cock in her sheath and she responded with exceptionally supple swivels of her hips and some enjoyable humping and hollowing of her back. He steadied himself by grabbing her hips as he felt his crisis approach and slammed against her buttocks time and again as he emptied his balls into her.

"Send the other one in," he ordered as he resumed his seat and waved the freshly fucked woman back outside. She tumbled down clumsily from the moving carriage but soon her lover clambered aboard, eager for a rare chance of getting some cock. Dunbar lounged at his ease with his trousers wide open and his slick, flaccid member lolling between his powerful thighs.

"Get your lover's cunt juice off my cock," he ordered and she fell to her knees and set to work hungrily with her tongue, licking him back into erection before taking him respectfully into her mouth and savouring every drop of the emission he soon spurted into her throat.

The auction was held that evening at the Sarum council house. There was a wide variety of women on offer; some wives, some slaves and one or two whores putting themselves up for sale in the hopes of being made a bought slave first of all and then maybe a wife. In any event every woman was desperate to wear a collar of any sort, it was the only security she could aspire to. Dunbar had them parade naked around the small stage, made them bend over as if for punishment and pulled their labia apart to expose their cunt flesh and reamed them with his fingers. If requested to he also drove them into their anuses to test the development of that passage as a fucking hole. Mostly the slaves were assessed for agricultural work and road haulage, this being a country town, but any female had to demonstrate that if she were lucky enough to be offered a cock she would be worth the man's trouble.

Webbley's two wives put on a good show, stripping naked eagerly and playing with each other's cunt while Dunbar gave them his personal recommendation. The whores stripped as seductively as they could and attempted to illustrate how many pleasures they could provide for an owner or a husband and were rewarded by being bought, Dunbar filled in the necessary paperwork afterwards and wondered whether they would cause any displaced wives to end up at his next auction. All in all it was a highly successful evening with all the lots fetching good prices and Dunbar retired for the night well pleased with his commissions.

The assizes were held in the town hall the following morning and only men were allowed to attend. There were plenty of empty seats on the benches these days and a fair scattering of scarred veterans among the able bodied men whose professions exempted them from military service.

The magistrate sat behind a high and intimidating desk to dole out sentences ranging from a lifetime's slavery to a few hours hung in the frames outside the courthouse. The prisoners were brought before him and were made to stand on a podium while charges were read out. They were allowed to make a statement before sentence was passed but few chose to.

There was precious little point.

Two whores who were accused by the sheriff of having assaulted a wife of whom they were jealous were sentenced to three years chained to an oar aboard one of the king's galleys. A wife who had been indicted by her husband for excessive cruelty to his slaves (who after all did have some financial value) was herself condemned to slavery for ten years and he marked her down for the salt mines. When she was released she would lose her rank of wife and have to return to whoredom and the search for an owner and then a husband. A haulage slave came up on a charge of idleness so persistent that her owner washed his hands of her. She was a strapping lass who still bore across her back and arse the welts of the man's final attempts to beat some work from her. As he was authorised to do, Dunbar offered the man the slave's basic value on behalf of the state and sent her to the galleys for an indeterminate sentence. Idleness was not an option there. The girl accepted everything with bovine indifference.

No fewer than three wives belonging to the same man were indicted for bickering and proved the case against them by quarrelling as they were led in, they were condemned to fifteen years each. One was sent to the mines, one to the galleys and one was sent for auction at a nearby town, in addition all three were sentenced to hang in the frames. The audience applauded the just nature of the sentence.

There was a whole string of whores accused of the usual things; theft, drunkenness, fighting, all the typical crimes of women who couldn't find a man to collar them. Some escaped with a few hours in a frame and a flogging but most of them were sentenced to wear slave collars for between five and fifteen years. Whores were the worst off of all women, they had neither master nor owner and slavery at least meant they were collared and belonged somewhere, an adopted slave rather than a condemned one could hope to aspire to wifehood. Enslavement also meant that they avoided the fate of becoming a renegade. That was the worst that could befall a female. Dunbar told them they should be grateful for the flogging they would get imminently and the useful life they would lead as slaves.

It was a fairly typical range of offenders and by the end of the day the king's mines and galleys were richer by twenty new slaves and the gibbets outside the hall would be full for the following day and all thirty miscreants would be flogged before the crowds. There was only one criminal who stuck in Dunbar's mind. She was a tall, good looking blonde whore who had been charged with refusing to have sex with a man. The man in question had been drunk and had been driving a slave-drawn wagon cross country for a week and so probably was filthy and stinking, but for any woman to turn down a man was an outrageous crime. However the icy, contemptuous stare she had fixed on him as he had begun to sentence her to ten years at an oar had caused him to stop and instead to reduce the sentence to seventy-five lashes and five years, followed by a referral to the Slavemaker. The girl had the look of a potential renegade and only one man could be trusted to cure her of that, and the sooner the better, she would fetch a handsome price once he had finished with her.

There had been applause for the sentence but the girl had been unmoved. She had probably dismissed the tales of what the Slavemaker could accomplish as myths designed to cow women into submission. Just how wrong she was, she would find out in due course.

First thing in the morning the gibbets were loaded. Ten women condemned to a day at the mercy of the crowd were paraded in front of the ten frames hanging from the arms of the gibbets and at Dunbar's command whatever clothes they were wearing were cut from them with knives wielded by the sheriff's men and sliced into ribbons, a walk home stark naked was part of the sentence. Then leather hoods blocking eyes, nostrils and ears were pulled over their heads and laced tight at the back, leaving only their mouths free. The crowd needed to hear the screams. The naked and trembling wretches were then roughly pushed forwards and fastened into rectangular frames that stretched them out into X shapes, wrists and ankles fastened at each corner. The sheriff's men availed themselves of the helplessly stretched flesh and the crowd hooted and cheered as breasts were mauled and groped harshly, nipples were pulled till they were twice their normal length and fingers were rammed unceremoniously into cunts. But finally the frames, hanging from a chain at the end of each gibbet arm were hauled up till they hung about five feet above the ground.

Ten naked and helpless figures faced the gleeful spite of the townspeople, the majority of whom were female inevitably, and as Dunbar gave the word and stood back to avoid the barrage of rotten food, mud, eggs and worse that was hurled at the women he was once again filled with admiration for the state he served. It had turned every woman against every other woman. It had made the collar – in days gone by a symbol of shame

– into the most longed for thing in a woman's life; preferably the lighter collar of wifehood, but even the thick collar of a slave was better than the semi nomadic and shiftless life of a whore. Women condemned for the most trivial of crimes were enthusiastically pelted by crowds of their own sisters who would ecstatically count the lashes of the later floggings.

The state ensured that however downtrodden the majority of women were, there was always another woman worse off than themselves and on whom they could look down.

There was an extra loud cheer as the sheriff passed along behind the frames once the first barrage had been exhausted and set the frames spinning. This made the sport more challenging as choice targets appeared and disappeared as the bodies spun.

Assize days were holidays. Even while the frames provided plenty of fun, up on the scaffold the whipping of those condemned to slavery began.

Leaving the frames with their naked occupants twisting and flinching blindly as missiles thudded home, Magistrate Dunbar climbed up onto the scaffold, pulled off his short tunic and bared his sizeable torso to an excited female cheer. The sheriff fastened the first of the slaves to the backward-sloping and sinister X shaped whipping cross and to a gasp of indrawn breath from the excited crowd below, he uncoiled his favourite whip. It was a braided length of hide about five feet long. About one foot from its end the braiding ceased and it became a single heavy blade of leather finished off by tassels that concealed small weights. It was the perfect implement to introduce condemned slaves to the rigours of the life ahead of them and for those condemned merely to flogging, it was far worse than most husbands and owners used. But then, a public punishment by a magistrate had to send out messages to the watching crowd.

By lunchtime, fifteen of the condemned women had groaned and screamed their way through their floggings. The crowd had counted every lash of each sentence and laughed as Dunbar had paused now and again to rest and to prod the pulsing welts with the whip handle to induce a sharper pain and get a sagging body to straighten up for the next few lashes. Frequently he would pause and auction off a few moments for any man in the crowd to step up and enjoy a public fuck. There was never a shortage of men willing to stand on the scaffold and display their wares to the cheering women before leaning against a well-flogged back, grabbing two handfuls of breast and slipping themselves up into a vagina which had been stirred almost to a froth by the severity of the flogging.

The blonde whore destined for the Slavemaker had taken some time to deal with. She had put up a struggle and it had taken two of the sheriff's men to bind her to the X and then there had been constant clamourings from the crowd for a chance to screw her. Dunbar had had to stop the beating no fewer than five times and it had taken each man some considerable time, fumbling inside her with his fingers to lubricate her enough for comfortable penetration. However, she had weathered her punishment without a sob escaping her, even when he had played his usual game of pretending to lose count of the lashes administered. The crowd would yell out numbers and he would pick one that seemed to him to suit the way the woman was bearing up. The blonde ended up taking over a hundred.

After lunch the magistrate handed whipping duties over to the sheriff for a while and took advantage of what every town referred to as the 'Magistrate's Tip'. As pretty a whore as the town could find would be made available to ensure that the magistrate was able to relieve himself of the inevitable stimulation his duties caused him. In this case the town clerk brought forwards a buxom, black haired girl with enchantingly big, dark eyes and bee stung lips. She wore a simple green gown which she had evidently been wearing for some time, for although it was clean, it struggled to contain the swelling breasts and rounded hips she had developed despite the hardships of a whore's life. She unlaced it and slipped it off with no demur when he commanded her to and laid herself back on the cleared dining table, leaving her legs dangling over the edge. Dunbar stood between them and rummaged his fingers inside the flooding, tight little channel of her vagina. Sarum had indeed found a gem of a magistrate's tip. How she hadn't been snapped up yet mystified him and he told the town clerk as much.

"She's just blown in a few days ago, been staying over the baker's and he's filed to take her to wife but the mayor said you was to have first refusal."

"Good man," Dunbar murmured as his thick fingers, swirling and clenching in the girl's innards while his thumb ground her clitoris roughly against her mound, fetched pretty moans from her mouth and hungry sucking noises from her cunt, its pinkly flushed lips stretching wide around his big hand. With his other hand he unlaced his trousers and guided his rampant prick home, steering the huge dome to spear her deliciously tight opening and disappear slowly inside her. He leaned over her and savoured the salacious grip she took on him inside her as he began to grope and torment her breasts, spreading his hands over the soft mounds and pressing them cruelly against her chest, then grinding the nipples under his palms. She arched up to meet his cruelty eagerly, her hands fluttering, unsure of where and how she could touch him. He thrust himself hard into her, making her body jerk on the table. She shouted in surprised pleasure and Dunbar gazed down at her softening face shrewdly, but could see nothing except genuine excitement. He pulled both nipples and twisted them hard. They were of a length and thickness that would take ringing exceptionally well. She covered his hands with hers, encouraging him to torment her tits even further.

"Do you want to be taken on as a wife? Is that your game?" he asked as he rammed into her again.

"Yes, yes, of course, lord!" she gasped as he jerked her again with the force of his penetration.

"I keep six of them and have them whipped each day, even while I'm away," he growled.

The girl's eyes softened as she spiralled up towards orgasm but she managed to control herself for a few seconds.

"A woman belongs under her husband's lash, my lord! Oh!" A series of spasms shook her slight frame and the magistrate himself passed the point of no return and began to ram her in earnest as he pumped thick strings of sperm deep into her.

He pulled clear after a few moments and looked at her, panting and undone on the table. Whores seldom gave such passionately enthusiastic service. She seemed quite genuine. He smiled, it had been a long time since he had had a natural in his household. Whereas all women were schooled to the lash to some extent or other and could find pleasure in any male attention they were lucky enough to get, a natural would welcome – sometimes demand – cruelty from her master and worship him for dispensing it.

As the girl peeled her sweating body off the wood of the table and regained her feet, Dunbar laced his trousers up and opened the purse he kept at his belt, tossing a few coins onto the tabletop.

"Go along to the saddler's, tell him to fit you with a collar with my initials on it and then pick out a horse whip. A slender and whippy one. Then come back here and wait in my chambers till I have time to thrash you."

The girl looked at him with bright, grateful eyes, then spread her legs and began to scoop up his emission as it trickled out of her and lick her fingers.

Dunbar made his way back outside, beginning to be mightily pleased with his journey. The crowd was becoming more boisterous as jugs of wine were passed around and whores worked the men present. Occasionally there were scuffles as wives and whores clashed but it was all part of a punishment holiday. Up on the scaffold it was the turn of the ten hapless frame victims to take their lashes. They had been sluiced down with buckets of cold water to wash off the worst of the filth that had been thrown at them and now the third of them was shivering at the cross waiting for her beating. The sheriff was glad of the rest but helped himself to a quick fuck before he left the scaffold. The woman took some fingering before she was open enough for him and provoked some ribald comments from the crowd about her being a 'tightarse' in any case.

There was applause once the sheriff had finished with her, he was a big man and took her to a raucous if reluctant orgasm before he pulled out and spurted his come up her back. Then the magistrate stepped forwards and shook out his lash and the crowd settled expectantly.

"Give her plenty across her arse! She only sits on it all day!" a woman shouted.

The condemned woman, now unhooded, craned her head round. "I'll punch your tits in for that, Flora Bethany! See if I don't!" she yelled.

Dunbar didn't let the exchange distract him and scythed in his first lash which reduced the woman at the cross to yelling of a more incoherent kind. The crowd counted the lash and shouted encouragement to the flogger. After thirty lashes he took a short break, the woman was tough, her body had shaken at the force of each lash, she was laced thoroughly from shoulders to waist, her ribs and the sides of her breasts were scored by dark red slashes where the ends of the lash had dug in, her chest was heaving for breath but no noise had escaped her clenched teeth after the first lash. Dunbar moved close and dug his fingers into some of the welts forcing grunts of protest at last. Then he delved down between her legs and found her groin a hot, damp mass of sweat, sap, semen and untrimmed pubic hair. He slid his fingers into her and she sighed in resignation as he discovered her wanton state. She had a capacious vagina and was easily fisted. Dunbar told the crowd this as he worked his entire hand inside her.

"It's where the robbing cow hides the money she steals!" the same woman called up.

The victim craned her head round again. "You wait….till his lordship's finished…..with the whip!" she snarled as best she could with Dunbar's hand wreaking havoc in her cunt. "I'll be down to sort you out!"

Dunbar joined in the laughter. It was not unknown for some excellent fights to erupt around a punishment and he set about finishing her sentence by welting her backside and thighs at a more rapid rate as, down below, odds were called and an impromptu ring was made by the husbands of the two women pushing the crowd back to give the combatants room to work.

The final floggings were carried out as the fight raged at the foot of the scaffold. Despite her welts and cuts, the naked woman held her own surprisingly well and as the final victim was taken down. Dunbar looked down to see that the heckler had been partially stripped and the flogged woman had a handful of her breast and was using the nipple to lead her around by.

"Not so cheeky now, are you?" she shouted at her victim as she struggled to loosen the grip on her nipple, then the flogged woman launched a round house punch to the other breast that downed the unfortunate heckler. As Dunbar made his way back into the courthouse he saw the heckler rolling on the ground trying to stop the shreds of her skirt being torn off by the naked and triumphant harridan who seemed to have shaken off her beating almost completely. Dunbar made a mental note to keep an eye on her in case her husband decided to get rid. She was good whipping stock.

A tall, cadaverous man was waiting for him in the courthouse, already enjoying a mug of ale.

"Sejanus? What brings you to Sarum?" Dunbar asked.

In reply the man drew a scroll from a satchel he had beside him on the bench and placed it carefully before Dunbar as he settled himself with a goblet of wine. Dunbar looked at the man, he didn't like him particularly but as reeve to the major estate in the area he was someone he had to deal with. He had day to day control over the running of the estate and its tenants, theoretically he ran it with Lady Tamara, but everyone knew her tastes lay in other directions. The man smiled, exposing large, discoloured teeth.

"Take a look there, magistrate."

Dunbar did look more closely at the scroll now and saw the seal on it. It was the royal seal of the island kingdom of Alba, the crown above waves. But it looked too fresh to have come all the way from Frankland where the king was fighting the unending war, it must have come from Tamesbury, the capital city and therefore from the queen.

Nervously he opened it and scanned the contents.

"An audit?" he asked aghast. "A royal audit of the estate accounts?"

"I had no choice but to report Sir William's fraud once I stumbled across it," Sejanus said with ill-disguised glee. "The trap is laid for the traitor and now we must wait for our quarry. As you know, Sir William is away at the war but he will return shortly and must face justice. You will of course be required to judge certain aspects of the case and Her Majesty expects your whole hearted loyalty, magistrate."

Dunbar's throat went dry, he was a good friend of Sir William but Sejanus was making it clear that he would be watched in case he made any attempt to warn him.

"I cannot believe that Sir William is guilty of any disloyalty!" he said as steadily as he could then raised his glass. "However, I am sure you have done your duty as you saw fit. Her Majesty's good health."

Sejanus smiled again, clearly aware of Dunbar's diplomatic choice of toast, took a drink and relaxed. Outside there was a roar from the crowd as the fight was plainly reaching a satisfactory and probably bloody conclusion. The townspeople had had a good day.

"Of course, once the case is proved against him, Sir William will be stripped of everything he owns. It is unfortunate but….."

The man's smugness was intolerable and Dunbar gripped his goblet fiercely. He could read his salacious grin. If Sir William was found guilty of the charges against him, all his possessions would be forfeit. And that included his wife and slaves.

Lady Tamara was famous for the quality and quantity of her pleasure slaves. Dunbar wondered how many of them Sejanus already had marked down for his possession.

CHAPTER TWO
Frankland; Castle Cevigny. 1251

The battle had been mercifully short and the Alban forces had prevailed. Now as dusk settled over the taken castle, the last of the fires sank into sullen smouldering, their light mingling with the red flickering of the pitch torches that the victorious soldiers had stuck into whatever sconces they could find. On the tops of the walls that were still standing intact after the undermining, the fires and the bombardment that had battered the defenders into submission, Alban sentries kept watch and envied their comrades the fruits of victory.

Sir William Courcey strode through the rubble strewn courtyards with his equerry trotting to keep up with him.

"Have the wounded moved back to our lines as soon as may be," he said. "Prisoners to be taken to Toubiere. They can labour to rebuild the walls their damned cannon blew down. Their wives and slaves.........." He stopped and looked through the main gate out to where his soldiers had camped. The drawbridge was down and with the equerry following, Sir William walked forwards until his boots thudded hollowly on the wood. He stopped and considered for a moment.

The open grassland fell away before him and he could see his army's tents, freshly moved up to the castle once it had fallen, spread out before him. The sounds of merrymaking drifted up and the hundreds of red glows from the cooking fires shone like a dropped ruby necklace around the castle. He could also see that the enemy's slaves were already being used. He nodded and smiled indulgently. The men knew the value of good Frankland slaves and freshly enslaved wives and would not damage the goods but they had fought well that day and deserved to play for one night. His Majesty King Edward had personally congratulated Sir William on his troops' valour.

He had even allowed them one month's leave back in Alba and tomorrow they would march for the coast and take ship to Southaven, bearing the women with them for sale on the quayside, the profits to be divided among all the men.

"Let them play with the women for tonight. Have wagons brought up to transport them tomorrow." He waved a hand to dismiss the man and walked down into the camp.

Over two hundred years of war between Alba and Frankland had severely depleted the male populations of both countries and the imbalance in the genders had made women simply cheap and plentiful and the surviving men aware that they had to work hard to keep them in subjugation, so polygamy and slavery had become the norm. The upshot was clearly demonstrated by the Frankland slaves – like Alban ones - all being female. Sir William's men had constructed T shaped crucifixes and tied the women to them with their arms pulled back behind the crossbar and a chain joining the wrists in front of the stomach. Some of the luckier ones had been given crosses with a bar for their feet to brace themselves on; some hadn't been so lucky.

They hung only a foot or so above the ground and the soldiery was entertaining itself by delivering lashes and teasing caresses alternately to the suspended bodies, making them jerk and writhe in their bonds. The women's cries rang out on the cool air and their long hair flew in the evening breeze like the tattered standards of the defeated army they belonged to.

The victorious soldiers' own slaves and wives laboured over cooking fires and looked on with sullen jealousy as, every now and then, a crucifix was lowered and its slave made use of. After a day's fighting and a stomach full of looted wine, the victors often took them where they lay, legs splayed either side of the crucifix's upright. The prettiest ones were the luckiest, they were taken by soldier after soldier and were spared being hoisted back up. Others were taken by just one or two men and put back up after a brief whipping.

Sir William caught sight of one of his lieutenants and called him over. The man was carrying a leather cup of wine but did not seem to be drunk yet.

"After midnight start taking the women down. Put them in the dungeon under the north tower until tomorrow. There'll be wagons coming for them."

The man nodded seriously and went to find a sergeant to organise things.

Sir William continued his stroll, waving and smiling to soldiers who recognised him, the news of the king's generosity had spread fast and the men were in high spirits.

He stopped to watch a group of them tormenting a big titted specimen who was writhing and crying out under a harsh tit whipping, her legs thrashing in the air helplessly as the thin tails sliced across the wobbling orbs in a manner guaranteed to have a man laughing in delight and doing it again; and again. Sir William joined in the laughter and applauded accurate strikes across the nipples that had her gurgling in shocked pain. He had no fear for her, they could all see that her cunt was leaking onto her thighs. A lifetime under the whip and a chronic lack of male attention made any woman respond well to a good beating. She would reach the auction block relatively unscathed.

After a few minutes he moved on and chatted to more groups of men around fires. Everywhere now, in the areas of shade away from the fires, naked male buttocks, pale in the weak light were pumping up and down between spread thighs or naked women knelt, their faces buried at the groins of the conquering soldiers. Female bottoms were upthrust as well and with their breeches round their ankles, soldiers who liked a woman's narrowest channel were kneeling behind them and hammering into them, heedless of the squeals of protest and grunts of discomfort.

At last, after draining a final cup of wine with one last group of men, Sir William began to make his way to where his equerry had had his tent set up. But as he went, stepping around and over the couplings his eye was caught by one slave still hanging on her cross. There were plenty of them still dotting the twilight scene but there was something about this one, although she appeared to be inert after the abuses heaped on her, that made him pause and look up a little more closely.

She was long legged and beneath her bent-forwards torso, her full breasts hung ripe and round. She was a tasty morsel alright and that probably accounted for the fact that she had been paid special attention to and had passed out in sheer exhaustion. But still there was something……..

Sir William reached up for the girl's face and as his hand approached her chin, she reared back, glaring down at him with pale blue eyes, ablaze with fury and hatred. All at once he saw what had been bothering him. Her hair. It was tousled and sweat-slicked but all the same bore the traces of where someone – almost certainly her personal slave – only that very morning had plaited her hair in the distinctive Frankish way. And only Frankish aristocrats could afford the time or the staff. And if her feigned unconsciousness and hair hadn't given her away, the fine bone structure and arrogant stare would have.

Sir William turned to the nearest group of men. "Get this one down! And go gently for you lay hands on the lady of the castle herself, Isabella Dulac." He was smiling in triumph as he spoke and the men picked up on his mood, handing the exhausted woman down with mock bows and tugging of forelocks.

She stood proudly before Sir William with her shoulders back and her head high, refusing to cower and try to hide herself however inadequately with her arms and hands. He stared back at her as she glared at him, head tilted back a little. She was a rare prize! Her thighs and legs were indeed long and shapely, joining at gracefully wide hips with a neatly trimmed blonde bush of pubic hair. Her waist was trim and flowed smoothly up to her ribs which supported breasts that would afford any man hours of pleasure, were he to want to stroke them and caress them or punish them for his pleasure. They were rounded and high yet they were deceptively large and swelled out sideways a little from the chest. Her shoulders were wide and her neck was long and smooth. Her face was graced by a wide, full lipped mouth and large blue eyes beneath her tousled blonde hair.

Sir William pointed to some dusky red stripes across her lower stomach and thighs. "I see some of my men have not treated you in the way you are accustomed to my lady."

She tossed her head. "They are pigs and sons of pigs!" she snarled in heavily accented Alban.

"But better them than the Slavemaker I have no doubt, my lady."

At once her fiery temper died and Sir William saw a slight tremor in her lower lip. "It was a bold plan and it nearly succeeded; to hide away amongst your own slaves once your husband had fled the field, then pray for a chance to escape," he said. "But I am afraid that now I have no choice but to hand you over to His Majesty King Edward and he will decide whether you are to be sent to the Slavemaker or ransomed."

Privately, Sir William had no doubt that the king would send her to the Slavemaker. Trained and conditioned by him, she would fetch far more for the royal coffers on the auction block than her wretched husband would be able to raise for a ransom.

"Bring her to my tent," he told the men and strode away, knowing full well that she was in for some more hard use before she made it to his quarters. Wives of the nobility were treated differently in law and they were the only women normally off limits to the common man's cock. Lady Isabella Dulac, once made a prisoner of war, was now fair game and there were many soldiers who would want to know what an aristocratic cunt felt like around their tools. And not just her cunt. But that was war; and that was what happened to the losers of battles.

His slaves had been busy and his quarters were clean and orderly. As soon as he entered the tent he stripped off his heavy leather jerkin, worn under the chain mail he had discarded soon after the surrender had been taken, then two of his slaves helped him with his linen vest and woollen leggings. They laughed and giggled lasciviously as they caught sight of the master's cock, now beginning to stir as the day's tensions eased.

The women had prepared him a hot bath and he relaxed into it as they stripped themselves naked and washed him.

Sir William lay back and closed his eyes, visions of the battle mercifully fading into more salacious ones of the tormented enemy women on their crosses. They would be sold for domestic drudgery or haulage or agricultural work at Southaven. The plight of women after constant war had decimated the male population had been worsened even more by the mysterious horse flu that had swept through the equine population of the whole of Northern Eropia some hundred years previously. Some held that it had been an attempt by Frankland sorcerors to cripple the Alban war effort but it had gone disastrously wrong. But whether it was duc to that or to natural causes the result was that men had turned to the nearest and cheapest beast of burden that was still available in almost limitless quantities. They were slower than horses and weaker than oxen but they were pleasant to whip and, with a slave team, a man always had a fuck available even when he was hauling goods across sparsely populated country.

A foal was worth more than a harem of ten wives and to make matters worse, every time the horses seemed to be recovering and breeding once more, the disease would erupt again. And so the familiar sight of teams of sweating, whip scored females struggling along the highways ahead of heavy wagons or highly prized pleasure slaves trotting in tooled leather harness between the shafts of a nobleman's trap, seemed set to stay for a long time yet.

Sir William's rambling thoughts were suddenly interrupted and he sighed in pleasure as he felt one of the women's hands under the water, begin to stroke and cup his scrotum.

"Did I tell you to do that?" he asked softly as the hand continued to explore him.

"No, my lord." The Alban was heavily accented, tainted by what Sir William thought was Hunnish ancestry.

"Then I shall have you beaten at supper. Now continue."

"Yes, my lord. Thank you."

He regarded the big titted slave from under half closed lids. He had picked her up at some village or other for a few coins, when she had caught his eye, taking a beating from her owner with supreme ease, despite the fact that the man was holding nothing back. She was a big boned girl, not bad looking and with not an ounce of spare flesh on her apart from at breast, buttock and hip. She was not classically beautiful but straightaway Sir William had spotted that she would be able to take any amount of punishment when he took her home to his dear wife, whose chief pleasure in life was sharing the torment of slaves with him.

Under the water he felt her strong hand close about his hardened shaft and begin to massage it. She was skilful at applying a pleasing amount of pressure and he felt his climax approach rapidly. He put his head back, resting it against the other slave's naked and warm breast as his sperm pumped out in long trails and the tension drained from him.

They dried him and dressed him in the usual short tunic and loose woollen trousers and then led him over to the low dining table for his supper. He reclined on his couch and domestic slaves, clad in short, roughly woven tunics served plates of bread, olives, oat cakes, meat and – his favourite – the spicy fish paste made on the Alban south coast. The far edge of the table in front of him had two semi circles cut in it and as the meal was served, the big slave had her hands tied to the ring at the back of her collar and she then knelt opposite him and shuffled forwards. Her upper thighs, slightly parted neatly fitted into the cut outs. Her colleague went to a chest and returned with a variety of whips. He chose a twenty tailed one with square cut lashes and at a nod from him, the slighter girl began flogging the bigger one on her back. Sir William lay back, chewing on choice morsels and watching as the slave was whipped.

She presented a delightful picture as the massive tits shook and shuddered while the leathers snapped and smacked heavily across her back. The slighter girl was a practised wielder of the whip and knew that nothing less than a full strength whipping would be acceptable to the master. Sir William watched as her lips compressed and her eyes blazed as she laid into her sister slave with no mercy whatever. Her own breasts swung and shook as she flogged and Sir William felt his cock begin to stir back towards erection. Gasps and moans began to escape the bigger girl as the whip continued to club and smack at her, Sir William felt it was time to make sure that the flogging was harsh enough to produce an abundance of what he wanted to harvest from the girl.

"You!" he cried, addressing the slighter of the two. "There's enough crosses out there for a regiment of sluts like you to hang on all night so if you don't put your back into beating this miserable lump of whoreflesh, I'll string you up on one of them!"

The girl had paused in her work while he spoke and now Sir William lay back to enjoy the spectacle he had created. If the big girl had thought she was getting flogged before, she was quickly disabused of the idea. Each lash was accompanied by a squeal of effort and the big body of the kneeling slave shook right down to the groin under each stroke. Her stoical silence provided a pleasing counterpoint to the squeals of the other girl.

Sir William ate happily as the flogging went on and only when the flogger was visibly wilting and the big girl had plainly orgasmed at least twice, did he reach out and pick up a blunt, round bladed knife, resembling a slightly larger than usual butter knife. As soon as he did so the flogging halted. The big girl tried to steady her panting and looked down at her crotch as her master reached forwards.

Sir William pushed the blunt blade between her legs and then drew it back towards him, pressing the flat of the blade up into the fleshy crevice between her labia. It emerged with several shining globules of her cunt sap on it.

He spread them lovingly over a piece of bread already spread with fish paste and savoured the rich combination of tastes. He spread another slice of bread and reached out with the knife again. Once more it came back with several smears and globules on it and once more Sir William enjoyed his favourite dish. The slave produced enough juice to spice up three more slices of bread before she needed beating again. Ten hard lashes produced enough to finally satisfy the appetite in his stomach but left him needing relief for the straining erection that was making him uncomfortable.

He beckoned to the slighter girl who came and unlaced his trousers then pulled them off completely. She eyed the thick and rigid cock appreciatively but knew that it wasn't for her just yet. She returned to her whipped colleague and unfastened her wrists. Without having to be told the big slave leaned forwards to rest her forearms on the table and have her wrists tied again to straps nailed to the wood. Sir William sat up and because the table was very close to the couch he spread his legs and rested them on the top. Thus his imperiously tall and thick length of cock with the tightly crinkled sac below it was almost in the slave's face and even before the next stage of her torment began, she was taking long, luxurious licks, tilting her head so that her owner could see her pink tongue lapping at him eagerly.

Meanwhile her sister slave had returned from the chest with a viciously thin and whippy length of cane. At a nod from Sir William she began to wield it across the girl's backside. He had a perfect view of how the wide curves of her buttocks buckled and shook and shock waves ran up the hips to the trim waist as the slender shaft whipped into the flesh. Even the normally impervious slave couldn't restrain a whimper and her soft breath caressed her master's cock. Sir William was delighted at his timing, He had had her caned some eight weeks previously and her skin had cleared just in time for this night of victory. He settled back to enjoy a lengthy fellation which would gather intensity as the caning progressed and her screams and moans would be music to his ears as well as exquisite pleasure to his cock as her mouth and breath bathed him.

"Don't hurry," he told the caner. "I want her to really suffer tonight."

The beating and the cock sucking went on for a long time, Sir William lifting her head away if he felt he was too close to coming. The slave's buttocks were a fiery mass of slashing double lines and in between strokes she was pushing her bottom backwards and sawing it across the cane by the time he finally allowed himself to be driven to his climax. The slenderer slave saw that he was about to spend into her colleague's mouth and suddenly threw in three especially harsh strokes in quick succession. The result was that Sir William's erupting cock was given a final treat as the slave screamed with her mouth full of it.

He held her head down as he thrust up in his orgasm and she failed miserably to get more than a few helpless gulps of spunk down her throat, she spluttered and snorted the rest everywhere.

As a punishment he had the wretched girl chained to a post outside the tent and took her companion to bed.

He knew that his dear wife, Tamara would have the time of her life with these two recent purchases.

Isabella Dulac also spent the night outside Sir William's tent, safely locked into a cage where neither the victorious soldiers nor her own ex-slaves could do her damage, thus the two beaten women, representing the opposite ends of female status, spent the night side by side, in chains, equal in the face of ultimate male authority.

In the morning the long column of soldiers with all the slaves who had either been brought along, or who had been purchased or captured on campaign, set off for the coast. The castle was still smouldering in places and the column of smoke rose high into the clear air as they crested the nearby hill and marched away. A small party broke away from the main column and in a caged cart pulled by two slaves, Isabella Dulac was taken a few miles south to the camp of King Edward himself.

The royal camp was in uproar as the cart entered by the narrow track through the gateway in the stockade. Victory meant that everything was on the move, the armies of Frankland had fallen back as a result of the loss of the castle and Alba with her Burghund allies was advancing. Isabella stared around her trying to see if there was anything of use she could note in the event of an escape being possible. Some females picked up sticks to prod her with as the cage passed by but the two soldiers who had been detailed off to guard her, whipped them away and the sturdy little slaves eventually delivered her to the door of the royal tent. A rather haughty man came out of the splendid tent and eyed her nakedness coldly.

"Bring her in," he said curtly.

The soldiers helped her down and held her securely as they hustled her inside. A short, rough tunic of nondescript brown material was thrown at her and she shrugged it on then was hustled onwards and straight into the royal presence. The soldiers bowed low and forced her to her knees on the luxurious carpets but she stared upwards defiantly as the king approached. He was a tall man, dressed in a simple, long green robe. But about his neck was a thick gold chain that alone was worth more than anything she had seen outside the Frankish court. His dark hair was encircled by a simple gold coronet. By his side was a man whose notoriety amongst women of quality made his title only ever whispered in hushed tones. The Slavemaker.

He was dressed in the simple grey robes of the Guardians, from whose ranks he was elected to the post of leader and had taken the title 'Slavemaker' his hood was drawn over his head and pulled so far forward that his face was quite invisible. There were Guardians in Frankland of course, they tended the great standing stones of Bretagne and conducted arcane rituals that were said to appease the gods and guard the kingdom. But also they had great skill with herbs and curatives of all sorts, being able to dispense blessed sleep to wounded soldiers so that their wounds could be attended to, potions to ease childbirth and cure dropsy. But only in Cambria, a Western province of Alba did they ally themselves so closely to the throne and render various services. Among them being Slavemaking, the secrets of which craft were known only to them.

Isabella felt her courage begin to melt as she stared into the impenetrable darkness of the cowl. The man stood with his hands joined in front of him and these drew her gaze at last. The skin was so pale as to almost be translucent and the fingers were long and delicate. They reminded her of a minstrel's hands but she shuddered as she recalled tales of what tunes this man could play on a woman's helpless body. The king looked down at her steadily.

"Do you speak Alban?" he asked suddenly.

"A little...... Your Majesty," she managed.

"She will do. Can you break her in time?" He turned to the Slavemaker.

"I will tell you in a moment, Sire." The voice was utterly unexpected, quite high-pitched, soft and with the distinctive Cambrian lilt. He stepped forwards and without warning placed a hand on Isabella's head.

She never did fully understand what happened next. It was as if a great light had been shone onto her and she was spread out naked under it. She actually clenched her eyes tightly shut but nothing could keep the light out of her head, the weight of his hand seemed to grow greater and greater, she started to cower under it and then it was gone, leaving her blinking and dazed.

"Yes. It can be done but it will be a close thing, Sire."

"It must be done, Owen! I have been away too long and that beldam in Tamesbury schemes against me every day!"

The two men turned and walked away from her. The king gesticulating angrily as he talked.

"We must push on and force Louis into one more retreat, then I can leave the Count to hold him over the winter while I return home."

"And in the meantime you want this one to do what we discussed last night?" The Slavemaker indicated her.

"Yes. If you can destroy them before I land, then Her damned Majesty Queen cursed Anneka will be left looking very foolish and with a mercenary army wanting to be paid!"

He spat out his words as he poured himself a glass of wine. "To think I married her to gain peace with the Deutsche Federation while I fought Louis! And now I find the back-stabbing bitch is trying to take the whole damned realm off me! Everywhere she stirs up trouble to foment resentment against me and when the time comes she will present herself as saviour of the nation! Hah!"

He took a deep draught and then turned to the hooded figure beside him. "Start on her now man! Do not waste a second! She is vital to us, and our fates hang by a thread…."

With sick horror Isabella realised that they were talking as she did in front of slaves. What these men were saying might be of huge worth to his Majesty King Louis of Frankland, but there was never going to be the slightest chance that she would have the opportunity to divulge anything. She didn't matter any more. She was a slave herself now, and the men knew it with complete certainty.

The hooded figure loomed over her and she gazed up into the darkness within the cowl. A darkness so deep that it seemed as if it would swallow her whole.

CHAPTER 3.
Southaven; Alba

Lady Tamara Courcey peered out eagerly from where two of the curtains that hung round her palanquin joined. Balanced on two large, elegantly spoked wheels the flat platform with its padded mattress and heavy curtains made a comfortable and private bed for a lady to lie on while her slaves pulled her, goaded by the whip from the driver perched on his high seat above their backs.

At present they were moving slowly through the crowded streets of Southaven, streets that were broad and well kept but nonetheless crowded. There were several ships due in that day and business was going to be brisk. Three days previously word of her husband's impending arrival had reached her and now, after hectic preparations, she had made the journey to meet him.

Lady Tamara risked pulling the curtains just a little farther open and spread her legs a little farther apart. She was kneeling over her current favourite slave's face with her thighs parted as widely as she could get them so that her cunt was pushed down onto the girl's mouth. Tamara looked down irritably for a moment as she adjusted her bunched up dress.

"Get that whoreslave tongue of yours deeper into me and make sure I feel those studs! You don't want to waste all that time and trouble I took over piercing you the last time do you?"

The slave shook her head with her tongue still stuck out and her mistress sighed as she felt it move inside her. "That's better. Now rasp my clit some more! Do it well or I'll add another stud!" She grinned as she felt the girl get to work with renewed vigour. She already had five studs through her tongue and the last had taken simply hours to put through, she had fussed so much.

Tamara settled down to enjoying the view as her cunt and clit were gently raked. However much she loved her husband's country estate and his wealth, she did so love the city! There were shops selling bolts of the most divine cloths, there were women of her own rank wearing gowns of a cut that must be fashionable in Tamesbury, but which were entirely new to Tamara. And the streets were thronged with people and slaves of all kinds. Her own palanquin drawn by four of her best matched slaves didn't look too out of place although as she peered around she saw a beautifully matched pair of blondes pulling a nobleman in a trap with vividly painted woodwork. He was just climbing down and tying their reins to a hitching rail. Two whores immediately approached him but he flicked at them with his whip and they backed off. A farmer was delivering vegetables to a shop, lifting heavy sacks out of a plain dog cart pulled by two naked and heavily built slaves, they had the mud of the fields plastered up their legs and sweat had carved runnels through the mud splashes on their skins. A little further on a grocer lounged beside the door of his shop and exchanged greetings with passers by as his slaves and wives laboured in the shop itself. On the other side of the street a struggling slave had been bent over a hitching rail and a wife was thrashing her naked bottom with a heavy leather paddle. Several men had gathered to assist the husband in deciding the extent of the punishment to be dished out. Tamara grinned, it didn't look as though the slut was going to be allowed up for quite a while. Outside the livery stable a saddler was fitting a new bridle to a noble's pony slave, who was prancing as he screwed her tongue into what looked like, to Tamara's excited gaze, one of the spiked, clamp bits she favoured for her own slaves. Her palanquin passed by a large wagon, drawn by a team of ten slaves who were waiting placidly to be whipped back to work, the long shaft stretched almost half the length of the street. Behind the wagon two oxen waited with equal patience until the time came when they would be needed to help the slaves. The two drivers – with a big team, one walked at the side to keep the whip applied all along the lines - were supervising as the tavern's slaves sweated and grunted with effort unloading the barrels. As she watched, one of the men selected a raggedly clad slave and pushed her up against the side of the building. Before her back had touched it, her fingers were fluttering at his leather britches, unlacing them, as urgent as he was. Tamara smiled; cock starvation, she called it, it made slaves so easy to control but she was suffering from it badly herself. Her adored William had been away for months, but at least she would be in his arms that night.

The palanquin rattled past the rutting carter, thrusting his pelvis back and forth with the slave's pale legs wrapped around his waist, and turned the corner into a street that sloped sharply downhill. Beneath her the slave's tongue worked steadily and she decided to help it along by rubbing her own clitoris. She rubbed her fingers harshly against it, using rapid little movements that sent shivers through her as the slave's tongue rasped at her inner tissues. She glanced outside as they passed a public whipping post, there was a naked slave shackled by her wrists to it with her back against the wood. An owner was entitled to administer summary punishment for trivial offences that weren't worth bothering a magistrate with and this one had plainly been quite vexed with the girl, her breasts, stomach and thighs were a livid tracery of pink and red lines. Her head hung down and a ragged curtain of curly brown hair hid her face but Tamara noted that she kept her legs well apart. Every slave knew that a freshly whipped female was attractive to men, and as Tamara watched, her own fingers and her slave's tireless tongue driving her on to orgasm, a drunk staggered out of a tavern and butted up against her even as he fiddled with his trousers, she roused as his clothes rasped against her and took her weight on her wrists as she wrapped her shapely young legs round the work hardened older man. Soon the couple were frantically gyrating against the post, the slave crying out in pain but only tightening her grip on his waist.

Tamara's orgasm broke and she felt her warm cunt nectar flood down over the slave's face and she retreated back into the shady privacy of the palanquin's interior so she could give voice to the moans of pleasure she felt bubbling up in her throat and collapsed half onto her front, half on her side and lay panting, listening to the sounds of the city outside. Her own driver cursed just outside as he hauled back on the reins as they headed down to the docks, she felt the brakes go on and trembled with a last shiver of excitement as admonitory lashes smacked onto the sweating backs to make the slaves haul back against the gradient.

"Jocelyn," she whispered to her slave. Jocelyn raised herself onto her elbows, her face flushed and shining, her hair tousled. She looked enquiringly at her mistress but made no move to speak. The weight of metal in her exceptionally long tongue made it easier to be mute.

"I shall have to put another stud in that tongue when we get home, you slut. It took you far too long to make me come. I may have you beaten as well."

The girl shivered with mingled apprehension and lust; if her mistress had her beaten rather than beating her herself, then that meant it would be done by Carlson, Sir William's trusted steward and he had a cock that every slavegirl on the estate dreamed of.

Tamara fumbled with her dress and smoothed it back down over her long, slender legs as the sound of gulls grew louder and the scent of the sea pervaded the interior. Jocelyn found a mirror and held it for her as she hurriedly ran a comb through her thick brown hair that cascaded onto her graceful shoulders. She bit her lips to try and redden them and then scrambled down the minute the palanquin halted.

The sunlight flashed and danced on the water of the harbour, dazzling her after the dusk of the coach's interior. She put her hand up to shade her eyes and gave a girlish squeal of joy. Just rounding the headland was the graceful shape of a bireme with its sail swelling to the following wind and its two ranks of oars swinging in well disciplined unison. Tamara thrilled to the thought of the ranks of naked, whipped girls straining at the huge oars as the overseers marched along the gangways, lashing them onwards to the relentless beat of the drum.

The graceful vessel sent sprays up at her prow as she ploughed the last of the rough water and then turned towards the harbour. As she watched, the sail wrinkled and collapsed then it was taken down and furled by sailors. The oars drove the boat on however until the master bellowed a command and the long shafts lifted clear of the water and were shipped. Gliding under its own momentum and with Sir William and his soldiers waving at the gathering crowds, the boat slid alongside the quay and hands reached for the ropes to moor her safely.

Tamara looked around her as the second of the ships carrying the troops rounded the headland. Seldom had she been so close to so many men. The dockers and sailors were excitingly muscular and tanned, and likewise the soldiers as they began to troop down the gangplank and greet the respective gaggles of excited wives who hadn't been taken on campaign. Almost immediately however there were squabbles as the soldiers introduced new slaves and even some new wives to their households.

"Every whipping post in Southaven will be full this night." The voice was deep and masterful and Tamara's heart did a somersault. She turned and looked up into her husband's face.

"My lord!" she whispered and fell into his arms.

An age later when she surfaced from the dizzying depths of his embrace, she started to babble inanely about everything she had done while he had been away.

"My dear girl," Sir William said, putting a finger across her lips. "You may ride home with me and tell me all the news. But for now there is an auction to be organised. Send Jocelyn home. You and I will follow tomorrow."

Almost skipping like a girl, Tamara scurried back to the palanquin and gave the master's orders to the driver.

"Expect us late in the afternoon and make sure you put out the slaves in just the way we planned," she whispered hurriedly to Jocelyn. "And tell Carlson we'll have you beaten for supper."

The driver whipped up the ponies and Tamara ran back to the quay where a sight so delightful met her eyes that she couldn't help putting her hands to her groin right in the open. The yard arm of the boat had sprouted a crop of ripely hanging fruit. She counted twelve naked Frankland slaves hanging by their wrists and bidding was already underway.

She picked out her husband and joined him, letting the press of the crowd push her against his hard, warm body.

"If you see aught you want, just say and we'll bid," he told her.

"My lord, I believe I have everything we could want waiting at home. And besides, I think I have what I want just now, right here."

She giggled and slid her hand around to the front of his trousers, pulling at the laces that kept his divine cock in check.

His hand stopped hers and he looked down at her, lust as naked as the hanging slaves in his eyes.

"We'll watch awhile because watching slaves makes you even more insatiable than usual in bed. And that's how I want you; utterly insatiable."

Tamara felt her breasts swell and her nipples thrust against her dress. At her groin the hot melting feeling of her cunt awakening returned. Up on the ship's deck the auctioneer was exhorting the bidders to greater feats of extravagance, by spinning the hanging bodies and squeezing buttocks and breasts, parting legs and describing the delicious moistness of the cunts, he seemed to be having some success and bidding was brisk. More people came to the waterfront as the second ship tied up and another auction got under way. The quay became raucous with the calls of the competing auctioneers, the squeals of the slaves and the calling of bids.

Sir William put his arm around his wife's shoulder and squeezed her left breast, hefting the soft but heavy orb in public with no compunction.

"We'll do well out of this, my girl," he told her. "There'll be a high old time in Southaven tonight, every one of my men will feel himself wealthy!" They watched as the second lot of slaves were led up on deck and hung from the yardarm before being sold. This time thc auctioneer whipped some of them to keep the bidders' attention. The third and fourth lots suffered even more as the bidders began to drift away, their purchases made. The auctioneers became more cruel as the competition for buyers became fiercer and even Tamara's boundless appetite for the sight and sound of slaves being whipped was almost sated as the men swung their whips in ever more vigorous attempts to prove the durability of the merchandise. The fifth lot were hung by their ankles and cunt whipped, some were prostituted to prove their worth before the bidding began but eventually all were sold and Sir William went back on board for his possessions, his wife following closely.

As they made their way towards the stern and the towering superstructure that housed the cabins, Tamara's attention was caught by the teams of galley slaves who had been allowed on deck for watering and rest. Their heavy chains, running from ankle to ankle, clonked and slithered as the welted girls collapsed gratefully against the ship's gunwales. One of the overseers banged a small barrel of water down and threw a few wooden cups after it. A free-for-all ensued as thirsty slaves fought each other for the means to drink. Tamara grinned as she watched the naked, struggling heap of bodies, slapping, spanking, punching and clawing at each other. The overseers let the fight develop for a few minutes before wading in with their whips and restoring order. And as some sort of queue formed for the cups, two of the men selected a slave each to receive a further drink. They wore short tunics which were easily raised for the women to duck their heads under and eagerly seek the erect cocks with their mouths. The third overseer moved some of the women by the barrel aside and raising his tunic began a leisurely masturbation, his massive hand only just able to encircle the girth of his huge shaft. With wide eyes the slaves watched until the monster began to jerk and spit forth thick ropes of creamy sperm that arced into the drinking water.

Tamara joined in the men's laughter as fighting broke out once more, every slave desperate for a taste before it dissipated.

Sir William returned and brought the shackled Hun slaves with him. Tamara was most impressed with the big one. She dug her little hands into the deep cushions of buttock meat and sampled the depth of breast flesh, concluding that she would certainly repay serious whipping at the first opportunity. The slenderer one was pronounced adequate.

"William! They're lovely but I've got such a treat for you at home, you'll never guess," she giggled after she had examined the new additions.

"Nevertheless, you'll have to wait till tomorrow to show me," her husband replied and taking her arm he led her away, leaving the slaves to join the wagons heading for his estate the next day.

He found them a room at a fairly reasonable inn and as soon as the door closed, they tore at each other's clothes and rutted frantically. Tamara screamed her release as his cock filled her to overflowing with its spend. His weight upon her and his hard muscled body squashing the softness of her breasts as he lay on her, had been the stuff of fervid dreams for so long. With the first storm passed, Sir William drank some ale and then dressed and went downstairs to hire a whore for the evening. He returned with a smiling, chubby young woman. She understood her purpose perfectly and undressed without having to be told. Sir William buckled her wrists into the cuffs on the end of the chain hanging from the ceiling, provided by the proprietor, and then took a heavy strap to her. It was an old strap that the landlord had lent him and had doubtless bitten deeply into many female bodies and had become soft and pliant over the years. The result was a pleasingly heavy sounding smack at each lash and a good width of pink weal quite soon after. While her husband dealt with the woman's backside, Tamara savoured the front, pressing her slender body against the full breasts, kissing the mouth that was open and panting as the lashes smacked home and delving her fingers into the plump lipped slot with its full and convoluted inner lips. Spitefully she pinched them and dug her nails in, making the woman's head throw back as a yell escaped her. Husband and wife exchanged smiles over their victim's shoulder. Sir William's long, thick shaft wagged as he swung the strap and the leather made the candles flicker as it swished back and forth. Tamara took one and grabbed a handful of the girl's hair, dragging her head up so she could see the way the candle hovered over her breasts.

"My lord, would you be so kind as to whip the strumpet's back? I want her tits to shake as I hot wax them."

"Of course."

Sir William moved a little closer so that the lash would wrap the body more and began to swing forehand and backhand so that the sides of both breasts soon sported diagonal brown stripes where the end of the strap had caught her. Tamara was working the nipples mercilessly meanwhile, pulling and twisting them then holding them stretched out as she poured on wax. The woman moaned and cried even as she blatantly thrust her hips back and forth, her chubby thighs rubbing together and shining with discharge.

"They're such lying little sluts," Tamara laughed. "They scream and yell but their cunts are flooding the whole time they're suffering!"

The quivering breasts were now covered in a rough coating of solidified wax and the whore's breath was rasping in her throat as she absorbed the thrashing her back and arse had taken while her tits had been scalded. Had they been at home, Tamara might have been tempted to don a strap-on and shaft the chubby little thing's cunt while William tested her rectum with his cock. But there was still too much lost time to make up for and, leaving the whore dangling from her chain, the pair launched themselves into a further frenzy of rutting on the bed.

After that they lay, panting and soaked, until they recovered enough to take an interest in the whore again. This time William held one of her legs out to the side while Tamara flicked the heavy strap up into the viscid and fleshy crease of the vulva. The tip of the leather snapped up onto her pubic mound with satisfying, loud smacks until a spray of thick moisture announced an orgasm. Sir William was all for seeing how much more fun they could have with her, but Tamara was sleepy after the journey and they dismissed her with a handful of coins then fell into bed. They woke each other several times in the night and by the morning, Sir William had renewed his acquaintance with all three of his wife's holes and she woke with her head resting on his thigh, where it had fallen after she had drained the last of his spunk from him and swallowed it before falling into a dreamless sleep.

After breakfast Sir William led the way to a livery stable and hired – for a horrendous sum - a horse. There was some fierce haggling before she was lifted up to sit side saddle behind him but at last they set off, Tamara holding her lord and master firmly around the waist as the horse's haunches rocked her back and forth. The debris of the previous night's celebrations was still on plain view and Sir William's prophecy that every whipping post would be filled, seemed to have been borne out. Slender collared wives, presumably those who had objected to new slaves or wives or who simply hadn't fucked as ardently as their husbands required, hung splayed in frames outside the sheriff's office or slumped against whipping posts, held by their wrists and left for the night after a flogging. Heavily collared slaves had shared similar fates, probably just for the amusement of owners and Tamara's blood began to stir at the sight of the hanging bodies, some beginning to wake and moan in protest, all of them sporting livid welts and crusted sperm. As they passed, a few were being taken down by bleary-eyed and hungover men who grinned sheepishly up at Sir William as they saluted him.

A couple of miles out of Southaven they passed the wagons that he had hired to transport all his belongings and those of his men who lived in the immediate vicinity of his villa. It was being pulled by two oxen and behind it walked the men with their chattering flocks of women, some of whom were vainly trying to make ripped clothes cover welted flesh, others of whom were smiling and enjoying the walk, plainly all the better for the attentions they had received the night before.

Right at the back came the two Hun slaves wearing red kerchiefs at their necks; the common signal used to indicate that an owner didn't want his property used by anyone else.

"Thought you'd want 'em kept clean my lord," the carter said when Sir William asked him why he had used it.

"No! Let the trollops be used as anyone wants. They'll be rusty from disuse by the time they reach home otherwise!"

The men laughed and cheered 'Good old Sir William' as they rode on ahead.

Tamara breathed in the musk of her husband's body as she leaned her head against his back, the sun was warm on her cheek and a soft wind was in her hair. Beneath her the horse's powerful body moved and memories of the previous night were awakening tingles at her crotch. She shifted slightly and pressed her nipples against William's back, the sharp thrill of the contact made her groan softly and her hands slipped down his body at the front, to where his legs spread apart. He chuckled throatily as he felt her small hands flutter and stroke his groin.

"You will have had all the cock even you can want by the time we reach home, my girl. And then you can have mine."

Tamara sat up straight. "Oh William, you wouldn't! Not today!"

"Especially today. Now jump down and get rid of those petticoats. You'll not be needing them these next few hours."

She knew that tone of voice; he would not be gainsaid in that mood and she slid obediently down when he reined the horse in.

The lack of underskirts didn't seem to affect the hang of her favourite gown too badly when she had finished unlacing them and had smoothed the skirt back down. It was cut low at the bodice and the gold edging on the scooped neck drew the eye to the broad swells of her breasts, standing deep and proud on her chest, crowned with smooth areolas and thick nipples that erected quickly and sizeably. There was also a girdle of gold thread that went round her waist, knotted at the front and its ends hung down at her crotch, drawing the eye there as well. It was tailored well to her hips and followed the smooth curves intimately. Tamara stooped and gathered up her underwear, secretly glad of the cool air circulating around her upper legs, then stowed it in a saddle bag. As a reward she was pulled up to sit in front of her husband, the pommel of the saddle creating agreeable havoc at her crotch as they resumed their ride.

Just a few minutes later the road began to pass through cultivated land. Teams of slaves were scything crops while wives whipped them on in the fields of wealthier farmers. In smaller fields, both wives and slaves worked under men's lashes. Sir William looked around him carefully, these were the fields of his estate.

"Sejanus seems to have kept everything in good order," he said. "Although I expect you helped greatly," he added with a rueful grin.

Tamara had the grace to blush. "I was too busy making sure the house ran smoothly," she told him.

“And our pony slaves, no doubt,” Sir William teased her.

“Well, we do have a reputation to maintain,” she insisted hotly.

Tamara’s family was a wealthy one from the Midlands and her dowry had been extensive lands, property and no fewer than twenty pleasure slaves. Now, however, with their lands and their wealth joined, the pair owned some of the most admired racing ponies and bed slaves in the country.

Sir William’s expression became serious. “Well in any case, it’s time I paid a few visits and I trust you will play your part as well as usual.”

Despite herself Tamara felt her vulva heat and moisten against the leather of the pommel as Sir William guided the horse off the road and into the courtyard of one of the wealthier homesteads on the estate. Chickens and geese ran noisily from under their mount’s hooves as it approached the thatched buildings surrounding three sides of the yard. In front of the main house to their right was the farm’s whipping post; a simple stout log stood on its end and driven firmly into the earth. From its top hung four ropes and as Tamara and her husband rode in they saw that currently one miscreant, arms raised and wrists bound by two of the ropes was undergoing correction at the hands of a pleasant faced man in his mid forties wielding a heavy, braided lash. The girl was naked and quite solidly built; to Tamara’s practiced eye she looked as though she could take sixty or seventy lashes without any problem but even so she was squirming and yelping, trying to twist herself away from the lash and occasionally taking one across her front for her troubles. The man halted long enough to tug at his forelock and wish them good day as they brought the horse to a stop. Sir William dismounted and lifted Tamara down, then the man put his whip down and came and took the reins. The girl at the post craned her head round and glared back at them over her raised arm, resentful blue eyes in a handsome, if grubby face staring through a curtain of thick hair. Her large breasts wobbled and shook as she panted and Tamara felt her naked loins moisten even more beneath her skirt as she smoothed it down. A large, smiling man had appeared at the door of the house and he and Sir William were greeting each other warmly, they turned and went inside, leaving Tamara to follow on. She lifted her skirts and climbed the short stone staircase to the front door. Behind her she heard the horse being led away and glanced back. The naked girl at the post sighed deeply and settled down to wait for the man to return and finish her punishment. Tamara smiled as she noticed the telltale rub of the thighs together to try and extract any frisson of pleasure she could. If she'd been Tamara's, she would have taken further punishment for that, but just then Sir William called and she remembered she had a duty to fulfil and went in.

The main hall was raftered and airy, a long table stretched for most of its length. A door at the far end led into the kitchens, already their host, had had ale served and he and Sir William were discussing how the land had been farmed while he had been away.

Her husband raised his hand and clicked his fingers at her. Gritting her teeth but taking two handfuls of skirt in front of her thighs, Tamara advanced. Sir William smiled infuriatingly at her and tapped the surface of the wooden table. She made to hitch up her skirts entirely and bend forwards but the tenant stopped her.

"My Lady, with Sir William's permission, I am partial to some breast meat before the main repast."

"Get 'em out, Tamara," her husband said easily and lounged back even more infuriatingly. Tamara bit her tongue, and shrugged the wide shoulders of her gown, one by one, onto her upper arms and slid them down until she uncrossed her arms and stood virtually naked to the waist before her husband's tenant. Proudly she thrust her breasts forwards and looked down as his big, tanned and work-hardened hands began to knead her soft, pale flesh; squashing it between his thick fingers, making cushions swell out as he gripped. Her nipples began to erect and send shards of excitement shooting down her body. He noticed and trapped them between the first and second fingers of each hand and squeezed them too. She gasped a little and the men laughed, then resumed their conversation.

The mauling of her proudly thrusting breasts carried on undiminished and she tried her best not to interrupt. It was the custom among some of the big landowners to share their wives with their tenants now and then; they felt it sealed the social contract between tenant and landlord. Furthermore it served to remind the wives that while the nobility were monogamous for reasons of dynastic stability, they were still their husband's chattels.

Tamara had closed her eyes and had surrendered to the constant stimulation of her breasts to the point of moaning helplessly by the time the tenant suddenly stopped mauling her, pushed her roughly in the back to indicate he wanted her face down on the table and, when she had urgently fumbled her long skirt up to her waist and pressed her pounding breasts down onto the wood, fished out a rampantly hard penis from his leggings and stuffed it unceremoniously into her seeping vagina.

Beside her face her husband helped himself to more ale and resumed the men's discussion of the water meadows and the yield of the north fields. Behind her the tenant was thrusting in fully and then withdrawing almost completely in a slow, relaxed rhythm that had Tamara purring even as she absorbed the insult of feeling him rest his ale tankard on the small of her back.

"Master Sejanus collected a full wagonload from just two of the north fields," the farmer informed Sir William as he pumped himself in and out of his wife's tight but slick tunnel. "Must've been more than a full load in fact 'cos one of my men told me that he had nearly half of it transferred to another wagon just up the road."

Tamara, rocking backwards and forwards as she was fucked, saw her husband raise an eyebrow.

"Well, I'll have reached home tonight and in the morning he'll no doubt render full accounts."

Behind them, Tamara heard the man who had been conducting the beating outside, enter.

"She'm had the forty you ordered, Master Turner," he said.

The man never faltered in his steady reaming of Tamara's body.

"My lady here is partial to the sound of the whip," he informed the man. "Give her another fifty or so."

Tamara couldn't hold back in the face of the remorseless penetration and the delicious cruelty, so as the faint smacks began once again to filter into the main hall and the coughing cries of the slave started again, she spiralled helplessly into orgasm and was still panting in its wake when the man inside her finally gripped her hips and spent himself in a series of teeth jarring slams of his pelvis against hers, driving her painfully onto the edge of the table.

One of the man's wives wiped her clean after a few minutes and she staggered upright as Sir William drained his mug and prepared to move on. Very aware that she was flushed and dishevelled and that her skirt was stained, Tamara tried to muster as much dignity as a well-fucked woman can who is still trembling inside and fluttering in the wake of orgasm.

Outside, the man was allowed to stop beating the slave who had slumped against the post.

"What was her offence?" Sir William asked once he was mounted and Tamara was safely gathered in his arms again.

The tenant farmer looked up and shrugged with a grin. "Can't recall just now. But she'll not do it again in a hurry!"

As they left, Tamara saw the man who had wielded the whip begin to fumble his cock free of his short tunic and take a grip on the slave's flogged hips.

They stopped at four more farms as they progressed homewards. One was at the substantial house of a landowner who nevertheless held his land in fealty to Sir William. He demanded entry to Tamara's back passage and she had to bite her fist to stop the shrieks of protest she wanted to emit as his enormously thick member ploughed her rectum back and forth before depositing its load as far inside her as it could reach and then wrenching her sphincters as it withdrew.

Again a wife was on hand to wipe the mess up afterwards but Tamara walked beside the horse, rather than face sitting on the pommel of the saddle, until they reached the next house. Here a man and his three wives plus four slaves wove brightly coloured fabrics from dyed wool and while her lord and master discussed the state of trade with him, she was required to kneel and suck his acrid tasting cock until it exploded into her mouth. But at least her stinging vulva and still throbbing anus got a rest.

Finally as the hot afternoon reached its height they rode over the drawbridge that spanned the shallow moat surrounding Sir William's villa. It had a wooden palisade inside the moat and a watch tower at one corner but ever since the imperial armies of Carthage had withdrawn some eight hundred years previously, Alba had been able to withstand the attacks from northern barbarians that had thrown Eropia into chaos and it had been a largely peaceful country until it had become embroiled in the convoluted power struggles between Frankland, Burghund and the Deutsche Federation. So Sir William's villa was fairly typical in being not too heavily defended, unlike the great stone castles on the continent that so recently he had helped destroy.

Tamara grew more and more excited as they approached, the surprise she had in store for her husband was almost too good a secret to keep. And having been given as good a helping of cock as a girl could hope for, especially in these man-scarce days, she could hardly wait to share with him what she had prepared; or what Jocelyn should have prepared. And then there would be the surprise!

Inside the high wooden gates, the horse's hooves crunched on gravel and Sir William reined it in as old Leonard hobbled over to take the reins. Once more Tamara was swung down to try and pull her ruined skirt out of the seeping crack of her bottom while urgently she scanned the expansive area before her and was relieved to see Jocelyn wave at her from over at the centre of the garden. At the far side of the enclosed space the long, low structure of the main house stood, it rambled into equally low wings that straggled almost the entire length of the far side, the Purbeck marble facing glinting in the bright sun. Apart from the lord and lady's accommodation they housed kitchens, dairies, breweries, dormitories for the staff who lived in and the domestic slaves they supervised, laundries, the bath house and the barracks for the small garrison. The rooms Tamara spent most of her time in were at the far end of the east wing. Here were the pleasure-slave dormitory and the dungeon where they were played with when they weren't running between the shafts of the wickerwork traps or serving in their owners' beds.

The wide gravel path surrounded an area of well-tended grass which itself was surrounded by tall poplar trees and in the centre of the grassed area was a marble fountain and pool. Around the pool were a series of arbours radiating outwards, formed by trellis fences supporting climbing plants and connected by arches in the trelliswork. It was towards this area that Tamara now led her husband. And once they had crossed the grass and entered an arbour through a clematis-fringed arch, Sir William stopped and looked about him in delight before bursting into laughter and catching Tamara up in his arms.

"You sly minx!" he laughed. "What a homecoming!"

Each trellis bore a hooded slave, either tied flat against the surface with her back outwards or hung by her wide spread ankles. Most of the arches likewise supported bodies in suspension and as Sir William and Tamara walked slowly along, stopping to sample a cunt here or a breast there, the decorative suspensions grew ever more exquisite. Finally, as they neared the fountain, they found two breast suspended slaves hung either side of an archway by ropes from a pergola. Their hands were tied neatly to the rings in the backs of their collars and they had plainly been hanging long enough for their initial struggles to have subsided. The bodies hung limply and the blind heads tilted upwards towards their tormented orbs, now stretched and distorted and turning darker red. Their legs hung slightly open and Sir William twirled his fingers idly inside a cunt that was dripping a steady drizzle of discharge. Tamara reached up to stroke the constricted and straining tits of the other. Although she touched them only lightly the slave groaned through her gag-bit. The two exchanged glances and Tamara, smiling and sultry fetched two pliable straps with wickedly narrow tips from where they had been hung on the arch.

Sir William knew the hoods the slaves were wearing with their attached wooden bits, they had been in his family for generations and the pads over the ears and eyes left a slave in sensation-heightening isolation that made them exceptionally sensitive. Maybe it was for that reason that the bits, buckled securely in the backs of the mouths, were pitted and scored by generations of slaves clenching their teeth as they endured their owners' pleasures. He also knew that they wouldn't hear anything.

"On the count of three," he suggested to his smiling wife. "One, two, three!"

In perfect unison they both launched the straps up and over the breasts. The pliable leather tips snapped down across the upper curves and bit deep into the curve of the breast farthest from the flagellator. The suspended slaves had no warning whatever and even through the bits the squeals of anguish rang through the arbour, their bodies convulsed, the stomachs attempting to clench and the legs trying to lift.

Tamara laughed in delight and biting her lip in malicious glee she lashed upwards again, striking across the impossibly engorged nipples with two strokes in quick succession. The result was a frenzied dance and more muffled screams, pale flesh flashing in the cool twilight under the trees as the slave kicked and twisted her legs. Sir William treated his similarly and then both tormentors waited until the legs had stopped thrashing about before delving upwards between the thighs. Again the suspended bodies shuddered from shock and fright at the touch but then in so far as their suspension allowed they relaxed and their legs parted farther to allow themselves to experience some less agonising pleasure. Tamara and Sir William worked on their respective slaves' cunts until they were squelching and the bodies' movements were becoming agitated again and then they left them to move on to the next arbour where Jocclyn waited with glasses of wine. Sir William, at last feeling that he was properly at home, pulled off his tunic and threw himself down onto a turf bench, resting his head on his wife's lap. She gestured to Jocelyn and the girl immediately knelt at her master's groin and began to unlace his trousers, she herself once more worked the sleeves of her gown down her arms to bare her breasts. Sir William propped himself up on one elbow and began to kiss the ripe swells of flesh and suckle at the thick and erect nipples presented for him while Jocelyn worked his thighs clear of the woollen trousers and began to use her prehensile tongue to lick his furious erection from balls to helm. He shifted slightly to open his legs farther and she obediently ducked her head under him and he sighed in pleasure as her studded tongue rasped at his anus and then licked its way forwards once more. She swept her long hair back and held it behind one ear as she took slow licks at the iron hard shaft, ensuring that her master got plenty of chances to see her long, pink tongue with its spectacular array of steel, working on him. Only when he was groaning in pleasure did she engulf him gently with her lips and begin to move her head up and down on him in long slow nods. He gripped one hand tightly in one of his wife's breasts and smothered the other with his mouth, making her yelp as she felt his teeth close round one tightly engorged tube.

It was Tamara who felt him tense as he prepared to ejaculate and she held Jocelyn's head firmly down on his cock as it jumped and spurted into her mouth, she choked once or twice but managed to contain the whole amount satisfactorily and the two women drew out every last second of their man's pleasure as his strong body bucked and thrust under them.

It was a few moments before Sir William could sit up and then stand to kick away his trousers and boots, he was lean, tanned and muscular so nudity held no peril for him and he was lord of all he surveyed in any case. Tamara more demurely covered her breasts again while Jocelyn, whose leggy frame was covered only in a short white tunic that ran to mid thigh, climbed to her feet and stood to one side licking her lips.

Husband and wife enjoyed another quick draught of wine and then arm in arm they went into the final arbour before Tamara's big homecoming surprise would be sprung. But even so this arbour delighted him.

Every noble house bought its children apprentice pieces to mark their transition into adulthood, she was usually an experienced pleasure-slave and acted as target practice for their whipcraft, training ground for their piercing skills and generally fulfilled the function of a living instruction manual for the owner of such a complicated mechanism as a woman.

In the next arbour Sir William's apprentice piece had been stretched out and he bounded forward to examine in detail what had been done to her while his wife looked on with an indulgent smile. The Courcey way with slaves didn't favour pet names, they just took the number of their pallet in the dormitory so the slave who had been with the family now for over fifteen years was still only known as Seven. Jocelyn, before Tamara had spotted the possibilities offered by her long tongue, had simply been Sixteen.

In her mid-thirties but still toned by hours of pony work, Seven had been wrenched into a spectacular display and Sir William congratulated his wife on her invention. The slave's wrists and ankles had been tied to an archway that stood at one end of a pergola, so that she was splayed in an X shape but she had additional pains to cope with.

An apprentice piece could look forward to repeatedly being pierced and then having the piercings removed and the holes left to heal before they were pierced again – frequently young hands shook with eagerness and sometimes labial holes took several goes to transpierce neatly. Nipples were sometimes pierced a little crookedly, or not quite tidily in line with each other. Currently Seven was sporting a recently inserted clitoral ring, a navel piercing and nipple rings plus a septum ring at her nose.

Tamara had had a chain passed through the clitoral ring and folded back to where two links could be slid onto one prong of a large iron staple. Smaller chains had similarly been passed through the nipple rings then passed up and over one horizontal beam of the pergola and down to slip onto the other prong of the staple. Then the staple had been pulled out into the centre of the arbour before finally being driven into the turf. The result was that Seven was not only spreadeagled but also forced to arch her body forwards by the traction on her nipples and clitoris. Dappled in shadow, her straining and helpless body presented a delightful tableau.

Sir William ran his hands over her quivering flesh affectionately. In deference to her long service she had been left unhooded but was still gagged. Her eyes were heavy lidded and her pupils dilated but she groaned her appreciation of the return of her master.

"Dear old Seven!" Sir William said as he looked at her. "I haven't seen her wearing that much gold for years. I had forgotten how well it suited her! I was hopeless with her to start with you know," he said, reminiscing to his wife as his fingers slipped down the bow-tight curve of the stomach, slid around the cruel chain and began to rummage inside the molten vagina behind the stretched clitoris. He moved closer to the slave and with his other hand casually toyed with her breasts. "The first time I tried her nipples I just didn't tie her down properly and she shook and struggled so much I made three false starts before I got the piercing tool through properly, Carlson said I could have made a better job with a shovel! I took her rings out and let her heal up twice before I did a halfway decent job. And her poor cunt, Tamara! I made a terrible mess of ringing her there. Mind you, it did teach me to make sure the needle was sharpened properly. But we got you done in the end, didn't we old girl?" He stroked the blonde head and then reached down to tug hard on the chain threaded through her clitoral ring, making her heave in her bonds, a long drawn out cross between a growl and a sigh escaped the gag.

"She had a slightly better time when I gave her this lot," Tamara told him dryly. Tamara's own apprentice piece had been sold by her parents before her marriage to Sir William, they had thought it better to move the girl on while she still had some value left.

Seven had been born into service as the daughter of another noble house's pleasure-slave. As such she was automatically a slave for life and had arrived at the Courcey's estate fully trained to the whip. The ensuing years had toughened her up to the point where her value to the family as whipping flesh and as a talented pony slave outweighed her value as merchandise and furthermore her experience would make her a demanding and capable slave minder when her usefulness under the lash was finished.

One day about a month previously Tamara had felt at a loose end. She had had an exquisite time a few days before that, boring a hole for a further stud in Jocelyn's tongue, Carlson had had to help hold her down but the resulting cunnilingus had more than justified the effort of the procedure but still the silence from Frankland was ominous and to relieve the tension she had decided to make some sort of start on preparing for Sir William's eventual homecoming. Seven with her large, well proportioned body and patient subservience had provided a suitable target. Jocelyn, by then settled down to life as a virtual mute and almost permanently between her mistress's thighs, provided eager help in working on the veteran slave.

Tamara looked at her husband fondling the trembling body in front of him and felt herself heat and melt as she recalled how, after an immensely protracted beating that had lasted most of the morning the sweat-gleaming and welted slave had been laid on the stone ringing-slab in the dungeon, tied down and left to recover while Tamara had taken Jocelyn to her bed chamber for some much needed relief. In mid-afternoon they had returned to finish the job.

Unfortunately Seven had gone off the boil over the hours she had been left and it had taken a robust thrashing of the sizeable breasts to make her cunt begin to ooze its sap once more and render her more amenable to further pain.

They had started with the septum, done the nipples and the navel and all had been accomplished efficiently, with little noise or squirming from the durable slave, but Tamara who had bent over the spread-open crotch, the cunt right on the edge of the slab and available for working on, recalled now how Jocelyn had held the clitoral hood back and the slave had tensed under her, knowing what was coming. The body had heaved at the piercing and even managed a slight twist to the torso. Only Jocelyn's own cunt, squashed down onto the slave's face had muffled the yell. That had displeased Tamara a little, it was hardly the first time she had been pierced there after all, but fortunately the thick needle was through and the ring had followed smoothly once the hole was established. This final passage of metal through the flesh had resulted in shivers racking the whole body and Tamara had held the cunt wide open to watch the thick, milky ejaculate pulse out of the vagina as Seven achieved an orgasm more powerful than most she had witnessed.

All this she now told her husband who admired the speed with which the skin had recovered from the beating and how well she endured her suspension and stretching.

Standing behind the slave, Tamara could nevertheless see that Sir William was being aroused by Seven's suffering and felt she had to make a move if her main surprise wasn't to be spoiled. He was likely to take her down and have her where they were. She reached for a slender riding whip hanging in readiness beside the arch and laid a scorching stripe across Seven's buttocks, slack but bunched by her posture. Somehow she managed to arch even further forwards and let out an anguished squeal through the gag. To make sure the spell was broken she cracked in one more buttock juddering lash and then stepped through the arch, lifting her skirt delicately to avoid the slave's right foot whilst ducking under her arm. Reaching her husband she encircled his rigid cock with her thumb and forefinger and then cupped his balls gently.

"If my lord will follow me, his real homecoming surprise will be revealed," she whispered and letting her fingers trail up his shaft she walked slowly forwards away from him.

He turned from Seven and laughed huskily. "My lady may lead me by the balls anywhere she wishes."

Leaving Seven to her own devices they passed through a further arch and out into the open lawn before the house's main entrance. Here there stood a long stone table at which meals were often taken during the summer. On this day, however, it was covered by a thick white sheet that was clearly covering something substantial, it was a something that was mounded and curved very curiously.

Tamara turned back to her husband as he emerged beside her.

"Now, my lord. See what I have bought for us while you were away."

His eyes ablaze with curiosity and excitement, Sir William strode forward and swept the sheet off the table. For a long second he made neither move nor sound.

"Two of them!" he whispered finally. "Two triple crowns! A brace! Never would I have thought we could own such priceless creatures!"

They lay, tied tightly down on their backs, head to toe, the curve of one's hip a perfect fit at the waist of the other. They were hooded but a tight pony tail of blonde hair spilled from the back of one and an equally neat tail of black hair from the other. Their breasts mounded softly up from the chests, hardly slipping to the sides at all. The long, thick nipples rose and fell as they breathed, lightly and evenly. Beneath the arch of the ribs the bellies were flat and ran smoothly down to shaven deltas between smooth-skinned, long and shapely thighs. And it was here that their crowning glory lay. High up on the inside of each woman's right thigh were branded three small crowns.

Sir William ran his hands lovingly over the smooth, unbeaten flesh then turned to Tamara. Laughing with delight he gathered her up and laid her down across the slaves, then lifted the skirt of her dress to reveal her long legs and her dusky lipped cunt with its mantle of sperm-crusted pubic hair.

"I see that your cunt is ready to entertain again. It would be churlish not to oblige," he said, smiling down at her as she wriggled atop the soft slave bodies beneath her until she was comfortable and ready to receive her lord.

"My body and the bodies of my slaves' are always at my lord's service," she whispered and once more bared her breasts for him then gasped in mingled pain and pleasure as her stinging cunt was invaded again and stretched wider than before as Sir William's massive cock speared her.

Three hours later, after a long bath and massage, Sir William and Tamara sat at their ease in the atrium and took a glass of wine before their supper.

"Master Sejanus brought me news of the sale and he said that the way the estate was performing we would have no problem in meeting the price," she shrugged. "So I just had to buy them! We'll be the envy of everyone who's anyone around here, William."

"They are a striking pair alright." Sir William agreed. "And I can't wait to get stuck into them later on but where is Sejanus? I need to talk to him."

"He said he'd be back tomorrow, something about needing to check on yields in the east. Now just relax and look forward to tonight!"

Triple crown slaves were the apogee of the Slavemaker's art. No one knew how he achieved such perfect submissiveness from women who had given the state problems in one form or another. Only the most intransigent cases were sent to him, noblewomen who refused to submit; renegades whose rebelliousness had become violent lawlessness; slaves who refused to bend the knee; women who had betrayed their country. Those who had been lucky enough to work on them swore that somehow the Slavemaker had contrived to leave them with memories of who they had once been at the same time as rendering them helpless to do anything but take perverse pleasure in submitting to those they had previously struggled against.

"Did they come with any provenance?" Sir William asked.

"None. They don't even have numbers. They're just blank slates for us to write on."

"Then come along, the sooner we sup, the sooner we can get started. I've arranged for Seven to be beaten at the table," he said, rising and making for the dining chamber.

Tamara made a moue of disappointment. "I was going to have Jocelyn. She took simply hours to make me come on the way to Southaven!" she said.

Sir William laughed. "Then have Carlson deal with her afterwards. We can stay and watch or leave him to it."

In the dining chamber, Thomas Carlson was just mounting Seven ready for the meal. She was kneeling with her thighs in the half moons cut into the far edge of the table, her hands were being tied behind her neck and Carlson who had run the house when Sir William had been a boy and had watched over his fumbling attempts to discipline and decorate Seven when she had first arrived, now inserted a wooden gag and pushed it hard into her mouth, making her rear her head and champ at it until it was buckled tightly at the back of her neck.

Once Sir William and Tamara were comfortably settled on their couches, domestic slaves brought in the various dishes and Carlson set about getting Seven to produce her thick secretions. Her rings shook and glittered in the lamplight as her body trembled under Carlson's experienced whip hand and gradually it began to shine with sweat as she arched and tried to twist away from the relentless lash. Muffled grunts began to escape the gag in answer to each thudding impact. Tamara ate with relish as she watched the display. She would have liked to lounge at her ease and watch Jocelyn suffer, but as long as some female or other was whipped for her, she couldn't find it in her to object to any particular one. With the skill borne of long experience, Carlson waited until Sir William was ready to move to the fish dishes before he wrapped the slave with the lash. Immediately he drew long drawn out groans from the woman as her breasts were targeted and the tip of the lash snapped round her ribs and vented its full spleen on her softest flesh. The nipple rings danced and sparkled in the light as the onlookers watched her shake and tremble in orgasm and Sir William reached forward to harvest the outpourings of her cunt. It was pungent and fragrant and complemented the dishes perfectly. Tamara had to admit that the flow was much greater than Jocelyn would have been capable of and pleasantly thick and sharp. Seven was forced to orgasm twice more and produced more sap than her owners could eat and when Carlson was told he could stop beating her, the strong thighs were streaked with shining trails of discharge. Briefly it occurred to Tamara to wonder what it must be like to be so desperate for a fuck that you would produce that much cunt sap under the whip and yet know that the whip was the closest you were going to get to a man. She closed her eyes in delight at the thought of how exquisite the suffering of slaves was and immediately knew she had to seek relief with the new purchases.

One look at her husband told her all she needed to know and as she stood up he joined her, his robes showing a definite bulge. She took his hand and began to lead him away but caught sight of Jocelyn hovering, not knowing if she was to be needed.

"Carlson!" Tamara called. "Give that idle slut Jocelyn fifty lashes for me."

The older man inclined his head. Tamara saw a look of apprehensive delight cross the girl's face. Of course, Carlson had often assisted at slave sessions and she was no stranger to the size of his cock. So the slut thought it would be worth a decent flogging for a subsequent fuck, did she?

Smiling with delighted malice, Tamara held the girl's eyes. "And when you've beaten her, Master Carlson.......fuck Seven will you?"

Jocelyn's face crumpled and, laughing happily, Tamara followed her husband to the bedchamber.

The floor was tiled and sported an exquisite mosaic of several satyrs enjoying women in a variety of positions. The walls were of marble facing on thick stone so that the underfloor heating kept it warm in winter but in summer it was cool enough to allow for vigorous sex and erotic cruelty in the hottest weather. The huge, four poster bed itself, which Sir William had had made especially as part of his wedding gifts to Tamara stood against the right hand wall as they entered. Spreadeagled between the posts at the foot of the bed the blonde slave had been mounted. The black haired one was knelt before the breast bars, her hands tied to the back of her neck and her ankles shackled to the floor. Both were now unhooded but were still gagged by the wooden bits.

Neither woman was a great beauty but both their bodies were more than acceptable, however their main attraction lay in the fact that any owner knew beyond any shadow of a doubt that there was simply nothing that could not be done with them. Sir William smiled at his wife as her hand lasciviously drifted across the aching hardness of his erection, then she walked across the room, loosening her gown as she went until it slipped off her shoulders as she reached the curtain of her dressing area. She blew him a kiss as she went inside to change and he, letting his own robe slip from his shoulders went to bind the black haired slave's tits. Two studded straps had been nailed to the lower bar and it had been adjusted to the proper height for her. She kept her eyes lowered as he approached and took her considerable weight of breastmeat in both hands then pulled and raised them slightly until she moved her torso forwards just enough so that her ribs grazed the side of the bar and the full extent of her breasts was on the top of it. Sir William gripped first the left strap and pulled it up then drew it closed over the top of the breast, located the tongue in the buckle and then paused. He could tell by the halting rhythm of her breathing that she was waiting nervously for the constriction to begin. So he left that breast and instead prepared the other one before returning to the left breast and suddenly yanking the strap tight. A strangled shriek greeted the pressure of the tines but one further yank and the buckle was fastened good and tight. The slave was panting as she absorbed the pain but was looking down at her right breast as Sir William went back to it. He tilted her head back and studied her face for a second. Her dark eyes were bright and clear, he could read unmistakable excitement as well as real fear – and maybe just a hint of anger at the bottom of the mix. How sweet it would be if the rumours were true and that even as they suffered and orgasmed, a triple crown slave was always aware that at some time in her life she had had dignity and free will.

Sir William smiled again as he gripped the strap and pulled it tight, then tighter still before buckling it. The slave was breathing in sobbing gasps as she looked down at her throttled tits bulging out from their constricted roots. He stood up and took down the whip he had requested be hung from the top bar of the frame and stepped back, then swiftly launched the first strike, the thin tails smacked down onto the tight skin and despite the maddening tines the slave attempted to rear backwards. The shocked groan that escaped the gag suggested that that was not advisable.

"Silly bitch! It's not as though it's the first time she's had them thrashed," Tamara said as she joined him. He gazed at her in admiration. Her thick, glossy brown hair flowed down onto her broad shoulders and she had on a wide, black leather collar, from the front a strap ran down between her breasts and then split into two when it reached her delta and the thin leathers passed between the outsides of her labia and her thighs, making the lips pout invitingly. He knew that behind her sweet little cunt the straps joined again and ran up between her invitingly round buttocks before being buckled to a waist strap. As they passed her anus, they supported a butt plug. Tamara loved being fucked by her husband while she was stuffed in her back passage. Her long legs were encased to the thighs in tight black, kid leather boots. Her cheeks had been rouged and her eyes were soft, the pupils enlarged by belladonna.

"I'm going to beat the slut by the bed," she told him and stalked away.

Sir William turned back to the job in hand.

After half an hour he paused for a rest. Before him the slave was dribbling helplessly around her gag, her head hung back and only strange gurgles emanated from her as the lashes bit into her. Her breasts were darkening from constriction and their upper surfaces were laced with thin but pulsing lines of darker red. Her thighs and stomach had not escaped either but Sir William knew that she would have to be released soon to enable the breasts to recover for further treatment but then Tamara approached, flushed and happy. She knelt before him without a word and took him into her mouth with smooth and well practised ease, then looked up at him and took her mouth off him for a moment.

"Beat the slut while I suck you, please, my lord."

The slave was watching Tamara with the heavy lidded eyes of the post orgasmic and the envy that could be read in them made him laugh out loud as he held his wife's head hard against his groin with one hand and recommenced the beating with the other. It only took the caress of Tamara's throat on his helm to trigger his climax and then he used both hands to hold her to him while he pulsed his spend out into her.

After that they released the breast constriction but left the slave where she was and turned their attentions to the slave at the bed end and both whipped her from opposite sides until her breasts and back were striped enough to have Sir William erect and ready for action again. Tamara knelt on the bed in front of the slave and supported herself by getting a grip on the woman's hips while she stuck her shapely bottom out. Sir William knelt behind her and worked his fingers inside her until she couldn't help mewing in urgent need. Only then did he move forwards enough to plunge his shaft between her open lips and sink into her sodden depths. The slight constriction of her opening, caused by the strapping only made the pleasure greater for him and he thrust in all the harder. She let herself be pushed forwards until her face was buried in the shaven cunt of the slave who lurched in her chains and moaned in delight but then yelped in shock as Tamara's sharp little teeth began to nip at her clitoris and her nails dug cruelly into the welts covering her haunches. Moving in long slow strokes, Sir William watched the women before him, the one being fucked into heaven the other being thrown towards an orgasm composed of agonised pleasure that she had no choice but to respond to. As he accelerated his rhythm he removed his grip from his wife's hips and took a firm hold on the shaking tits of the slave. He gritted his teeth as he felt his climax approach and sank his fingers into the soft cushions. The spreadeagled woman threw her head back and screamed, thrusting her hips savagely at Tamara's face, careless of whether she was tongued or bitten. All three climaxed together, Tamara giving her characteristic short gasps as she came, the slave screaming with all her force and sluicing thick ropes of come onto her Mistress's face.

When she recovered, Tamara made her pay for her impudence in besmirching her so. She drove a long, multi-tailed whip up between the spread thighs until the slave couldn't come any more and her head slumped onto her chest. Only then did Tamara lie on the bed and open her legs for her lord who had enjoyed a refreshing glass of wine whilst watching his wife at work. With her back passage already stuffed and a thoroughly whipped slave hanging at the bottom of the bed, she was already gasping her way to orgasm as Sir William's cock slid into her, squeezing against the plug and sending rippling shards of ecstasy running through her. The rutting was urgent this time and Sir William pounded into her until he came as she was sliding down the slopes of post orgasm. This time the aftershocks went on for a long time and they lay together panting and happy. Sated for a moment.

But after a few minutes Sir William stood up slowly and Tamara joined him, together they went to assess the slave who had been breast bound. She was still whimpering softly from where the blood was flowing back into squashed flesh and intensifying the pain of the beating. She was clearly ready for some more treatment. Tamara unshackled her ankles and had her stand, then she led her across to the rack. Normally even a slave as resigned to her life as Seven would try and hang back and, if ungagged, beg for mercy when faced with being stretched out for a merciless beating. But to Tamara's delight, with her hands still tied behind her neck the slave contrived to climb up onto the flat, table-like top and kneel patiently awaiting the order to lie either on her face or back. Tamara simply tapped the wooden surface in front of her. Immediately she lay face down and Tamara untied her wrists, instantly the slave reached out to have them chained to the drum by her Mistress while her Master dealt with her ankles.

Tamara stood back and admired the way the solid wood of the rack's surface forced the buttocks into their full roundness and emphasised the graceful curve of the back with the pale swells of the breasts squashing out to the sides of the chest. However a few turns on the drums had improved matters still further, now the body in full extension revealed its full beauty, not so much in its physical form but in the way the thighs, buttocks and back were pulled into total immobility by the tension, only a rearing of the head was possible to acknowledge the lash.

Tamara selected a single tailed, heavy but pliable strap whilst Sir William chose a whip that split into many thin tails about two feet from the end and wielded it across her back. Tamara relished how her strap smacked loudly into the quivering mounds of the buttocks, leaving bright red flares on the skin. Across her back a network of thin lines criss-crossed right across the full expanse and round onto her breast. Under the double assault the slave held her tongue until orgasm began to claim her and odd bird-like cries began to issue from behind the unforgiving wooden stopple.

Tamara took a rest and watched her husband's now re-hardened cock wag as he belaboured his new slave.

"Do you think it's good for them to be allowed so much pleasure?" she asked.

Sir William too stopped, a little red in the face from his exertions. "No. But tonight I wanted to hear how they orgasm so that in future we'll know if they disobey an order not to come. They'll have plenty of sessions devoted solely to our pleasure, don't you worry."

"My lord is indeed a wise and cunning man. I would not have thought of that," Tamara said.

"You're too fond of your own pleasure!" her husband agreed grinning widely at her across the welted slave.

Tamara giggled and reached out to delve between the parted thighs, her fingers found a hot and sticky vulva still leaking its nectar onto the stained wood of the rack. She withdrew them and went to the bottom of the rack to release the tension slightly on the drum so that she could then release the chains that held the ankles.

She slapped one thigh. "Up, you horny bitch!"

Obediently the slave shuffled her knees up under her so that her bottom stuck up in the air.

"There! All ready for my lord's pleasure," she said.

"And once I've fucked her?"

"Oh then I'll have no choice but to cunt whip her till I have to come."

"I wronged you. You are generous and unselfish to a fault!" Sir William said, grinning as he climbed up behind the slave.

He knelt on the hard wood behind the slave and savoured the sight of the helpless arousal before him. The promise of a cunt whipping had wreaked havoc with her and her sex flesh sported pearls of thick juice. He plunged into her and, bracing himself on her hips, simply rammed himself to his climax. Then he returned to the bed and watched as Tamara stood over the slave's head at the rack and did exactly as she had said she would. The slave, having been well fucked by him was now helplessly crying out an acknowledgement of each lash that splatted down into the morass of her groin. But she made no move to try and change her position from the one in which she had been fucked. Her bottom stayed raised, wriggling from side to side as Tamara sighted down the buttock cleft for each stroke. The lash was sending up sprays of his own spend mixed with her juices as his wife masturbated, her legs spread wide, her hand almost up to its wrist inside herself as she spurred her new slave ever onwards.

Too fond of her own pleasure? Of course she was, but that was what had attracted him to her. There was not a shred of dishonesty about her. She loved whipping slaves and cared not a jot who knew it.

As he watched, his cock slowly pulsing back to life, she halted the beating and shrieked as she achieved yet another orgasm and fell to her knees. Sir William roused himself and stood up, then approached the spreadeagled blonde, his come-slimy cock now fully rearing up once more. He went to stand behind the slave and reached under her to dip his fingers into her seething little sheath, extract the juice and use it to soap her tighter entrance. Then he grabbed his hard shaft and positioned it, then thrust in. There was just a pleasing amount of resistance before she surrendered and he watched the tight mouth stretch wide to receive the full length as he plunged in up to the hilt. Vaguely he heard a gag-muffled groan but it was of no interest to him, the caress of her inner tissues and the way she relaxed as he went in then gripped skilfully as he withdrew was what he was after. It was a divine feeling, almost as good as mouth fucking, to his mind. Tamara came and knelt on the bed to bite and chew on the engorged nipples and torment the clitoris until the slave finished a shattering climax just as Sir William filled her backside.

Soon afterwards they summoned Carlson to return the women to their cell to be chained for the night and then husband and wife slept deeply and peacefully in each other's arms and dreamed of further sessions of delicious cruelty. So deeply did they sleep that even the unfamiliar sound of horses' hooves on the gravel outside the house didn't disturb them. The first they knew of their arrest was when troopers from the Queen's Household marched into the room.

Interlude.

On board 'The Wayfarer' bound for Alba from Frankland.

"Fifteen!" Isabella's voice sounded harsh and rasping even to her own ears but that was hardly surprising considering the combination of stinging pain and unbearable longing that slammed through her suspended body as the whip smacked down between her wrenched open legs. She was hanging by her ankles from the ship's rigging and undergoing a twenty lash beating on her wide spread thighs and crotch. Her arms had been pulled down and apart, her wrists shackled to rings set into the deck. At each lash her stomach convulsed and her legs tried vainly to close. The reaction was instinctive and she resented it. She desperately wanted to offer up everything she was and everything she had to the man who was the centre of her universe.

“Uh!.........Sixteen!” The call was late as the sailor who was whipping her from behind her back must have moved forwards, making the tails of the whip smack heavily into her lower stomach. Her voice was a croak and she was still choking a little at the next impact.

“Seven…..teen! Seventeen!” she managed, shaking her head to clear her face of tangled, wind blown and sweat-matted, blonde hair. Her cunt stung unbearably and at the same time ached for something to fill it. She knew that if He ordered it she would stand, spread legged in the middle of the deck and bring herself off with her own hands. The Lady Isabella Dulac had become a slut and she knew it. In the dark desolation that were the hours without her lord, the Slavemaker, the voice of Lady Isabella shrieked and screamed inside her head even as her hands, if she was lucky enough to have them free, roved around her battered body, reliving every exquisite torment that had been visited on her and she would masturbate until she obtained some kind of peace. Even the certain knowledge that she had been administered some kind of potion in her food or in her water could not affect her headlong rush into passionate subjection to his every whim. The crueller and more humiliating it was the more pride she took in submitting to it. But still somewhere inside her the woman she had once been looked on in tortured disbelief.

“Eighteen!” Involuntarily her stomach clenched and her thighs tried to close once more as her cunt was stung by the heavy leathers. She craned her head up, looking through the valley of her breasts and feeling her insides melt at the blatantly lewd way her legs were parted in the brightness of broad daylight, the sinews drawn tight by her suspension. There were bound to be salaciously grinning sailors standing around watching her lap up the pain inflicted on her. She let her head fall back and sought the robed and hooded figure of the man who had come to mean more to her than her own life. He stood motionless a few feet away from her and his presence stilled the shrill screaming of Lady Isabella's voice. In his presence she found complete peace with herself as an abject and devoted slave. Without him she was guilt-ridden and horribly confused.

"Aah!.........Nineteen!" It was the hardest lash of this current beating and the tails landed smack on her throbbing clitoris, making her jerk painfully against her bonds even as she felt her cunt spasm in delight. She tried to relax as she waited for the final – and surely the harshest - lash by fixing her eyes on her beloved lord. The ship was making good speed ahead of a brisk breeze that had the sail above her booming and snapping, and yet nothing about him, neither his body nor his robes moved. It was as if he existed in a slightly different world. And never, not even in this bright light, did any chink of it seem to penetrate the gloom within his cowl. She had often heard tales of the Guardians' mysterious powers. She now believed everything she had heard.

"Uh!.......Twenty! Twenty taken, my lord!" she managed to gasp as the final lash cracked across her exposed groin, the leathers gleefully digging deep between the obligingly parted inner lips of her cunt.

She felt the sailor who had administered the whipping release her hands and then she cried out in shocked pleasure as she felt the ball handle of the whip rammed unceremoniously downwards into her. She knew what her lord required; a show of complete and utter abandonment to any humiliation a woman could imagine. Eager to show him how obedient she was she reached her nearly numb arms upwards and ignored the ironic cheers of the onlookers as the fingers of one hand slipped over her clitoral hood and began to rub at the inflamed stump while the other hand seized the whip handle firmly and began an urgent masturbation.

It didn't take her long to attain a rippling climax that tore through her making her almost curl up until her face was on a level with her tormented crotch. She pummelled her insides with the whip handle and rasped her clitoris mercilessly hard even as she shook and trembled like a victim of the ague. She never even felt herself being taken down; the thump of the decking against her face bringing her round to find herself held by one leg by the sailor who had flogged her.

Her lord gave the slightest of nods and she was allowed to fall in a heap at his feet. He crooked the index finger of his right hand and turned away. She picked herself up, suctioned the whip out of her viscous cunt and crawled after him. He went into his cabin in the stern superstructure and she followed, by the time she entered he was seated in a throne-like seat and another woman was kneeling by his side, looking up adoringly at him.

Instantly Isabella was consumed with the bitterest hatred she had ever felt. It swept over her in a dizzying wave that almost made her sick. But then her lord spoke and just as instantly it was swept away as she drank in his every mellifluously pronounced word whilst daring only to fix her eyes on his waist.

"Over the past weeks you know you have been given something that alters the way you experience pain and pleasure?"

"Yes, my lord," she whispered respectfully.

"The effects, if I stopped administering it now, would wear off in time and you would be free."

She shivered in terror of that thought. He spotted it and laughed softly. That laugh she had learned to love and dread. It usually presaged an escalation of whatever torment she was undergoing into scarlet realms of blinding sensation that left her limp and trembling in its wake, wondering if a woman could die of ecstasy. He had laughed like that the first time he had hung her by her breasts over a ring of candles and watched her dance on air. That laugh had preceded the addition of a clitoral piercing to a session that had already seen her breasts run clean through with long steel needles, placed with expert care and knowledge.

But on that day he merely gestured at a glass of clear liquid standing on a low table beside him and the kneeling girl.

"But if you were to drink of that……now that would make all the changes I have brought about in you permanent, see. Irrevocable. And the part of you that is the slave will be much more powerful and will be able to control the voice of Lady Isabella. Also it will mean that I will forever be your lord. Whoever you are given to, ultimately I will know that it is me you serve. And you will of course never doubt it for a second."

He paused and Isabella waited for the resumption of his lilting Cambrian voice and his strangely accented Alban.

"You are quite free not to drink it, Isabella," he said, leaning forward in his chair. In vain she searched the darkness of his cowl for a gleam from his eyes, any clue as to what he looked like or to what his expression was.

"Freya here has drunk it." He administered the coup de grace. Isabella's eyes flicked over to the hateful girl who was smiling pityingly at her.

"I will drink, my lord. I want only to belong to you and submit to your will in all things."

"Very well. The mixture needs only one more ingredient." He sat back and Freya reached for the glass, then with her free hand she groped the folds of the Slavemaker's robe apart until she had freed his long slender cock. Isabella had known the robe opened that way, on plenty of occasions she had seen his divine shaft spearing other women's bodies as he sought relief from the arousal of mistreating her, his robe was never removed and his cock, long, slender and with a gentle curve to its veined length and a superbly shaped helm crowning it, was the only part of his body she had ever seen, apart from the hands that worked such careful devastation on her body. If sacrificing the rest of her life to his service was the price of seeing more and perhaps getting to touch what the detestable Freya was now vigorously masturbating, it was one she was willing to pay.

As she watched, spellbound, the Slavemaker sighed deeply and relaxed as thick creamy spunk spurted hard from his cock and Freya skilfully held the glass at the correct angle to gather every drop. Then, as Isabella shivered with gut-churning envy, she bent her head and put out her tongue to lick the quivering helm clean. It was clearly done to enrage Isabella and it succeeded perfectly. Freya climbed to her feet, her linen gown rustling as she walked forwards, her breasts gently swaying beneath the light material. She held the glass out to Isabella who knelt up to receive it, the clear liquid now clouded and laced with strings of sperm. She glanced over at her lord to ensure he was watching and drained the bitter tasting liquid in one gulp.

The Slavemaker sat back and made an infinitesimal gesture with his index finger again. She stood up and as haughtily as she could handed the glass back to Freya.

"You two will entertain the crew tonight by wrestling for them, the loser will be heavily flogged. It will be you, Isabella. The job I have for you starts tomorrow and you will need to be clearly marked," he said. Freya smiled broadly and stuck out her tongue before going to the cabin door and summoning a crewman to return Isabella to the cage she was kept in below decks.

It was an hour before dawn when her lord and master came for her. Isabella stretched and groaned as she awoke, every move reviving pains from being thrown round the deck by Freya in front of cheering men, pains from the subsequent beating which had been one of the longest she had ever undergone and aches and stings from her abused anus and vagina, still complaining from the crew's attentions. Still at least she was handed a rough weave, mid-thigh length tunic and some crude sandals before she was let out and led along the main gangway between the ranks of benches the galley slaves usually sat on.

Up on deck a cool breeze was blowing and the Slavemaker, unusually brisk and businesslike, led her to his cabin. On the way she was delighted to see Freya hung by her wrists from part of the rigging, her gown ripped and her spread thighs caked in dried sperm. So she had not been the only one who had entertained the crew.

In the cabin was a simple breakfast and as she shamelessly scoffed as much bread and honey as she could, the Slavemaker showed her a large map of southern Alba and gave her detailed instructions.

Then they had to clamber down a net slung over the gunwales and take their places in the ship's boat which was then rowed towards the shore that Wayfarer was now anchored close to.

As the keel scrunched onto the shingle of the shore, Isabella leapt into the shallows and waded to the beach. She turned briefly to watch her master as the boat took him back out to sea. She had sat next to him and even the cold of the water and the dawn breeze couldn't penetrate the warmth that wrapped her, the warmth of the thought that she had been so close to him. Part of her wondered how much effect the previous day's drink was having but most of her just basked in the glory of doing her master's will. She watched until the boat was just a speck that disappeared against the bulk of the Wayfarer and then she turned inland. She scrambled off the beach and made for a track that wound through heathland until it met a road she had been shown back on board ship. But just before the sea was out of sight, as she had been told to do, she lifted the front of her tunic and reached up under it until her fingers encountered her clitoris. She pressed her forefinger hard against it and rubbed it as she would when masturbating. But instead of concentrating on the physical sensations which that produced she concentrated on forming a vivid mental image of the robed and mysterious figure of her lord.

And instantly she was with him.

Whether or not it was some property of the elixir she had drunk to bind her to him, she had no idea. But it was as if she was sitting beside him as the boat came under the lee of the ship and moved into its shadow. Entranced she kept her finger rubbing at herself and gasped in amazement as the hooded head turned towards her; he knew she was there beside him. Her heart leaped for joy as she was suddenly quite certain that somewhere inside that impenetrable darkness he was smiling. Again she was bathed in an inner warmth. Her master was pleased with her.

"Go and do my bidding, Isabella. And when you return I shall reward you." His voice seemed to explode into her head, as though he was speaking directly inside it.

Weak from a combination of pleasure and shock, Isabella Dulac tottered inland, determined to play her part in whatever would benefit her lord.

Owen Daibron relaxed in the stern of the boat as it came alongside the Wayfarer and he let slip the glamour he had wrapped himself in while he had trained Isabella. It was not an easy thing to keep in place but he found that making himself almost invisible helped instil awe and trepidation into females in the early stages of enslavement. However it was pleasant to feel the breeze in his hair and on his face once more.

The contact from this slave had been a good one! Vision had been crystal clear and he had almost been able to taste her pleasure and excitement. The king was luckier than he knew, barely one in ten women broke so utterly, so quickly - but Isabella was one of them. She was permanently under his spell now and would give her life in his service if it was required. That gave the king's plan a good chance of success and in that case it would be advisable to keep the Guardians' allegiance to him, for the time being at least. If the Queen began to get too powerful then there was plenty of time to rethink that policy.

He swarmed up the net and vaulted easily over the ship's rail at the top then strode up onto the poop deck to talk to the captain.

"How many teams of galley slaves do you carry?" he demanded.

"Six. We keep two spare," the man replied.

"Rotate the shifts as you see fit but I want this ship rowed all day and all night until we make harbour at

Deeping Pool. You can commandeer fresh teams there. I must get word to the king and ride overland to be in Cambria inside a week! Go to it man!"

He watched the startled captain run down the stairs and begin to shout orders.

All the pieces were now on the board and the game was afoot. The king was an astute tactician and he would almost certainly be able to bottle up the Franks and leave them to the Count of Burghund. But could it be done in time? It was down to Owen to rendezvous with his brethren. Then they would have to muster what forces they could from the military academies in Cambria where all young Alban men were sent at the age of fifteen to learn the longbow and all the arts of warfare. Having done that they would then need to stand ready to march south and east in case events didn't go as the king hoped. In only a few months, the issue of who ruled Alba would be settled one way or the other.

Below decks the drum began to beat out a brutal rhythm as the oars were unshipped and the whips began to crack. He made his way down onto the main deck and surveyed the dishevelled form of Freya, still hanging in the rigging, bound by immensely complex nautical knots. He grabbed the arm of a sailor hurrying by.

"Take her down, sluice her clean and bring her to my cabin," he said.

"But the captain's just ordered me to........"

Owen tightened his grip and the man went pale, he made an attempt to struggle and then sagged to his knees.

The Slavemaker smiled down at him pleasantly.

"My cabin. Five minutes."

He held his grip for a second longer and then let the man go. He scurried away towards the limp female figure, rubbing his arm and casting terrified looks behind him.

Feeling that the day had got off to a good start, Owen strode on towards his cabin, noting that the rhythm of the drum had accelerated and the ship was already making good way. He allowed his mind to turn to making a choice of implements to pass the time with on Freya's willing body.

CHAPTER FOUR.
The Courcey Estate.

By mid afternoon the trial of Sir William Courcey had been concluded. He was convicted of having withheld taxes due to the crown in times of war and was thus a traitor. Magistrate Dunbar had sat glumly and helplessly as the reeve, Peter Sejanus had produced damning evidence of consistent fraud, culminating in the purchase of two valuable slaves from an agent who worked for the Slavemaker himself with money that by rights belonged to the crown.

He had been unable to do any more than make some mild examination of what he knew to be false accounting, because the queen had sent one of her judges down to supervise the case and Dunbar didn't fancy incurring the queen's wrath, Sir William was to be taken to Tamesbury in chains and have sentence passed on him by the queen herself.

Of course Lady Tamara should have taken a much more active interest in the running of the estate but in her defence, Sejanus had been highly recommended by several previous employers. Dunbar could only think that someone had promised him the pick of Sir William's property – and he felt he could safely wager his own life on the two triple crown slaves being Sejanus' property by sunset that day.

Sir William had treated the proceedings with the contempt they deserved and had contented himself with a shout of 'Long Live the King!' as he was hustled away to spend the night in his own cells.

Now the judge turned to Dunbar, a grim smile on his face.

"The Lady Tamara Courcey is to be judged and sentenced next. I am of the opinion that we do not need to bother the excellent Master Sejanus any further, we have heard all we need to so I propose we move directly to sentencing. I believe the need is for galley slaves currently, do you think she is sturdy enough for a couple of years at the oar before being sent to the Slavemaker?"

The phrasing was carefully designed not to allow him any leeway to protest her innocence – if not her financial acumen.

He sighed.

"I believe she is in good health, my lord, but beyond that I cannot comment." It was poor recompense for the long nights of delicious debauchery he had frequently enjoyed at the villa. The Courceys were generous hosts and never stinted on the availability of slaveflesh when guests came calling. Somehow he would help them, but just at present there was nothing he could do.

The judge gave him a sharp look.

"We shall see how her health is," he said. "I shall pronounce the sentence. You will carry it out. I hear good reports of your abilities as a flogger and look forward to watching you at work. Of course I always travel with my own assistant."

The judge paused and Dunbar followed his glance, a huge man was standing at the back of the room. "But I'm quite sure he won't be needed today," he concluded.

The meaning was plain. A flogging was inevitable and if he didn't satisfy the judge that he had carried it out thoroughly, Tamara might end up taking a double dose. No one cared much how the wife of a traitor fared at the whipping post.

Tamara was dressed in a green satin gown cut low at the neckline and with a full, flowing skirt. She was pale but held her head up proudly, even though the rise and fall of her prominent breasts betrayed her anxiety.

The soldiers brought her to a halt directly before the two chairs the judge and the magistrate occupied. Dunbar tried not to meet the imploring look she cast him when she saw him.

"Lady Tamara Courcey, the court is satisfied that the wife is at least as guilty of these heinous crimes as the husband. The evidence of fraud is incontrovertible and therefore, by the authority vested in me by His Majesty King Edward of Alba, I sentence you to one hundred lashes of the standard punishment whip and to a day in the village stocks, two years' enslavement at the oar of one of His Majesty's galleys and finally you are to be sent to the Slavemaker. The price you fetch at auction when he is finished with you will be paid into the royal treasury. Have word sent out that the Lady Tamara Courcey will be placed in the stocks first thing tomorrow morning."

Tamara gave a cry of despair and started towards Dunbar, her hands held out; begging for help. The soldiers dragged her back and he found himself under the gimlet stare of the judge again.

"Chain her up for the night in the stables," he managed. "Stand guard and don't let her talk to her husband."

Nothing was as pleasing to the downtrodden female population of any town or village than the plight of a noblewoman come to grief. And the next morning, as Tamara, dressed only in a rough woollen shift, crawled out of the cage in which she had been driven from the villa and stood up, she saw a dense crowd, mainly female, with bags full of goodies with which to pelt her before the flogging commenced. The stocks stood on the green, just beside the scaffold with its sinister gibbet. They consisted of two simple, heavy beams with four semi circles cut in them. They were hinged at one end, bolted at the other and would hold the ankles and wrists of the victim. One of the soldiers mockingly dusted off the grass before inviting her to sit. She tried to adopt a disdainful expression as she made to take her position but the judge intervened.

"The prisoner will strip," he said.

"My lord!" Dunbar butted in, shocked into an outburst. Usually a noblewoman was allowed to keep a scrap of clothing through a public punishment – even at the whipping post or frame a loin cloth of some sort was usually allowed.

"You wish to defend the wife of a traitor, magistrate? I shall be sure to inform Her Majesty of your desire to lessen her deserved humiliation."

Dunbar subsided and Tamara had no choice but to stand quietly while her shift was ripped from her and a ribald jeer went up from the crowd. One of the soldiers pinched a buttock and from the laughter she assumed he was leering. Another one grabbed a nipple and led her forwards by it. He pinched so hard that tears half-blinded her and she was grateful for the curtain they drew across the faces of scornful, jeering peasants, even now beginning to fumble in their bags for rubbish to fling at her. They were the first tears she had cried.

Although the night had been long and horrible she was more fearful for her beloved William than she was for herself. She knew enough about the whip to know that Dunbar wouldn't wreak any lasting harm on a fit young woman, even if – as she suspected – he would have to use it at full strength. Slavery and the thought of the horrible things the Slavemaker was capable of terrified her but she was determined she would escape. But William? The queen was known to be moving against her husband, King Edward and she had some support in the country from those fed up with the war and with the roving bands of female renegades now at large. She would want to pass the Courcey estate to one of her followers and so William would have to be disposed of permanently, but Tamara had faith that somehow he would escape and join the king, whose favour she knew he had. That was probably why Sejanus had been bribed to perjure himself, in order to ruin one more of the king's supporters. Her thoughts had whirled on and on all night as she listened to the soldiers taking the haulage slaves again and again. Some of them leaned over the door of the stall in which she was held and gloated over her from time to time. But there was obviously an order out that she was off limits. The judge probably wanted her to savour the full depths of her ruin and face her day's punishment with a fairly clear head.

The grass tickling her labia as her wrists and ankles were locked into place brought her back to the present and she looked up to see Dunbar give her a look of helplessness before he rode off behind the judge. Two soldiers were left to make sure that no lasting damage was done her and as the riders left, the fusillade began.

She was bent nearly double, her knees bent, her legs spread wide and her arms out straight for her wrists to be held between her ankles, even so the accuracy of some of the throwing meant that her lower stomach and even her groin got a fair pounding from rotten potatoes and tomatoes. The dregs of cooking pots were emptied over her head and the filth massaged into her hair gleefully. The soldiers didn't mind if her breasts were tweaked and mauled as they swung beneath her torso. Cabbages and heavy balls of mud rained down on her dazed head and all the time there was the deafening noise of jeers about her being not so stuck up now. Someone found a stick and began prodding her between her spread legs with it; the soldiers didn't seem to mind people coming right up to the front of the stocks. Tamara became increasingly disorientated as the mob grew bolder in the face of the soldiers' cheerful acquiescence; her head rocked from blows from mud balls that had stones embedded in them, someone kicked her in the side. She even began to think that the rest of her sentence would be irrelevant; it would all end here and now. But at last the soldiers moved in and made sure she was saved for later. From then on the abuse became more sporadic and controlled. One of the men came forward and to delighted cheers from the crowd, pulled out his cock and began to masturbate.

"Give her a full load!"

"Bet you can't get it on her tits from there!"

And from a woman; "Get yer hands off that, John Brooks! Let me do it. I'll fetch more pints out of you to pour over that spoiled rotten bitch!" That drew the biggest cheer and as Tamara blinked her eyes clear and gazed out from under the filth-clogged veil of her hair she saw a heavily built woman give the cock a really hard wanking and soon gobbets of thick, slimy spend splatted onto her cheeks and slithered down her face. Another man stepped forwards to see if he could hit her tits. From behind her another load spattered her back.

It was only a matter of time, she realised, before she got more than spunk and it didn't really surprise her that it was a woman who first hoisted her skirts and squatted over her from behind so she could piss all down her back. All Tamara could do was lower her face and screw her eyes up in disgust as the men began to step forwards.

At midday the crowd withdrew to the local inn for lunch and Tamara was left a shivering wreck, dripping and stinking. Unrecognisable from the soignée, cool Lady of the Manor she had been only the day before.

Spitting and spluttering, she at last dared look up to see the holiday in full swing across the green, a fiddler played and people danced and drank. One of the soldiers came to stand in front of her.

"I was thinking I might let you suck me, but I wouldn't insult my cock now," he said and laughed as he walked off to join the villagers with his companion.

Throughout the long afternoon, Tamara was pelted with more refuse and beaten with sticks. The slops from the inn's barrels were poured over her – and in second hand form she became acquainted with all the ale and wine the villagers had drunk over lunch. Then there was more spunk. And when every last ounce of malice and envy had been worked out on her, the riders returned and she was taken to be flogged.

Of course it took several buckets of clean but cold well water to return her to a state in which she was deemed presentable enough to face the whip but at last she staggered up the steps and Dunbar raised her arms before fastening her wrists to the end of the chain that hung from the gibbet arm.

"I can spare you nothing!" he managed to whisper as he tied her.

"I know!" she hissed back. "Just make sure William escapes back to the king."

"I will. And I will do what I can for you tonight."

He stood back and Tamara heard the expectant hush of the crowd settling down to enjoy the last part of the day's entertainment.

She gritted her teeth against the bitter, stinging pain about to assault her. She well knew the way the whip would drive her to skip and spin at the chain's end; any girl was helpless to prevent herself from doing that in the face of a sturdy length of pliable leather wielded by a skilful and strong man and so the villagers would have their fun.

Dunbar did not disappoint her or the crowd. He laid into his work with every indication of pleasure. Tamara was screaming after only ten lashes and dancing so wildly that she was given a brief rest at twenty. She had had no idea of how much the whip hurt. Now she understood why she was always obeyed so instantly by her own slaves. But as she hung by her wrists, her chest heaving as she panted and sobbed all at once, fires raging from the backs of her thighs right up to her shoulders, with outlying conflagrations reaching around her ribs and coming dangerously near her breasts and crotch. She briefly wondered how her slaves always managed to find a reason for arousal in the midst of such blazing pain. It was probably because they were born to expect it, she decided, whereas she was far more refined and therefore suffered all the more acutely. She flicked away some hair from in front of her eyes and saw Dunbar standing in front of her, the whip was coiled in his powerful hand and he stood with his thickly muscled legs slightly apart. He was waving and smiling to the crowd; oblivious to her pain. And like a hammer blow in her chest it hit her that that was how she had used to enjoy seeing him when he had been a guest at a session in their dungeons. He was a powerful and steady flogger equipped with a divine length of cock that William had graciously allowed him to sink into her depths on occasions. But now the whip-seared, naked and desirable piece of womanhood hanging in chains before him was herself and she had eighty lashes still to take and he had a huge erection.

He started in again. This time, as he was working from in front of her, she saw the lash drawn back and then snap forwards, obscenely eager to bite into her flesh. She screamed and lifted her left thigh, trying to spin away and shield herself but Dunbar knew his business well and at the second lash the whip cut into the inside of her right thigh. Instinctively she lifted it too, taking her weight on her wrists and the lash bit again across her lower back. She shrieked and spun back, putting her feet back down and trying to flee to the fullest extent of the chain. Dimly she realised that she was completely defeated, Dunbar was choreographing her every twist and turn and the crowd was lapping up her abject fear and her every scream.

At thirty he rested her again and this time relieved the arousal he had built up. Tamara was shaking and sweating so much she hardly felt his big hand push between her trembling thighs and his thick fingers start to pry her open. To start with, that was what he had to do; she was dry and hostile. But after only a few seconds of probing he had gained quite a deep penetration and Tamara began to be aware of him through the fog of burning pain. But when he eventually took her properly from behind to cheers from the onlookers she was still tight and difficult. He had to thrust into her and haul her back onto him before he could penetrate to his full length and she cried out in pain once he began to fuck her in earnest.

It was as she hung sobbing from her chain, her legs still reluctant to support her and the magistrate's sperm oozing out of her, that she saw him carelessly shake out the lash and prepare to go on beating her and she got a sudden bolt of arousal that shocked her to the core. It was the very cruelty that was being inflicted on her naked, helpless form that was the key. Driven beyond any region she had ever visited before she got a brief glimpse of how slaves felt. Suddenly Dunbar was pure maleness, all strength and arrogance and she was helpless woman, a toy to be beaten or fucked as it pleased him and a shameful surge of pleasure in this thought ran through her.

The moment passed however as the whip bit into her again and didn't stop until she had taken forty lashes. Then one of the men in the crowd paid handsomely to fuck her. This time she was much wetter and almost came when he did.

She was fucked again at sixty and although too pain-racked to bc fully aware, she thought she came.

From then on she was scarcely aware of anything, but Dunbar used all his skill to prevent her sinking into a sort of half-conscious stupor that would rob the crowd of its entertainment. He altered the pace of the lashes, he flicked at her between the legs to make her jump. He landed excruciatingly accurate blows across her nipples, making her try and draw in her chest and spin away in the aftermath. At seventy, eighty and ninety lashes she was fucked again and the judge pocketed the proceeds for the crown. At the end of the sentence Tamara Courcey was a sad remnant of the woman she had been only twenty-four hours previously. Sobbing helplessly she dangled at the end of the chain, her head sunk down between her agonised arms, her feet trailing on the planks of the scaffold, she was a mass of narrow scarlet welts, skilfully and cruelly applied to every inch of available flesh. Dunbar took her down and hoisted her over his shoulder. The last thing she could remember was the sight of the steps, lurching past below her dangling arms as she hung down his back. Strangely, her last thought was to wonder if she had come during the last times she had been fucked.

A soft metallic noise woke her. She sat up and nearly screamed through her parched throat and lips as her body exploded into a firework display of different aches and pains. Fortunately it was her parched state that prevented a scream from penetrating the dark. As her eyes became accustomed to the moonlight she looked around at the grounds of the villa, where the cart with her cage on it had been left overnight. Nothing stirred, but then she caught sight of the tunic and sandals lying just by the door and she scrambled towards them to cover her nakedness. As she gingerly pulled the tunic on, wincing as occasionally she touched a welt, her hands nudged the door which swung slowly open. Hardly daring to breathe she stared round again. She could see no one. In furtive haste and stifling her groans, she scrambled to the ground on stiff and uncertain legs.

Perhaps this was Dunbar's promised help and then again perhaps it was a trap but in any case Tamara was past caring and she tottered weakly across the lawns towards the wicket gate that the washer women used on laundry days and which led out to the moat. From there she could swim quietly across without disturbing the lookout and disappear into the night.

From the deep shadows beside the house's main entrance, magistrate Dunbar watched her go. She would have to fend for herself somehow until the king returned and put the realm to rights. If he didn't or couldn't, then they would all be swept away on the tide of the queen's greed and power lust and she would be no worse off than they. His main priority now that his energetic thrashing of Tamara had relaxed the watch being kept on him was to organise a raiding party to ambush the group taking Sir William to Tamesbury and then escape back to Frankland with him. There were enough loyal soldiers in the area and he would recruit them just as soon as the party set off in the morning. Across from where he stood, he saw Tamara's delicious thighs, pale in the moonlight, gleam as she eased herself through the wicket gate and vanished.

CHAPTER FIVE.
Southern Alba.

Slowly her stiffness eased as she walked and the chill of the night began to clear her head. Tamara assessed her situation as she tried to put as much distance as she could between herself and her erstwhile home, limping along as quickly as she could manage. She had only the rough tunic and a pair of sandals to her name now. Unfortunately the tunic was typical of the ones condemned slaves were given and somehow she would have to ditch it. But how to find any other garments? There was just no obvious answer to that one so she moved on. She had no collar which was not entirely a bad thing. Once she had been condemned she had had her wife's collar taken from her but had escaped before the heavy collar of a slave had been fastened around her neck so anyone seeing her now would think she was a whore, which was better than a runaway slave. But a whore had to sell her body and do any jobs that needed doing to earn her keep and to try to get adopted as a slave, be properly registered as such and hopefully be taken on as a wife in due course. Ruefully she reflected that William – and her heart ached at the thought of her lord being kept in chains – had in effect prostituted her only the day before, so there was no reason she couldn't play the willing harlot and skivvy. Most important was to get far enough away from the villa so that people were unlikely to recognise her. Already a grey light was beginning to suffuse the darkness and she hobbled on more quickly, trying to massage the more stubborn of her bruises as she went and trying to ignore the itching of the dried semen around her crotch. In some of the fields scarecrows had been forgotten and left out overnight – probably overlooked in all the excitement of seeing Lady Tamara stocked and whipped – and their bodies hung on crosses and frames, the bright coloured ribbons that did the actual bird scaring hung limp and colourless about them. Using flesh and blood slaves to scare the birds away was an affectation of a well-to-do estate, they were no better at it than straw-filled effigies but were much prettier and afforded welcome relief and entertainment during a hard day's work in the fields.

As the time passed a breeze sprang up, heralding the dawn and gradually Tamara became aware that she could make out the outlines of hills and woods to quite a distance. She shivered and tried to hurry her pace but just as she was passing the gate to a field on her right, something caught her eye, a flash of yellow, not much more than a brighter tint of grey really, fluttering in the dawn light, inside the field. She stopped and went over to discover that it was a hurriedly discarded, ragged yellow gown, it probably belonged to the scarecrow who had been made to strip when her owner had sprung his delightful surprise on the girl. She looked up and saw the hapless slave hung up in a rectangular frame from yesterday, but even as she looked she saw the breeze begin to stir the ribbons attached to the girl and to her horror she began to stir and groan pitifully. Hurriedly Tamara grabbed the godsend of the gown and scuttled away quietly, changing in a copse a little down the road. The gown was more or less a fit and much less likely to attract attention than the tunic.

She buried the tunic under some leaves and went on walking until it was broad daylight and then slipped into some woods and slept for most of the day. She awoke in the late afternoon and was even more wretchedly stiff and sore. She found a stream and dared to strip off, bathe and drink. She also examined her wounds and concluded that Dunbar had done a very workmanlike job on her. There were very few cuts despite the verve with which the lash had been applied; that bespoke a good aim and a knowledge of female flesh's durability. A knowledge he had partly acquired in her own dungeons.

Despite her hunger Tamara lay low that day and dozed as best she could, husbanding as much strength as possible. At dusk she set off once more and by midnight had passed the last farm she recognised as being on the Courcey lands. Her stiffness began to lessen but hunger gnawed at her and cramped her stomach so that in the early light of the following day when she saw a smithy by the side of the road she curled up in its doorway and waited until the smith was up and about, determined to try and get herself a billet here whilst praying she wasn't recognised.

The rarity of horses had forced blacksmiths to diversify and while still able to shoe mail ponies and the occasional warhorse, they mainly worked leather for harnesses for slaves and oxen. Many, like this one, had also seen a lucrative sideline develop in fashioning restraints and punishment implements for pleasure slaves. And so when the door finally opened and Tamara was allowed in, she found herself already familiar with many of the whips, crops, straps, tawses and cuffs she saw adorning the walls of the smithy. The smith himself was a tall burly man by the name of Bickham; Harold Bickham.

"Mostly they just call me Black Harry," he informed Tamara as he inspected her. Two quite presentably good looking wives stood behind him, glaring at her with open hostility. Tamara could see his eyes assessing her body lustfully and made her plans accordingly.

"Where you from?" he asked, coming close so he could stare down her cleavage.

"I had a bed back up the road aways, I don't know the name of the place, sir," she quavered in what she hoped was a fair imitation of the voice of an ignorant peasant girl. "The master there said he was going to register me as a slave all proper and legal if I worked a month, but at the end of that time he just give me a thrashing instead of my wages and cast me out."

Black Harry caught her chin and lifted it slightly. "Well you've no mark of a slave collar so you might not be a runaway," he said. A wife's collar was softer than those worn by either registered or condemned slaves and Tamara knew her neck was unmarked. "But if you was thrashed, you'll still be carryin' I reckon."

'Carrying' was the slang for a whip-marked woman and by the look of Black Harry, Tamara thought both his wives would be carrying, but at least she was on safe ground here. Slowly she unlaced the ragged bodice of her gown and drew it down to bare her breasts and stomach. She took care to breathe deeply so that Harry should be in no doubt about what else she was carrying, apart from welts. Both wives murmured in shock at the density of the latticework that covered her chest. Harry gave her a long and uncomfortably calculating look.

"He took his time thrashing you.......this man," he said eventually.

"Yes Sir. He hung me up most of the day. Kept coming back to give me more......." She glanced up and saw he was still suspicious but the wives' mood had swung around and they looked openly sympathetic. It was probably that, coupled with hunger and fear that made her burst into tears and fall to her knees.

"Oh please! Let me stay and work a few days. You don't have to take me on, just give me a few pennies and I'll be on my way after a week if you like...."

Perhaps it was because Tamara was kneeling before him or perhaps it was because the two wives began to give him looks that boded ill for domestic tranquillity, but in any event Harry relented and Tamara became a skivvy for the smith's household. Adopting the name Bess she slept over the smithy itself, worn out each evening by her constant labours in the smallholding and vegetable garden at the back of the small house. She wasn't badly treated by the women, they even gave her some ointment to help heal her wounds but she found it hard to work at the rate they seemed to think perfectly normal. She helped with cooking as well as gardening and sometimes helped in the smithy by modelling some of the lines of disciplinary wear Harry was making, or plaiting leather. Sometimes she operated the bellows and pumped until she was blinded by sweat as the fire turned white hot and Harry's big hands fashioned needles for the rich to torment their slaves with, some were short and suitable only for nipple play, some were long enough to transpierce both a girl's breasts or run the entire length of a labial lip. All of them Tamara knew well and she could feel her own fires igniting as she watched. She longed to be able to take the fresh, shiny steel from Harry's hands and feed it into the dangling, helpless body of Jocelyn or Seven and watch as they absorbed the pain and the erotic impact of seeing what had been done.

"Bess, you're a deal more pretty than them two oxen I got for wives so you'll do to model for posh folk at the fair in Southaven," Harry told her one day as he fitted her with a steel chastity belt and then made her drink water until she had to pee, in order to check the opening was correctly placed. She had to keep it on overnight to check the other orifice and being watched in the morning by Harry and his wives was even more shaming than the stocks. Somehow she coped however and that night Harry climbed up into the loft she slept in and stood over her while he stripped off his shirt and britches then he lay down beside her. Tamara sat up and pulled off the old linen slip one of the wives had given her for sleeping in. She knew he was entitled to take her and if she was entirely honest with herself, she was in need of a decent length of cock.

His hard, rough hands immediately began to stroke and feel their way around her body in the dim light that filtered in from a grubby skylight above the straw she slept on.

"Just wanted to let them welts go down a bit before I tried you out," he whispered and she caught a rich scent of alcohol on his breath. "Tomorrow, you and I will set off for Southaven, so we'll get a bit acquainted before we go, how's that?"

"Of course, Sir. Do what you want. It's what my body is for," she whispered back. It was an answer she knew a whore should give. One of his big hands squeezed her right breast cruelly hard and she gasped. Harry chuckled and squeezed the other then reached the hand down between her legs. She had opened them in readiness and his fingers slid down along her crack, rasping over the stubbly pubic growth. The nakedness of her cunt had caused some comment, it was an affectation of the wealthy and their pleasure slaves but Tamara had passed it off as one of her previous master's cruelties. Now however, Harry's thick blunt fingers, each one feeling about the size of a hard cock to her, began to poke about inside her moistening sheath, stretching its tissues and occasionally scratching them.

"Mmm. You're a rare piece to wash up on a man's doorstep," he whispered. "Nice, tight and juicy. Those old trouts downstairs can take an axe handle up 'em," he chuckled again and Tamara realised with a jolt of horror that he had probably pushed the axe handle up them himself. Fortunately he was in a hurry and her thoughts were pushed aside by his weight crushing her as he rolled onto her and she felt the huge helm of his cock begin to barge its way into her. She moaned a little as she felt herself try to accommodate it and its very girth came to her aid as it dragged some of her tissues with it and pulled at her clitoris. She felt herself respond inside and with one last shove she was stuffed to the hilt and gasping for breath under his rib-crushing weight. Black Harry was no subtle lover and under him Tamara could only pant and moan as she felt every inch of her vagina reamed by the monster and her cervix pounded repeatedly until he stayed at maximum penetration for one long moment and she felt him pump into her then he sighed in pleasure, rolled off her and immediately got to his feet. He bent to gather up his clothes and loomed over her as he smiled down, his massive chest heaving in the aftermath of his orgasm.

"Can't have you marked up if you're modelling for all them posh folk. So now I've taken the top off the milk, I'll just have to give my two bitches their rations of marks in advance. It'll keep 'em from straying while I'm away." He threw his head back and laughed, then, still naked he climbed down and Tamara heard him stamp across the smithy and enter the small house. There was silence for a while and then the unmistakable slap of a heavy strap being plied on flesh. It went on for a very long time and towards the end was accompanied by female wails and sobs.

Tamara tried to wriggle down into the straw and block the sounds but even in the silence that followed the beating she could envisage Harry's bulk covering the thrashed, naked form of one of the wives bent over the simple bed all three shared. In days gone by the sound of a beating would have had her reaching between her legs and eagerly pleasuring herself to the sound of another female's suffering, but now she had first hand experience of the whip, her feelings were more complex. A few minutes later there was the sound of raised voices and a door slamming and then Harry was dragging the second wife into the smithy.

"Please, Harry. No! You know I can't walk for days after you do that!" she pleaded.

"Good, then you'll still be here when I get home!" Harry roared.

He reversed his grip on her waist as Tamara squirmed over and peered down through the loft hatch and he turned the woman upside down as easily as if she had been a doll, then with just one hand he looped rope around one ankle as she kicked her feet desperately at the level of his face and then he reached up and passed the rope over a hook in one of the beams over to Tamara's left. Then he held onto the rope and let the woman go so that she hung by one ankle. He made the rope fast to a hook in the wall and returned to treat the other ankle in the same fashion. From Tamara's vantage point she could see almost directly into the wide-open crotch with its thick pelt of black pubic hair through which the pale labia peeped, the crack between them firmly closed. The woman's nightgown had fallen over her head and Harry eased it off her slackly hanging arms then spent a few moments massaging the sizeable breasts and tormenting the reddening nipples. The woman kept up a dirge of soft pleas for mercy until suddenly Harry strode away and took up a whip Tamara had been helping him with earlier in the day. It was a thick bundle of square cut leather tails about a foot long, joined to a phallic handle.

"No, Harry! Please….." the hanging woman intoned as she saw what he held. The door opened and the other wife came in, naked and sporting a rich weave of heavy red flares where she had been strapped.

"Stop whining, Sarah," the newcomer said, leering down at her. "Harry's got every right." She came to stand close behind her husband and rubbed her breasts against his back, stroking his strong shoulders and arms.

"Let the silly cow have it, Harry," she crooned.

Harry did just that. He held nothing back, bringing his mighty arm well up and back and then sweeping it down to land between the spread thighs with a heavy Smack!

The suspended woman heaved and twisted, her torso trying to curl up but her face only encountered Harry's balls. He struck again and the woman's thighs flexed desperately, the rods of the tendons standing out like ropes. The other wife applauded the strength of the blow. Two thick bundles of pink ridges now adorned the insides of the thighs. The standing wife's hands now came round Harry's body and began to caress his flaccid member.

"She can take it harder than that, Harry. Remember how she egged you on with the strap just now? She was right wasn't she? I could take it harder. So can she, believe me. She loves being cunt whipped."

Harry grinned and went up onto tiptoe on the backswing for the next strike which cut down onto the buttock crease. Some of the lashes buried themselves gleefully in her crack, others splayed out and made the generous globes judder. The woman's body arched backwards and the arms flailed helplessly up her back. Harry pounced and sliced the whip down square onto her cunt. An ululating wail tore through the night as the woman twisted and bucked so much the beam creaked.

The other wife chuckled throatily. "Well, *I* love her being cunt whipped anyway" she said.

Up in the loft, Tamara's heart pounded. She had always adored hanging slaves by their ankles and whipping the crevices that split them, making them scream and jerk in their chains. And she had always loved seeing the way the labia spread apart and in some slaves quite thick, liver coloured inner lips blossomed around the vaginal entrance, in others, pink, wavy lips protruded from between the outer lips and then the dark hole of the vagina was revealed as the slicked nubbin of the clitoris stood proud from its hood. And below her she could see Harry's whip working the same magic. She didn't care if she wouldn't want to be whipped like that herself. Just here and now she wasn't being. She dug her fingers into her thickly oozing cunt and urgently masturbated as the first wife sank to her knees behind her husband and began to probe between his powerful, hairy thighs with her tongue, licking his balls while her hand caressed the stiff giant of the cock, the purple helm gleaming beneath Tamara's face. The whipping went on until the woman was nearly inert and merely gurgling incoherently as she swung to and fro. Her thighs were lividly ridged as were her buttocks and increasingly her groin. Harry seemed to be targeting the clitoris now and as Tamara approached her climax, she saw the woman's hands reach for her husband's thighs and draw him towards her as yet more lashes stung her crotch and the inner cunt lips shivered and shook in their wake.

Suddenly Harry ceased the beating and his hanging wife's hands reached for the thick shaft of his cock, and bending it slightly downwards she fed it into her mouth. Tamara just had time to wonder how she got the thing in before she exploded into a rippling orgasm that left her limp and sated, lying where she could watch the end of the session below.

With her mouth upside down the wife couldn't lick at the sensitive spot on the underside of her husband's cock and so just had to let him mouth fuck her in his own time. But despite the size of the thing that must be choking her she managed a long droning moan of pleasure as the shaft drove in and out slowly. Then Harry leaned forwards and buried his head in his wife's groin, taking long rasping laps at her clitoris and plunging his rolled tongue into her cunt itself. She gave a muffled shriek and Tamara saw her stomach and thighs clench and ripple as she orgasmed. Harry let her finish before he stood up again and went back to fucking her. Behind him, her head bent sideways to get at his balls, his other wife laboured to please him and at last he grabbed the hanging woman's head and thrust in and out of her mouth furiously until Tamara saw a look of bliss smooth his features and as his wife spluttered and choked on his spend, he pleasured himself in her before he withdrew his glistening shaft and turned around to allow his other wife to clean him. The hanging one swallowed and sniffed before kissing his buttocks and telling him he was a lovely, black hearted bastard.

He laughed in delight, looked up over his shoulder to where Tamara crouched, and he winked broadly.

CHAPTER SIX
Southaven.

Three days later, Tamara and Harry set up camp just outside the port of Southaven.

"There's no point in paying an inn for more nights than we need," Harry explained as he lay at his ease and Tamara knelt over a cooking fire, stewing rabbit he had trapped the previous day. On the journey she had proved hopeless at skinning and gutting and had been sick once or twice. She had been certain that Harry would realise that she was no whore but he just seemed amused by her attempts with the flensing knife. She had learned quickly though and she felt the stew was coming along nicely. She needed it too. For three days she had been pulling the cart that held all Harry's goods, their tent and bedding. He had walked beside her as the cart wasn't big enough for him to ride in, and in any case she wouldn't have had a chance of pulling it if he had. She had been allowed to retain her ragged gown, albeit with the bodice unlaced and pulled down to her waist. That way if he needed to, Harry could lash her up any hills, or – as he had done on several occasions – simply yank her up by her nipples. Her wrists were encased in heavy leather restraints that clipped to the cart's shafts.

Walking had been uncomfortable. The final night's session at the smithy, far from quietening Harry's libido seemed to have awoken it. Several times on each of the days they had been on the road, he had steered them to the verge, freed her wrists and taken her into the undergrowth to fuck her. Then, hardly allowing her time to wipe herself clean he had dragged her back to the road. On two evenings they had camped with other traders heading for Southaven and Harry had sold her body quite profitably. She was more shapely and slender than the average slave or wife, who tended to have been thickened up by hard work. One after another they had taken her into the woods and had her. She had counted ten on the first night and seven on the second. She had barely had time to sit up and wipe one man's sperm out of her before the next was on her. By closing her eyes and thinking of her husband she had managed a couple of orgasms, in despite of the men fucking her rather than because of them.

She didn't dare ask for a share of her earnings but was content that Harry seemed happy and she seemed to have got away with her deception.

Her entry into Southaven the next day could hardly have been more different from her previous one. At least Harry allowed her to cover her breasts but other than that everything only served to exacerbate the misery of the comparison. There was no cool palanquin pulled by her own slaves, there was no passionate, studded tongue to pleasure her. Instead she sweated and strained to pull the cart over the wide flags of the streets, kept clean by gangs of condemned slaves equipped with brushes and driven by the inevitable whips. The rich shops were not for her any more, nor were the gorgeous gowns of satin and silk that rustled and swept by her as she waited, shackled to the cart outside an inn door, a chain running from the hitching rail and locking around her ankle keeping her in her place. Occasionally a passing man would notice her and pause for a moment to grope a breast or feel up under her gown. For the first time she felt the lack of a collar acutely. Without one she could be traded on the spot. At least as a registered slave there had to be a legal transaction and the slave had to sign her agreement to the sale. If she didn't she immediately returned to the rank of whore and would promptly get a beating to boot, but at least a registered slave existed legally. A whore was just a fuck looking for someone to have it.

Eventually Harry came out and told her he had got them a room. He unclipped her wrists, unlocked her hobble chain and told her to start unloading but before she could, one of the men who had groped her earlier approached them.

"She for hire?" he asked.

Tamara's heart sank, the man was not unpleasant, in his early forties she thought, like most men in Alba not excused military service. His face was marked by a long scar that ran from his brow to his chin on the left side. However, her cunt still burned from Harry's final fuck on the way into town. He had backed her up against a tree and rammed himself into her, finishing before she had had any chance to become excited herself, and she wasn't sure how she was going to cope with being used the way she had seen so many whores and slaves used, just bent over in the street and penetrated in whichever hole the man chose while the world passed by.

Her thoughts were dragged back to the present by Harry grinning broadly and going to lounge against the inn's wall, idly jingling the coins she had been bartered for.

"Down over the hitching rail, girl," the man said as he came to stand behind her and pushed her firmly in the small of her back. Tamara glanced right and left, hoping that by some miracle there would be no one about, but with the spring fair about to start there was small chance of that. On her right there was a wagon of hay with its team of twenty naked and dusty slaves manacled to its shafts. Beyond that a two seater trap pulled by two beautifully groomed and naked ponies was parked outside a milliner's shop. On her left a farmer was unloading cuts of meat from a cart pulled by four sturdy slaves. Beyond the hitching rail people were moving in an almost solid stream, nobles in richly coloured robes with their wives in fine linen and silk gowns mixed with tradesmen and farmers in plain jerkins and britches. And amongst them moved women with the heavy collars of slaves on, their clothes usually just dull coloured rags, the skirts no longer than knee length, the bodices frequently torn and showing pale breastflesh. Then again there were wives with softer, smaller collars of finer leather. They were soberly dressed in floor length gowns but with bodices that were cut low at the neck, exposing as much breast as they dared; it paid to advertise after all and they never knew when they might catch the eye of a man richer than their current husband.

But Tamara was the only uncollared whore.

She bent forwards and spread her arms along the top of the rail. Straightaway she felt her skirt being lifted and shoved unceremoniously onto the small of her back. She felt air circulate around her crotch and thighs and screwed her eyes shut to block out the thought that everyone on the other side of the street, or whoever cared to step off the pavement and walk round her could see her bottom and her cunt. In the stocks she had had no choice; she had been imprisoned, but here she had no physical restraint. The temptation to stand up and refuse to participate was overwhelming but recollection of the stocks and the flogging came to her rescue. That had been nothing compared to what she could expect as a recaptured runaway. She felt the man's hands run across her hips and buttocks and then delve between her thighs to find her sore cunt, she suspected it would be firmly closed and the discomfort his first fumbling penetrations caused her confirmed that. With a tut of disapproval the man withdrew his fingers and with no warning landed two thunderous spanks, one on each of her cheeks. Tamara jerked upwards in shock as, in the wake of the noise a hot, burning sensation deep in her flesh seared through to her belly. Two more heavy blows landed and before she could protest the man's hand was back and under the hot seething his smacks had caused she realised that he had slipped easily inside her and was stirring her up with no problem.

"That's better!" he said and Tamara had to agree, it was the first foreplay of any kind she had had since her arrest and her cunt was responding enthusiastically. The fact that it had responded exactly as she would have expected a slave's to respond was blotted from her mind by the sounds of laughter from passers by as she began to squelch loudly. The fingers withdrew again and the man's cock barged into her, making her gasp with the speed of its penetration. She felt his hands settle on her hips as she began to swivel them and hump her back to maximise her pleasure. She quite forgot about being taken in public until suddenly a pair of leggings appeared before her eyes. They were joined by Harry's and above her, as she wagged her tail and was fucked in long, delicious strokes, she was sold off once more.

She was panting and crying out as she ascended towards climax and didn't pay attention to what was being said but suddenly the man behind her withdrew almost to the point of disengagement and held himself there. Tamara looked up in distress and saw another man's hands in front of her, undoing his laces and pulling free an impressive, rock hard length of cock. He pulled the foreskin back fully and grasped her hair.

Harry's heavy hand patted her on her back. "Suck it well or I'll take a whip to you!" he said.

With her throat stretched tight by her posture, Tamara tried to open up all she could and was just able to let the bulbous helm slide gently between her lips and fill her mouth right to the back. The man had clearly not washed very recently and the cock tasted a lot more acrid than she was used to.

"You in okay?" the man behind her asked the newcomer.

"Yes, she's a tight fit though," he replied.

"At this end as well," her vaginal ravisher replied and slammed himself back into her with all his strength and length so that she was rammed forwards and the cock in her mouth was forced into her throat. She gagged and spluttered before the men settled into a rhythm and she was able to control her breathing through her nose. As soon as they felt her accommodate them, the man in her mouth grasped her breasts and began to thrust in earnest while the man behind her began to punctuate his inward thrusts with hard spanks.

Tamara felt the rise towards orgasm become irrevocable and forgot everything except the cocks that possessed her, she hollowed her cheeks as she sucked with all her strength, while she swung and undulated her hips, tightening her internal muscles she caressed and encouraged the plundering shaft in her vagina. She came in muffled shrieks around the mouth-filling cock and she was still spasming and fluttering when the man behind her came in a sudden series of savagely hard thrusts and then the cock in her mouth swelled and began to pump out thick, choking sperm that blocked her throat before she could swallow it all and she had no option but to snort some through her nose. The two men withdrew abruptly and Tamara was left to collapse to her knees while amused onlookers went back to their own business.

Harry came to stand over her.

"Get up! There's work to do, you can't just lie around and enjoy yourself all day."

Slowly Tamara got to her feet and tried to re-arrange her skirt and tidy herself a little before she set about unloading. Her bottom stung and her vagina was really complaining now, but it had been a shatteringly intense orgasm and she felt that she had adopted the role of whore maybe a bit too easily and completely for comfort.

The spring fair was held in a series of streets just behind the harbour itself. Harry rented a small shop space with an open front and a table to put outside with samples of his wares. He made no bones about the fact that she had earned him the money to rent a bigger shop than usual. They were up not long after dawn on the first day and by the time the first passers by began to stroll between the shop fronts and stalls, Tamara had laid out an attractive display of Harry's best whips, restraints and harnesses. Almost immediately she was required to model various items, it seemed that Harry had a reputation with the local nobility for good quality tack and Tamara found herself buckled into a bridle, stripped naked and then harnessed into so many straps she lost count. The one she really didn't like however was the crupper strap that ran between her legs and was buckled up tightly above her backside. Once again she got an insight into the lives her slaves had led. Almost daily she had driven out in a trap pulled by a ponyslave in similar tack.

Harry was keen to have his customers note how he padded the bits on all his bridles so that they would withstand a lot of chewing and champing. He smacked in several hard slashed across her bottom with a riding whip to make her prance and bite onto the bit to illustrate his point and made several sales by lunchtime of the first day.

In the afternoon, most people seemed to want manacles and restraints so Tamara modelled those more comfortably but was aching to point out that the manacles Harry was selling would chafe and spoil a slave's wrists if she was hung by them for too long, they needed much more padding.

That night he locked her into the room at the inn and went out, returning very late. He undressed, slipped into the narrow bed beside her and roused her when he settled his bulk closely beside her. She woke to find her face pressed against his shoulder, then he turned to face her and grasped her breasts, squeezing them viciously and making her whimper. He chuckled nastily in the dark and lay on his back, released her breasts and instead put his hand on her head.

"Get down where you belong, you whore." His voice contained a nastiness she hadn't heard before and the hand on her head was inexorable. Obediently she slid down the bed and found his cock fully erect and challenging her by its sheer size. She grasped it gently in one hand and began to masturbate him until her head was rocked by a blow from his fist.

"Get it in your mouth! And if you spill one fucking drop of my spunk, I'll hang you up and flay you tomorrow."

Suddenly alarmed at his change in mood, she abandoned all attempts at subtlety and opening her mouth till her jaws ached she dipped her head and fed the huge helmet between her carefully tightened lips so it wouldn't scrape on her teeth and then she set about rasping her tongue at the sensitive underside.

Again she got a blow to her head.

"Don't hurry me! Just give me a mouth fuck!"

Slowly and carefully she began to nod her head, trying to give him the feeling of fucking an exquisitely tight vagina. She was rewarded by a contented sigh from above and in a few minutes she felt his hand grip her hair and his cock swelled in her mouth and started to pump. Desperately she tried to swallow everything he was spurting into her but with her head rammed down hard onto him she had no chance. He was laughing even as she choked and snorted in the aftermath and he had withdrawn.

"We'll sell out tomorrow, my girl," he told her. "You'll make a lovely model for them to try out the whips on."

He slept with his great arm slung across her chest and Tamara knew she had no chance of escape.

The next day was a nightmare for her. As soon as he had opened the shop he tied her hands behind her back and roped one ankle to a table leg. Then he hammered a nail into the door lintel and freed her but only to tell her to strip naked. She could see the harsh light of cruelty in his eyes and obeyed, then held her wrists out to have his thick leather cuffs attached and chained together, then he lifted her with no visible effort and hung her from the nail. She scrabbled about desperately with her feet but could find no support. Straightaway her arms began to ache savagely and as she had correctly predicted, her wrists began to chafe painfully.

Harry paid her no heed however and instead stepped out to stand in front of the table and began to shout his wares to the crowds who were examining bolts of cloth, furniture, ornaments and crockery on adjoining stalls.

Slowly a crowd began to form and Harry retreated to come and stand beside her suspended body.

"I've not only got the finest whips and clamps in all Southern Alba! I've got the finest little whore for you to try them out on! You sir! You look like a gentleman who knows good value when he sees it, try any whip you want and if you don't think it's worth my price – I'll flog the lovely little bitch's hide off! How's that?"

There was good natured laughter and a man in gaudy red robes stepped forward. He picked up a flogger which had a score of long thin tails depending from a phallic handle. He hefted it a couple of times and Tamara felt the wind of its passage on her face then he stepped behind her.

"She is a comely little piece, Harry," he said, running his free hand down her back and squeezing her buttocks. "I'll buy what's left of her when you close tonight."

"We'll see, sir. For now, don't spare the whip, she can take a lot more than she lets on," Harry said.

The man did as he suggested and Tamara screeched as thin stinging lashes wrapped clear across her back and bit at her ribs and breasts. He gave her no quarter and tested the whip to its limits immediately, swinging it in a steady rhythm that would cause the clearest marks in the minimum amount of time. Tamara's body was merely a place for welts to form and be examined. She understood this quite clearly even as she screamed under the relentless assault and tried to twist in mid air. It was no more than she would have done with her own slaves – but she wished she could find the trick of orgasming freely under cruelty alone like they did.

The beating stopped as abruptly as it had started and hard fingers prodded and poked at her burning skin.

"It's a fine implement, Harry. As good as your best," the flagellator decided and brushed past Tamara as he returned to the table and purchased the whip. That seemed to break the dam and from then on there was an almost non-stop queue of people wanting to try out riding whips, dog whips, heavy, broad bladed floggers, narrow sharp bladed, spiteful floggers. Two women held her legs apart while their husbands sampled what Harry called his best 'cunt cutter'. It was a small whip whose lashes were hard and narrow and did indeed cut into her cunt. The men took a great liking to her screams and pleas for mercy while the wives exchanged comments about which of their slaves would suffer it first. Harry had only brought two examples with him and sold both. He locked her into the shop, tied up and slung in a corner while he went for lunch at last and in the afternoon he tied her down to the table and introduced his latest nipple clamps to another avid audience.

"The finest steel you'll find anywhere, forged into an implement of exquisite pleasure!" he cried. "Just see how much I enjoy putting them onto my charming little whore here!"

The clamps were indeed of fine steel; bent into a narrow U shape, very nearly closed at the top. And at the end of each arm was half a tube bristling with sharp tines on its inside. The sprung steel kept the two halves pressed tightly together but it could be prised open for long enough to slip it onto a nipple and allow the tines to embrace its full length.

Unfortunately Tamara's nipples refused to erect as she gazed in terror at the evil appliances.

"Anyone care for a free fuck? Compliments of the management?" Harry hit on an elegantly simple solution. Tamara was tied down on her back with her legs already spread and all it took was an eager sailor to drop his britches and climb aboard. All Tamara could see was his weatherbeaten face leering down at her as his weight pressed her hard down onto the wood and all she could hear were shouts of encouragement and general laughter as he slowly forced his way into her. Once he was in it took only a couple of thrusts before he was able to move back and forth comfortably. He looked up and grinned at his audience then thrust in hard and Tamara's body took over. Just as at the hitching rail she bucked her hips up to meet him and intensify her pleasure in being so publicly screwed. It was a brief and crude rutting but at its end, as the sailor slithered off her, it had achieved its purpose, her nipples stood proud and hard at the summits of her breasts and with no warning Harry opened the clips and slid them over the tender little tubes.

Tamara screamed immediately and Harry stuffed some revolting old rag into her mouth so he could go on with his sales patter. She had never dreamed of such pain. The clamps were new to her and she had never tried them on a slave, let alone suffered them herself. Their pain was intense and grew by the minute as they bit into every inch of the length of her nipples. She heaved and twisted desperately on the table until Harry had finished his sales pitch and suddenly turned, removed the gag, opened each clip and removed them. Applause broke out among the onlookers as there was a moment's silence followed by a howl from Tamara as the blood surged back into the crushed tissue. When at last she could blink the tears from her eyes she saw Harry pocketing handfuls of coins as he parted with the last pairs of clamps. Some of the crowd departed with their purchases, some newcomers pushed closer to replace them.

"Now then My Lords and Ladies!" Harry boomed cheerfully at his audience. "If someone would be so good as to help me have this slut sit up and tie her hands, I'll demonstrate my latest breast press and the refinements that can be added to make sure your slaves are always obedient!"

Tamara let out a whimper of dismay as she realised that her torment was far from over. In fact she had to sit for an hour or so with her tits flattened mercilessly by the two horizontal wooden spars of the press, screwed down severely hard while members of the public tried out various whips on them. The worst of it was that she could see why she had always enjoyed tit whipping her slaves while they were pressed, the strangely shaped elliptical tits, squeezed out from between the bars shuddered and trembled exquisitely under the lash and she found she couldn't take her eyes off her own suffering breasts. To make matters worse – or better, she couldn't decide – her nipples were achingly hard and beckoned to every conceivable cruelty the knowledgeable crowd could devise. When her tormented tits were bright red and pounding with pain from the constriction and the lashes, Harry finished her off by piercing each nipple horizontally. Tamara watched in fascination through her tears as an action she had performed a thousand times before on slaves was performed on her. To her own amazement, despite the pain she kept quiet during the whole procedure. She couldn't exactly take pleasure in the sharp spears of pain but at the same time they were excitement of a kind.

Harry released her hands from behind her back once the piercing had been done and then went to take the orders and purchases she had made for him. Dimly she heard him making last minute reductions to clear his stock while she gritted her teeth and eased the needles out of each nipple then set about unscrewing the press and releasing her poor tits. As the last of the crowd disappeared and the market began to pack up she was slipping weakly off the table, having untied her ankles. Harry appeared, beaming but still with the spiteful gleam in his eyes he had had the previous night.

"Right that's me cleaned out so the cart'll be no trouble to pull on the way home. Although I might buy a new slave to save myself the trouble, and I can well afford one now!"

Tamara stared up at him, puzzled and alarmed. "But…." she quavered.

Harry reached out and clamped a huge hand around her bicep. "I got a good price for you!" He came closer and whispered. "Lady Courcey."

He roared with laughter at Tamara's look of surprise and horror. "You puked up at skinning a rabbit! You'd got no idea how to make a fire! All I had to do was ask around for a noblewoman recently flogged……and then decide whether to sell her or turn her in! Fortunately for you, someone made me a very handsome offer."

With these final words he jerked her after him as he set off through the market without letting her dress.

"Please, Harry! Please let me go! I fucked well for you didn't I?"

Without slackening his pace he turned a fierce grin on her. "You fuck like a born bed-slave and take the whip like a common haulage slave…….My Lady!"

He made a mocking bow as he came to a heavy door set in a wall that stretched the length of the alley they now stood in. It was opened by a woman dressed in britches and tunic, her face was almost masculine in its hardness and only the swell of her tunic across her breasts betrayed her femininity. She nodded at Harry and stepped back to allow him to hustle Tamara inside.

She found herself in the atrium of a smart town house with a fountain in the centre of it and couches and tables arrayed round the edges, under the projecting roof. Two women of about her age and dressed only in simple white loin cloths were busily engaged in sweeping the stone flags. Like her they wore no collar.

"Lady Tamara Courcey," the woman said. "Yes, you fit the description alright. If you make any attempt to escape from me I'll report it to the sheriff and claim the reward. If you work hard and earn me back all I paid Harry for you and then some more, I might – *only* might – allow you to stay here and stay alive. But your life will always be in my gift. Understand?"

Tamara didn't at all but as she looked wildly around her trying to work out where she was and what was going on, she saw another, older woman approach the two younger ones who were cleaning. This one had her hair cropped short and like the one who had opened the door, wore britches and a tunic. She had a whip coiled at her waist and as she approached the younger women she slid it out from her belt and flicked it out with practised ease and then brought it down across the back of one of them, before helping herself to a big handful of breast. The young woman had twisted back under the lash but now held herself steady while her breast was groped and mauled by the leering, older woman. Suddenly Tamara knew where she was and what her future held in store. Her heart plummeted into despair. Whatever happened to William now, if he escaped and returned with the king, he would never find her. Black Harry had sold her to a cock house.

As she watched, the nearly naked young woman was led away and as her companion went back to cleaning, from a room somewhere inside the house there was the sound of a whip being plied and peals of female laughter above the groans and cries of the girl being flogged.

CHAPTER SEVEN.
The River Tame

The boat was exquisitely carved into the likeness of a huge swan. Its graceful neck arched up to form the prow, its beaked head faced down into the dark brown waters of the river which reflected the dangling body of the slave who hung by her wrists from its beak and swung gently to and fro as the oars propelled the vessel onwards. Towards the stern where the sides of the boat, carved into the likeness of folded wings curved up to form the sides of a deck, Her Majesty Queen Anneka lay at her ease on a couch beside the lean and grizzled figure of Captain Otto Berghaus, clothed in travel stained leather. They were attended by four slaves, clothed only in the most diaphanous of robes that the sun shone through quite easily, revealing the tantalising outlines of the supple bodies beneath.

Below and ahead of them the overseers walked up and down the gangway between the ranks of the rowers and plied their whips to keep the rhythm set by the drum master, who in deference to the queen was wielding muffled hammers. There were two slaves to each oar and ten oars to a side.

The two passengers sipped their wine and studied the ranks of hooded, blind and anonymous rowing slaves before them. The queen did not relish being watched by her galley slaves and always had them hooded.

As they leaned back and drew the oars towards them the overseers swung their lashes at the breasts and as they leaned forwards to start the next pull, the lashes fell on the backs. Flesh shone, sweat-slicked in the hot sun as the graceful boat sliced through the water and the brilliant meteors of the kingfishers flashed and sparkled under the trees that shaded the greatest river in Alba.

"I have laid on some entertainment at a delightful island a few miles further upriver and there you may disport yourself to your heart's content, my dear Captain," the queen purred, leaning over to lay a long, manicured hand on his thigh.

Otto stirred uncomfortably, the sight of straining galley slaves under the whip always excited him. Any slave undergoing discipline was a fine sight as far as he was concerned but the sheer number of bodies available to the whips in the galleys was always something special.

"That there will always be plenty of entertainment to be laid on is worth drinking to, is it not Your Majesty?"

The queen laughed and waved two slaves over who replenished their glasses.

"You," the queen commanded the slave attending the Captain. "Administer relief."

The girl dropped to her knees and began to fumble the Captain's laces apart so that she could draw out his cock and suck it.

"So, you understand. All your men have to do is overcome a ragtag army of renegade female slaves on my command and the kingdom will fall at our feet in thanks! And from then on there will never be a shortage of slaves for either of us," she went on as the mercenary from the Deutsche Federation lay back with a sigh of contentment while the slave's lips gently closed around the head of his cock.

"A ragtag army that you have nevertheless kept well armed, Your Majesty," he whispered.

"Of course! They have to pose a real-seeming threat or there will be no renown in our victory. My agents tell them where there will miraculously be some poorly guarded weaponry. Then they tell them which estates to raid and make sure that there is sufficient mayhem and damage caused to alarm opinion locally. I have watched them carefully as they have made their way down from the north, pillaging and looting as they went and growing in number."

"And how many are there.........uh ....now?" the Count paused while he emptied himself into the slave's mouth and then slumped back.

"Four or five thousand, I believe."

"But Your Majesty! I have but two thousand men!"

"Mercenaries, Otto. Men of experience and guile up against mere women who have fed themselves by stealing chickens and burning a few farms. You will slaughter them just when the rich Southlands lie at their mercy while Edward's armies are all at war in Frankland.

"The nation will revile Edward for having left the kingdom to its fate; they will turn to us as saviours of the country and they will support every measure we take to ensure that the country's women become even more deeply enslaved. After all discipline can't be allowed to slip again!"

The Captain, tired from his forced march through the Lowlands in answer to the queen's summons, lay back on his couch and considered. She had not said anything about an army of that size; of course his men were battle hardened but even so a desperate force of that size with a leader of even only moderate capability could be a problem.

"Ah! We're here!" The queen's voice broke into his thoughts and he sat up.

They were approaching an island where lawns swept down to the water's edge. There was a pier stretching out for them and on the greensward, couches laid out around tables piled high with delicacies from across Eropia. From amid the trees there came the sounds of harps being played but best of all, from many branches of the trees surrounding the lawns slaves hung and behind the tables stood tall posts with slaves already attached and ready for whipping.

The queen stepped up onto the pier, her skirt parting at the front as she did so, revealing long, pale thighs. Her figure was tall and slender, her face undeniably handsome but her dark eyes were cruel and hard. Her hair fell in waves of deepest black about her shoulders as she stood and gazed about her.

She smiled a slow, dangerous smile as she took in the careful preparations that had been made for her and noticed the way that the soldiers of her household straightened up when they saw her. They knew that a posting to Frankland could be arranged very easily and slaves were not as easily available over there. The extent of the Alban Royal Family's slave-holding was known only to the royal auditors but King Edward's forebears had been keen collectors, that much was known and his alliance with the Slavemaker and his brethren in Cambria had kept the dormitories and dungeons filled to an extent that taxed even Queen Anneka's ingenuity when it came to keeping them all fully employed. However, she tried her best.

The walkway on the top of the pier was covered by the traditional red carpet. However, this one was clearly laid across the backs of slaves tied at full stretch across the wood. The inviting shapes of the buttock mounds could be discerned to the left and the curves of the shoulders to the right.

The Queen turned to her guest as he absorbed the sight before him, his face alight with the realisation that he stood on the threshold of a paradise of perverse delights.

"As many of them as even you can use," she whispered and stroked the front of his britches, laughing as she felt his cock harden and fill under her touch.

Together they walked along the soft and giving pathway to the shore. She taking delicate steps that allowed her high heels to wreak havoc across girls' shoulders; the Captain's heavy boots squashing the buttocks.

As they stepped onto the grass the Queen turned and addressed a sergeant, standing guard at the end of the pier.

"I distinctly heard at least three of the wretches groan when they were stepped on. I will not have my guests disturbed like this! See to them, man. And I'll hold you personally responsible if I hear a sound from them on my return."

While the pair walked up the sloping lawns, the Captain heard the sergeant order his men to pull back the carpet and as he glanced back over his shoulder, he saw a row of soldiers standing on the naked buttocks and beginning to work whips across the shoulders of the slaves beneath them. The trees rang to the swish and smack and the desperate attempts of slaves on the receiving end to keep their yelps and screams to a minimum.

The queen slipped her hand onto the Captain's arm.

"I can see the importance of the job in hand, Your Majesty," he said. "Alba must be protected from the bane of free women. Except, of course, those not born to suffer under their masters' whips."

The queen acknowledged the neat verbal footwork. Alba, Burghund and Frankland were the countries with the greatest wealth of slaveflesh in Eropia due to their enthusiastic pursuit of dynastic war and the Captain was not used to navigating through the diplomatic niceties of addressing a free woman in a country so heavily burdened with female slaves.

"I have arranged some entertainment for your men in Tamesbury and I'm sure that they too will come to see the importance of your commission and its potential rewards."

The Captain thought of his crude, tough soldiery and hoped that the royal household really did have plenty of slaves. They were going to be needed.

He followed the queen up the grassy slope to the couches and reclined at his ease while slaves served him with black bread and honey. The delicacy of having fresh cunt sap whipped from the slavegirl at the table was not a Deutsche one and it was something he always looked forward to on his visits to Alba. He was allowed to make a choice from twenty delicious girls, all of whom paraded before him with downcast eyes and who were clothed only in thin robes that were no more than two long panels clipped together at the shoulders. One after the other they passed in front of him and made their reverence to him. All of them were stunningly beautiful and he was at a loss and told the queen so.

She laughed and told him he could sample all of them.

At a click of her fingers the slaves unclipped their robes and provided the captain with a panorama of female flesh that even his long and cruel military career had not prepared him for. And it was the longest, most deliciously decadent and cruel meal of his life. The Queen was as good as her word, she had each and every slave whipped at his table until he could push a slide between her cunt lips and spread her juices on his tit bits. When he could eat no more, the Queen had a leggy blonde suspended by her ankles from the bough of a tree and suggested he work off his meal before enjoying as many of the other delights on display as he could. Indeed the cunt whipping was the perfect foil for the meal and he was soon eager for more. As he lay on his back on the cool grass and watched the naked, black haired beauty squatting over his cock and caressing it artfully with well trained interior muscles, he felt that the Queen was quite right, the renegades were just a rag tag army and would present him with no difficulty. He also had no doubt that she would provide his men with sufficient incentives to fight like they had never fought before.

Off the Southern coast of Alba.

Dunbar leaned back against the railing of the poop deck of the trireme and cast one last look over his shoulder at the receding coastline of Alba before he gave the gently nodding head at his groin his full attention. Jocelyn's mousy brown hair stirred in the sea breeze and she paused in her fellation long enough to sweep it to one side of her face irritably before resuming work on Dunbar.

The magistrate reached down and pushed her head back so that she had to stick her tongue out to continue caressing him. He sighed in pleasure as he watched the studded and almost prehensile organ, glide and swirl around his helm, shivering sometimes at the intensity of the frissons of delight it caused him. At last he gave in and released her head, relaxing against the rail as she gently engulfed him once more and he allowed himself to spend.

"It is a generous gift, William," he said eventually as his spurts subsided and Jocelyn's swallowing could slow a little. "And one I would not allow myself to accept were it not for the fact that the queen will strip me of my rank, my house, my wives and slaves. So the gift of a pleasing slave to start again with is a fine one."

"My dear Dunbar," Sir William said. "I owe you vastly more than even the gift of Jocelyn can repay you. If you had not rounded up enough of my lads and led them in the ambush, I should probably be dancing the hemp jig by now in Tamesbury with Her Majesty toasting my demise as she watched me die. I just wish you had been able to liberate more of my property and I could have been more generous."

Dunbar had had no trouble recruiting men for a rescue mission. Sir William was a popular commander. The fight had been brief, the Queen's escorting force being no match for the battle hardened troops of the Courcey regiment. Sir William had immediately made for Southaven and taken ship for Frankland to rendezvous with the King. Most of his men had elected to accompany him and were even now lounging comfortably on the poop deck and sharing the favours of those Courcey slaves that had been liberated by their action and who had now been gifted to them by Sir William. For himself he kept only Seven who now knelt at his feet, passively awaiting the next command to serve him as she had been doing for all her adult life. Of the two elite Triple Crown slaves there had been no sign. They were doubtless enjoying Sejanus' attentions in the Courcey dungeons, where they would need all their training to find any pleasure.

Sir William gazed down at Seven's blonde head and his mind wandered to Tamara. Where was she? Dunbar had told him about seeing her escape, but was she still at large? Could she stay out of the authorities' way for the months it might yet take for the king to return? He just had to hope so. In the meantime.........he clicked his fingers and instantly Seven raised her eyes and saw what was required. She reached up and began to unlace his britches.

Her soft lips stroked over his rapidly hardening shaft and in a few practised nods she had given him good enough penetration to harden him up properly. As her tongue went to work and she continued to nod and let him slide deep into her throat, the three rows of oars dipped and pulled, driven by the remorseless drum. Sir William began his exquisite climb towards orgasm, and it seemed to him the scene was symbolic of all they were fighting to save, a passionate, soft and obedient mouth was preparing to swallow every ounce of his sperm while he was being carried towards help by the straining, naked bodies of over two hundred, flogged women. The distant smacks of the whips filled his ears as he achieved his climax and felt Seven eagerly swallow every spurt of his bitter tasting emission.

They would succeed and Alba would be saved, Sir William felt as Seven licked him clean. It was impossible to believe in Alba falling under the rule of a woman.

CHAPTER EIGHT.
The Cock House

Tamara blinked away the tears caused by the stinging and the shame. She was on all fours in a puddle of dirty water and a greased strap-on dildo was being rammed up her rectum by a woman kneeling behind her. She tried her best to stay still and endure the penetration but it was one of the house's biggest strap-ons and she had never been very wide in her back passage. Moreover the woman to whom the thick, leather sleeved monster was attached was belabouring her back with a whip made from many thick leather tails in time with each vicious thrust.

"You lazy slut!" she shrieked. "If you don't finish scrubbing this floor by the time I finish fucking you, I'll flay your worthless hide!"

"Yes, Mistress!" Tamara quavered and made a few token attempts at scrubbing while trying to give the woman a good ride and stay steady under the onslaughts.

The only thing that would come to Tamara's rescue was the clitoral rasper set at the base of the dildo and just as she felt sure she would faint if the buggering didn't stop, she felt the woman's hands grab her hips and the strap-on come to rest at full penetration before making rapid jerking motions as the woman grunted and growled her way through an orgasm. Once she was finished, she merely unlaced herself and stood up, leaving Tamara to pull the thing out herself. She reached behind her and began to try and slide it out, her arse stinging from the abuse.

"Leave it!" Matilda Pevensey's voice echoed along the hall. "There's two more want that arse yet. Stay as you are!"

"Mistress, please! I can't take any more in there!" Tamara wailed. The stocky woman, who ran the house, walked forwards menacingly and glared down at Tamara who cowered before her, knowing what was coming.

"You'd rather sample the queen's mercy? The rope necklace – after half the garrison of Tamesbury have dipped their wicks in whichever of your worthless holes they want?"

"No, Mistress," she whispered miserably and hung her head. She was beaten and she knew it. She had known it every waking moment of the weeks she had been kept here. William would never find her now and he probably wouldn't want the cowed wretch she was becoming even if he did.

"You'll be providing the entertainment this evening, so make sure you don't scream yourself hoarse. You know the guests like a good noisy one at the table."

"Yes, Mistress."

Cock houses had gradually spread throughout the kingdom as the lack of men had become ever more acute and the rules on female subjugation ever more stern. They were not officially sanctioned but neither were they persecuted. They fulfilled a useful function by providing relief for wives whose frustrations might otherwise spill over into rebellious activities, they also provided employment for some soldiers returning from the wars, who could trade on their abilities as swordsmen of a more pleasurable kind.

At a cock house a wife could rent the services of a female employee – sometimes a runaway like Tamara - or sometimes a slave who had been sold by owners down on their luck or bought by the house from bankrupt stock.

Most cock houses couldn't charge very much for their services and so only bought cheap slaves.

In a cock house a wife from any social stratum provided she had ready cash, could turn the tables on life for a little while, she could beat and fuck women the way her husband probably did her and the rest of his household. She could recline in comfort and be served by slaves but most important of all she could have herself fucked by the Mistress or one of her cronies with a strap-on. These butch women were nicknamed pizzlers as the coverings of the phalluses they used were fashioned from the skins of bulls' pizzles. In short a wife could buy the sexual attention she might not get from a husband who had too many wives to satisfy and she could also lord it over the lowest of the low, the cock house slaves. They were usually gaunt and listless specimens for whom service for life as the butt of every other woman's desires was at least life of a sort. A runaway was always welcome as they were not normally as downtrodden as the other slaves. Tamara was one of three runaways held at this particular cock house and was much in demand.

That afternoon, by the time she was able to return to the cell she shared with another runaway called Suzanne, Tamara was hobbling, her back a raging inferno and her rectum stinging viciously. Suzanne had had a relatively quiet day and was considerate and kind. She bathed Tamara's wounds gently with cool water and kissed the welts on her back.

"They're harder on you because you're the prettiest," she whispered.

Tamara didn't protest at the compliment, she was shivering with delight at the delicate touch of soft lips on inflamed and welted flesh. Over the weeks she had been there she had begun to find ways of extracting pleasure from whatever life threw at her and was becoming adept at finding satisfaction of a sort even under the whip, if she was fucked soon after the beating. Memories of her life at the other end of the whip were fading fast.

Suzanne's lips and tongue trailed down Tamara's back as she lay forward, cradling her face on her crossed arms and let the other girl kneel astride her. The gentle kisses continued and Tamara couldn't help making muted groans of delight, especially when one of Suzanne's hands found its way under her hip. She made a little bucking movement and spread her legs wider as Suzanne's fingers groped their way into her and began to rub harshly at her clitoris, the counterpoint to her gentle licks and kisses to her back. Tamara groaned again, loudly and Suzanne shifted so that she was kneeling beside her, then withdrew her hand from under her and instead plunged it in from behind. This time her fingers thrust deep into her cunt and she clutched at it, as pleasure starved as only a plaything for other people could be. Suzanne bent lower and ran her tongue over Tamara's buttocks as she worked her hand inside her, flexing and clenching her fingers so as to stimulate as much of Tamara's internal tissues as possible. For her part, Tamara cried out in delight as Suzanne's clever tongue ran ever deeper between her scored buttocks, tracing the twin creases that defined her as female and therefore subjugated. Suzanne's fingers dug into her ever more intrusively even as her face delved into her crotch and Tamara's own fingers clenched about the wood of the bedstead and she began to climb towards another of the climaxes she was beginning to become used to; darker and more intense than the ones she had had as a mistress. These orgasms whose first stirrings increasingly began under the whip, now regularly devastated her, thrusting her deep into realms where pain was no more than a part of her pleasure. Dimly she was beginning to realise that she was becoming what she had always been on the lookout for as an owner – a good piece of whipping flesh.

Quaking and sighing, Tamara eventually began to calm down as Suzanne lay beside her, whispering to her.

"I just wanted you to have some pleasure, you poor thing. We're both riding the horse tonight and you've already taken a battering."

Tamara's groan this time was one of dismay. At the evening meal each day, if there were guests, two or three of the slaves would be detailed off to provide entertainment. This invariably meant a feast of suffering for the greedy eyes of the paying guests to gorge themselves on. Riding the horse, which was one of the most testing pieces of furniture the house had, was dreaded by the inmates. It consisted of several planks fastened together to form a long tri-angle and it stood on legs about four feet tall. It was a simple and effective way of ensuring a slave had an entertainingly agonising time. She was perched astride its summit with her arms roped to hooks above her and then weights were progressively added to leather straps knotted around her ankles. The summit was only an inch or so wide and the wood inevitably cut painfully into the soft slot of the girl's sex. She could relieve the pressure by pulling herself up on her wrist ropes, but as time and weights went on, those periods of relief would become shorter and she would have to spend more and more time with her cunt pressed down onto the wood.

Tamara had often employed a similar device in her dungeon but after three or four evenings spent riding it herself since she had been in the cock house, she was well aware of its slow burning torment. But what she didn't dare to admit, even to herself was that as she listened over her moans and cries to the casual banter and laughter at the tables, she was beginning to experience the other side of cruel pleasure. She was beginning to react as a good slave to casual cruelty and the juice that seeped out of her left an undeniable stain on the wood when she was taken down. Madam Pevensey had commented on it after the last session and had sneered knowingly at her.

On that particular evening Tamara and Suzanne were lifted onto the horse by one of the pizzlers and a soldier who was passing through - a veteran who never the less could still sport an impressive erection and was earning good money in tips from the guests. As an extra humiliation the girls were hooded.

"The guests say they only want to listen to you. Not watch you," the veteran said with a nasty chuckle as he held Tamara above the narrow ridge. "Probably put 'em off their food!"

Then he lowered her onto the device and she immediately whimpered in discomfort.

The hoods were, Tamara suspected, of Black Harry's making. They were of hard leather with just a hole for the mouth. The laces at the back had been pulled tight and Tamara had felt the now-familiar rise of panic in her chest as the leather had been cinched tightly against her face. But with increasing ease she was able to force herself to calm down and concentrate on settling herself on the horrible apparatus. However, there simply was no way of being comfortable and behind her she could hear Suzanne whimper in her turn as her soft, plump lipped cunt came into contact with the unyielding wood. No sooner were both girls mounted than their arms were raised by the ropes that had been tied to their wrists and fed through rings in the ceiling before they were mounted. Tamara also felt straps being tied at her ankles and then fastened under the horse so that pulling her legs up was not an option.

She wound her fingers around the ropes and pulled herself up that way immediately, to ease the pain at her cunt and felt Suzanne do the same. The other slave's back touched hers and in her hard leather prison, the simple human touch was exquisitely pleasurable. But pleasure was cut short as she felt a strip of leather touch her thigh.

"They want your tits roasting ahead of the main meal, as well," the voice of the pizzler rasped and Tamara tensed herself for what was coming, behind her she felt Suzanne do the same. There wasn't even a whisper in the air before the whip landed, just a scorching burn across both breasts. She yelped and tried desperately to pull her chest in to spare it the next stroke but whoever was whipping Suzanne laid the lash on her just as Tamara tried to shrink back, the two slaves' backs collided with the result that they were both slammed back into the path of the second lashes. With expert timing the two flagellators had the helpless girls wrenching painfully at their wrists, rocking on their cunts and getting absolutely no respite from the whips.

Tamara abandoned herself to the long night's torment and sank beneath the whip's burning caresses across her poor, bouncing and swinging breasts. Gradually she began to rock her groin against the hard wood, it would only make the torment worse later on but for the moment bright lances of pleasure speared through her body from her clitoris as she ground it with fierce intensity.

But just as suddenly as they had started, the whips stopped and Tamara and Suzanne's rasping breathing and whimpering were the only sounds.

Tamara's pulse thundered in her ears as the stinging in her chest and stomach eased but the ache at her groin didn't. She pulled up on her ropes for a second and dimly heard footsteps walking away and the doors to the long, low ceilinged dining room open and shut.

Suzanne must have heard the flagellators leave as well and she whispered over her shoulder.

"I hope they'll let us come!"

Tamara nodded her agreement. After an hour or two on the horse with weights at the ankles and occasional whipping, a finger giving a hard rub at a throbbing clitoris would mean an eruption of slavish ecstasy that would leave a girl sobbing her need for more whip. Most guests enjoyed seeing that display of helpless submissiveness but some just wanted remorseless pain while they themselves came.

Suddenly the doors burst open and several sets of footsteps sounded loudly on the polished wooden floor.

"But cock house slaves are gutter sweepings!" a male voice brayed. "Everyone knows that!"

Tamara's hooded head jerked up and she went rigid with shock. Her eyes stared frantically at the blackness in front of them. She knew that voice!

"Most are. But sometimes you can find some quite good runaways. If they haven't gone renegade like so many these days. My father was so mean that I had to buy my own apprentice piece and I got her from a cock house. She lasted quite a long time." This second voice was female and less familiar but straining every sinew in her dark prison, Tamara was certain she recognised it too.

"Well, if it pleases you we'll take a look at the stock. But we've got the triple crowners still." The male voice again, the hated voice. The voice that had perjured itself to secure her downfall and her beloved William's imprisonment. By some strange quirk of malevolent fortune Peter Sejanus had found her and now all that stood between her and the queen's vengeance was a leather hood.

"If you want to impress my mother, you'll need more than them! Good though they be! She expects any man who wants my hand in marriage to have a full complement of pleasure slaves," the female voice went on, becoming increasingly shrill and petulant. "And anyway we wouldn't have to hunt round auctions and cock houses if the queen had sent a proper escort and hadn't let Sir William escape with nearly all the slaves. Honestly! The king may be losing his hold on the country but if that's how the queen intends to run it then may the Gods help Alba!"

"Josephine! Be quiet!" Sejanus hissed. "That's dangerous talk!"

In the claustrophobic dark of the hood, all pains forgotten, Tamara's heart soared. William had got away. Dunbar had been as good as his word and now whatever hideous fate awaited her, she would try to face it calmly. The female voice she now recognised as belonging to Josephine Delacourt. They had met occasionally at dances and on some feast days. Her family were openly supporters of the queen and plainly a union was being planned which would bring a big swathe of the country over to her party.

"You there! Why aren't these sluts weighted? I specifically ordered that the meal should be served with full vocal accompaniment and these ones aren't even groaning yet!" Josephine was plainly speaking to one of the pizzlers or maybe Madam herself. In any case Tamara felt hooks slide in between the leather straps and the flesh of her ankles, then the hands which were manipulating them were removed and weight pulled down at her cruelly, crushing her cunt even more fiercely. Another weight was added to each ankle and the whipping resumed. Tamara had no choice but to give Josephine what she wanted, tossing her head and yelling as her body was consumed by the various pains. Dimly she was aware of the sound of food being served even as she was dimly aware of rubbing herself desperately on the wood trying to find relief.

At some point she and Suzanne must have reached a volume of noise that satisfied the noblewoman for they were left to recoup their failing strength, hanging from their ropes, gasping in their darkness, submitting to the pain at their crotches.

Through the long evening, as she recovered she could once again listen to the casual conversation and laughter her distress was giving rise to. Then the whip would start again. Then she would be left to try and hold herself up. She could hear wagers being taken about how long it would be before she had to lower her - by now - almost numb cunt back onto the wood. More weights were added and more wagers were laid until Tamara was in a haze of pain and frustration.

Then at long last she felt a hand stroking her thigh and to her delighted amazement felt the fingers slide up until they came achingly close to her pounding clitoris. She thrust her pelvis forwards begging for relief and heard Josephine's husky laugh from just below and beside her. All of a sudden her awful predicament, driven from her mind by the whip, returned and she held herself still and rigid, listening to the conversation.

"You see….Sire?" Josephine was clearly talking to Sejanus and was weighing her tone with heavy sarcasm. He might now be lord of the Courcey estates but the Delacourts would take a long time about accepting him into their ranks. "This one is no common peasant girl driven here by ill-luck and hunger. Look at her hands, the work here was probably the first manual labour she's ever done. Her limbs are clean and long and those breasts have never been suckled from. No, this one's a runaway of fairly wealthy origin I'd say. She's probably fallen foul of the law so won't be keen on being seen in public. She's learning her slavery well, she screamed very prettily I thought. Take her down and let's have a look at her."

Tamara's gorge rose in sheer terror as the woman gave the order to a member of staff. But there was nothing she could do as strong hands lifted her and the ropes slackened off. Relief from the pressure on her cunt briefly flooded out the terror but then she felt the laces at the back of the hood being eased open and suddenly it was off.

Tamara blinked in the reddish light of the dining room, coming from the torches burning in their sconces.

"By all that's……! It's her!" Sejanus broke the shocked silence as Tamara finally focussed on the faces around her.

"Tamara Courcey!" Josephine Delacourt's shrill voice chimed in. "We'll take her! Pay the Madam whatever she wants, Peter!"

Madam came striding in as Tamara collapsed once the veteran took his hand off her arm. She lay curled up on the floor as she was haggled over. Her mood was still swinging wildly between euphoria and stark terror as she heard Sejanus pay a price for her that she would not have paid for a triple crown slave. But then she was uniquely valuable as Josephine made clear to her.

Bending down the blonde noblewoman whispered in her ear as Tamara's stomach turned to water.

"Peter's shown me the cellars at the villa. That's where we'll keep you. In chains. We'll take you out for our guests to play with." She reached down and dug her fingers into Tamara's whip scorched breast. "They'll love seeing my long needles go through those," she hissed venomously. "The queen can have you........eventually. But by then you'll be nothing but gallows fodder!"

As Tamara looked up she saw Sejanus' face with its horse teeth and leering smile appear above Josephine's shoulder.

"We will hold entire evenings' entertainments devoted to your torment. Maybe whole days if you can last the pace. Then when everyone has taken their pleasure with you, you'll be slung back into the cellars until the next time we want to hear you scream. And the only time you'll ever leave the villa again will be when you're dragged behind a cart to Tamesbury where we'll tell the queen we've just found you skulking in a cock house."

Tamara was all too well aware of the security of her cellars, having frequently used them to pen unruly slaves. She also knew that the couple didn't dare let her see the daylight again until they were ready to send her to her probable death. But she reminded herself that William had escaped. And he had more chance of finding her at their own villa than of stumbling across her in some cock house. As soon as he was able he would aim to retake his estates, so somehow she had to hold out until then.

"Take her away and lock her up for the night," Josephine called out to the staff.

"No! Wait!" Sejanus said, stepping forwards and straddling Tamara as she lay on her back. His hands started to unlace his britches and his smile broadened.

"There's something I've been meaning to do to the stuck up bitch for a long time!"

Tamara suddenly realised what he intended and tried to squirm away but the veteran soldier was too quick and his hard hands pinned her shoulders down. Sejanus kicked her legs apart and stood between them as his britches fell to his ankles and his rampant cock sprang free. It was long and thin, curving up from his groin like a scimitar, its purple helm was already gleaming and exuding the first drops of his pre-ejaculate.

Tamara's eyes were fixed on it. Here was the core of the man who had betrayed her trust and wrecked her life. And like the scimitar it resembled, she was going to be impaled on it. She writhed in disgust, trying to close her legs but two of the pizzlers laughed and wrenched her thighs apart.

"Go on, Sire!" Josephine cackled from somewhere beyond Tamara's sight. "Stick that to her! It won't be the last time!"

Tamara's struggles grew more violent as her disgust grew and Sejanus knelt between her legs and then lowered his weight onto her. She felt sick with horror at having his treacherous, cowardly body on top of hers. His breath stank as his face sank towards hers, she twisted away and screamed in revulsion at the thought of taking his body inside hers.

She stiffened as she felt him nudge at her entrance, still stinging from the horse. Her whipped nipples hurt as they rasped against his tunic when she arched her back and tried to throw him off. She felt him thrust with his pelvis and to her absolute humiliation she felt him begin to slide into her. The long evening's suffering had done for her, her body was beyond her mind's control. It needed finishing and Sejanus' cock was a good as anyone's.

She screamed once more in horror as she felt herself accept his full length and heard him laugh in triumph.

He began to ram himself into her, slamming his pelvis against her and pummelling her bruised clitoris. Tamara gritted her teeth against the urge to buck her hips back at him and increase the friction inside her and for some time she held out, lying inert beneath him. But finally he wore her down and with the ironic cheers of both him and his fiancée ringing in her ears, she began to fuck the man who had ruined her and who had sent her husband in chains to Tamesbury.

She had been made a slave of. Life could hold no worse for her.

CHAPTER NINE
The South Alban Coast.

The sun was hot and the dust blew up from the road into Tamara's eyes. She turned her face away and tried to wipe it on the shoulder of the short tunic she had been given to wear. Her hands were tied to the back of the cart that followed the Lady Josephine's palanquin both of which were pulled by similarly dressed slaves and beside which Peter Sejanus rode on horseback. She recognised the horse as one of William's cherished stable of three. They had been on the road for several days now, following the coast road, heading west back towards her own villa and brutal imprisonment there. Her two captors made repeated use of her, revelling in their superiority and power. They had whipped her until she had obeyed a command to lick Josephine's cunt. She had been hung by her wrists from a branch only the previous night and again thrashed with a birch until she had obeyed a command to kneel before Sejanus and suck his cock. Her cunt however was still burning and stinging due to the fact that she had then been hung by her ankles and whipped between her legs for having failed to swallow his entire emission smoothly. Shamefully she had felt herself moisten under the lash as she realised how often she had done the self same thing to slaves who had failed to take William's spend.

She looked down at herself ruefully as the day drew to a close. Her long legs had thinned and become even more coltish over the course of her enslavement and the tunic only covered the tanned thighs to just below their junction. The men who escorted the party frequently took advantage of that fact to grope at her and get a feel of a 'noble' cunt. Surprisingly her breasts had remained unaffected by the slimming down of the rest of her and remained proud and high, tenting the low-necked tunic

and inviting further intrusions and molestation. Josephine was not especially well endowed and in the evenings would torment Tamara by dripping hot wax onto her breasts and then using a birch to whip it off.

"Just a little taste of what lies ahead, my lady," she would say mockingly. "But of course you know how divine transpierced breasts look. I promise you I will make pin cushions of these.....and then I'll hold a torch to the ends of the needles and make you really hop as the metal heats up! Oh, we'll have such fun!"

On those occasions she tried to not to look at her tormentor in order to hide her fear that she might not be able to stand the torment for long enough. If she once stopped giving them pleasure by putting up at least token resistance to her mistreatment and became listless and broken instead, she would lose her entertainment value and they would ship her off to Tamesbury and she had no doubt what would await her there.

As dusk began to flicker under the trees that shaded the road on the left, Sejanus called a halt and while the men pitched the tents and the slaves began to prepare the evening meal, Tamara was left tied to the cart. It was rare that she found herself idle and she used the time to look around. Ahead and on the right the land dropped away down to a bay in deep folds of green, punctuated by copses of low growing trees permanently bent before the prevailing wind off the sea. Squinting against the sun, Tamara gazed out and wondered whether William had made landfall in Frankland yet. She was certain he would return to the king with tidings of the queen's growing confidence. The light of the bright, setting sun shimmered and danced on the waves, dazzling her and making her squint even more and turn her head slightly. Just as she did so she caught sight of something. She looked again, eyes screwed up, and just caught a glimpse of a ship, outlined against the glare, disappearing around the headland that jutted out maybe a mile or two ahead of them on the far side of the bay. Its sail was furled which meant it was intending to make landfall. She frowned in puzzlement. There was no port of any size up ahead. The road turned inland from here and headed towards the rich farmlands of the Courcey estate.

Soon however her mind turned to more immediate things as the air became fragrant with the scent of woodsmoke and roasting meat from the cooking fires. No one made any attempt to hide the smoke. There was no need.

Tamara was tied, standing with her back to a tree after she had been fed and between her spread legs, the men of the escort enjoyed themselves while they exchanged banter with the other slaves about Tamara's cunt being much more refined than theirs.

For once Sejanus and Lady Josephine seemed to find pleasure in each other's company and left her alone. So it was fairly early and the moon was still rising when she was able to slide down and sit on the turf, uncomfortably leaking sperm from between her legs and try to get some sleep.

The last she ever saw of Peter Sejanus was as a silhouette against lamp light, closing the flap of his tent for the night. The last she ever knew of Josephine Delacourt was a soft laugh in the dark as Sejanus went to her bed.

She woke with a start to near complete darkness as a man's body toppled over her legs. There was just light enough from the dying fires as her eyes adjusted, for her to see that an arrow was sticking out of his back. She jerked against her bonds in futile panic. More arrows whispered past her in the dark and the men who had jumped up from sleep and were silhouetted against the fires, cried out and fell. More men leaped past her and she shut her eyes to try and blot out the slaughter that ensued.

Eventually the horrible noises stopped, footsteps approached her, a sharp blade pressed against her chin and she had no choice but to look up. A tall black haired man with a beard stood over her, holding his sword under her chin, she could just make out his sharp features as the fires were banked up again. Men were working efficiently and methodically, going through the pockets and the packs of those they had slain. They worked in silence and the only sound was of female sobbing coming from the slaves rounded up and crouching by one of the fires.

Tamara gazed up. Her mind took in the fact that Sejanus was probably dead and so was Josephine, hence she was no longer under sentence of torment in her own villa but she knew from the windswept appearance of the man and the crossing leather belts that held a ferocious array of swords and knives that she had fallen prey to slavers.

With an economical motion so fast she hardly saw it, the man sliced away her bonds and gestured with his head towards the other slaves. She had no option but to obey.

By the time it was full daylight, Tamara could see that her immediate future lay as a galley slave. The surviving women had been marched down towards the sea, and as the light had broadened, they had been able to see columns of smoke rising from different places inland. As they neared the shore, they began to encounter other gaggles of ragged and bewildered women being shepherded in the same direction they were. And like Tamara's own group, each was surrounded by dark skinned men, mostly bearded and all carrying deadly arsenals of bows, knives and swords about them. They wore short kilts and jerkins of animal hide. Some had their beards plaited but all were lean and well muscled.

Seeing a large number of men always had an effect on Tamara – and she suspected on other women too – it was a rare sight in any case and to see so much strong, lean, male flesh on view as well was even more uncommon. These were men from the south of Frankland, she guessed, and maybe from beyond there. The great Middle Ocean was surrounded with dark skinned races mostly descended from Carthaginian stock. The man who had taken her prisoner was clearly some kind of chief and as he indicated they should hunker down and wait, he strode away, shouting orders.

Tamara looked out towards the bay and saw there were actually two ships. One was a trireme with its three banks of oars shipped and its sail furled. From the masthead fluttered a strange flag that she did not recognise, it wasn't the Frankland emblem but instead it bore a simple depiction of a blood red hand. She shivered at the sight of it and recalled the sounds of the brief battle in the night. The other ship was obviously a prize the pirates had taken from a mooring somewhere. It was a slender and graceful bireme, definitely Alban in origin but now flying the same bloody hand standard. It seemed unmarked and she could only presume that somehow the pirates had managed to spirit the ship away from its mooring, crewed by themselves and now they were looking for a slave crew. And had found them.

If they weren't Frankish – or in the pay of the king of the Franks – then probably she and the other women would be made to row across to wherever in Eropia the men were heading for and then the ship and its crew would be auctioned off. If they were in the pay of the Franks, then the women would be gifted to various soldiers who had served the king well – an Alban slave in Frankland could be done with as her owner pleased and had no recourse to law, so they were highly prized possessions - and the ship would be used to prowl the waters between Alba and Eropia and disrupt troop and cargo movement.

Whichever was the case, fate seemed to have intervened yet again to make it impossible for William to ever rescue her. But Tamara was beyond any despair now, it seemed to her that she was a permanent piece of flotsam, doomed to drift and be at the mercy of anyone who found her. But there was no mercy, no kindness, just a life of endless slavery ahead of her…

Her thoughts were interrupted by the return of the tall pirate. For some reason he ignored the rest of the women and came to stand directly above her.

"You bad girl. They tie you, no?"

Tamara stared up at him and shrugged non-commitally. A hopeless lethargy seemed to have engulfed her. He would beat her or fuck her, maybe sell her, or work her till she dropped and suddenly it didn't matter to her which one he chose.

He smiled, his teeth white against the jet black of his beard. "I bad man! I like bad girls!"

He bent down and effortlessly dragged her to her feet, holding her close against his side. Tamara could feel the hard sinews of his body, her right thigh brushed the muscles of his left one. He shifted his grip from her upper arm to holding her round her waist. Her feet were hardly touching the ground and yet he seemed to be making no effort at all. All of a sudden Tamara realised that it had been weeks since she had been taken by any man other than Sejanus. The veteran at the cock house had regularly fucked and drunk himself into oblivion by the time the last guests left and so the slaves had had to make do with their own, or their cell mate's fingers and the pizzlers' strap-ons.

The man pressing her against his body was impressively strong and smelled of sweat and the sea. Despite her gloom, Tamara felt a stirring in her lower belly at being once more in the presence of a powerful man.

He grinned down at her and smiled again. "I like bad girls!" he repeated and hefting her slightly higher he strode down towards the shore where several rowing boats had been beached, shouting orders as he went in a language Tamara didn't recognise.

He threw her unceremoniously into the stern of one of them and then took up a place at the helm, standing over her as he organised the captured slaves being piled into the midships and guarded while the rest of his men ran out the oars. Once the boat was afloat, Tamara attempted to sit up but the pirate simply put his boot on her upper back and stepped firmly on her.

As Tamara had foreseen the new slave crew was unloaded onto the stolen ship where they found that the slavers had already made some other raids and collected about half a crew, so Tamara's group now brought them up to a full complement and allowed the rowing crews to work shifts, which would improve the vessel's speed and endurance.

It took several trips back and forth to the shore before all the slaves were embarked. In the meantime they were kept on deck in a huddled, fearful mass of near-naked femininity, while Tamara's captor shouted and laughed with his crew. But once he was satisfied all the booty was aboard, he caught a long stock whip, thrown to him by a colleague and cracked its lash loudly in the warm afternoon air. Instantly he had the attention of every woman aboard.

Tamara, squatting not far from where he stood, looked up as he coiled the lash and noticed the muscles of his arm, knotting and ridging under the tanned skin.

"You row good! You my slaves now. Slaves of Pepito! I feed you, I let you sleep below decks, I treat you good! But you got to be good to Pepito and row fast as you can. Fast as whip make you. If not, you bad girl. And Pepito punishes bad girls!"

Tamara's heart sank as with those words he turned to look in her direction and strode across the deck. She tried to wriggle away but he leaned forward and picked her up by her upper arm with steely strength.

She had barely got her feet under her before he pushed her backwards and sent her reeling into the arms of two of his crew. He gave them incomprehensible orders and turned back to the other women.

"That one is bad girl," he said pointing to her. "So watch what we do to bad girls!"

Someone rammed a foul tasting rag into her mouth as she opened it to scream and then tied it in with coarse rope. Meanwhile she was pushed to the ground face down and a network of the rough rope was woven skilfully around her arms and legs. Her tunic was sliced off with a knife and moaning in fear Tamara felt herself being lifted into the air by the ropes and painful tension come onto her limbs. She was hauled up in a spreadeagle shape tilted sharply forwards. She tried to scream as the deck swung away below her and she seemed to hover over the ship's prow. Then to her relief the ropes began to lower her. But her relief was short lived. As she descended a sailor appeared with a long pole on the end of which was a phallus. He looked up at her, grinning a gold-toothed smile and as she swung down he dextrously inserted the fingers of one hand into her cunt and followed it up with the pole. Tamara made a gag-muffled grunt as she felt herself stuffed to capacity and then there was a jolt inside her and craning her head down she saw the other end of the pole had been driven into a hole in the decking. The ropes lowered her further and she registered another stifled protest as more of her weight bore down on the shaft inside her. And then there came a final jerk and she stopped. She was above the prow and spreadeagled in the air, impaled on a dildo pole.

"We in a hurry now, so we just whip her a bit!" she heard Pepito announce to the other slaves. "But when we got time, bad girls get wet leather round their titties and then we let it dry and listen to them as the leather squeezes and squeezes. Tighter and tighter!"

Pepito surveyed his cowed audience and then administered the coup de grace. "And then we whip them! Now get these bitches below and chain them!" The final order was to the slaver crew who immediately hauled the trembling slaves to their feet and hustled them below. From her position as makeshift figurehead, Tamara heard them go and heard the sailors begin to haul on the sheets to unfurl the sail. From below came the smack of whips on flesh and the rumble of the oars being run out. Soon the drum began to beat as the sail filled and Tamara could see the ship begin to move out into the bay.

Suddenly she felt Pepito's big, hard hand on her thigh as he came to stand beside her. A hand which then moved up and across her until it was at her spread-open groin and there it found her clitoris. Tamara moaned in forced pleasure as the rough skin of the finger rasped and rubbed at it.

"I like bad girls!" he repeated, coming to stand in front of her but keeping his relentless frotting up and using his other hand to maul and squeeze her left breast. "Hey! Diego! Mind my hands when you whip her!"

Tamara tried to shriek in protest but was too late, Diego must have been standing right behind her and a line of fire scorched across her entire upper back. She arched in her bonds, thrusting her body onto Pepito's hands.

"That's my bad girl!" he chuckled. "Just fifty, Diego. And then we leave her for the rest to see."

Throughout the whole fifty lashes, Pepito kept up his massage and by the end Tamara was drenched in the sweat of pain and multiple orgasms. Her head lolled drunkenly as the ship rolled and she hung inert. She was never aware of the sun beginning to set and the slaves being brought on deck for an evening feed. She also never heard the gasps of dismay from them at how wrecked she was and how Pepito told them it was due entirely to the severity of the whipping.

She really only revived when she was taken down and had some kind of fiery spirit tipped down her throat and once she struggled up to a sitting position, she was given some unleaven bread and some kind of salad with ground nuts and yogurt in. It was surprisingly good and she wolfed it down as she looked about herself. The sun was setting almost directly astern, so that must mean they were heading east and towards Frankland, and the trireme could be seen sailing in line behind them. The crew were hunkered down and at ease around a brazier, relaxed about escape attempts now they were in open waters.

Familiar, heavy footsteps sounded behind her and she spun round to see Pepito's silhouette looming over her. He clicked his fingers imperiously.

"Come on bad girl. Follow!" he said.

Instinctively responding to the power of a man in command, Tamara crawled after him to the superstructure at the stern of the ship. His bunk was narrow but it was the closest to a real bed she had experienced for months and she revelled in having a strong man take his pleasure with her once more. Pepito was an insatiable lover with a magnificent cock. She felt not an ounce of guilt as she cried out under his thunderous lunges into her and unalloyed pleasure crashed through her abused body. He was the closest thing to Sir William himself that she had experienced since her arrest. Once he had assuaged his immediate thirst for a woman by taking her on her back with her legs spread and raised till her feet could brace themselves against the ceiling, Pepito slid out of the bunk, magnificent in his nakedness, poured himself a glass of wine and to Tamara's horror opened the cabin door. Then as he swigged down the wine he casually bantered and joked with any crew men still on deck. She wrapped the sheet around herself and huddled down, hoping he wouldn't want to share her around. But soon he slammed the door and came back to the bunk, sliding his massive body in beside hers.

"They say you squeal like a pig when you fuck," he told her, chuckling.

The relief of it seeming that he intended keeping her for himself, at least for this night, allowed Tamara to laugh a little. He caught her in his arms and turned her just enough to deliver a resounding spank to her right buttock, the report of the smack seemed deafening in the narrow wooden confines of the cabin. There was a faint cheer from the listening sailors on deck and then his hand was pressing on her head and, still delighting in the feel of bed linen next to her skin, Tamara slithered down to attend to his semi-tumescent cock. He lay back, parting his heavily muscled thighs for her and she began licking at the massive ball sac that lolled beneath the veined and throbbing shaft of his cock. He still smelled of her own juices, just as Sir William had when she performed this service for him. She took long slow licks as the hairs on his thighs tickled her face and the pungent taste of him filled her mouth. She glanced up to see the thick shaft pulsing back into erection, growing, hardening, promising a girl all the pleasure she could want. She wriggled up the bed a little and began to lick up the shaft itself and fetched a sigh of pleasure from Pepito. She stretched a little further and lapped the smooth skin of the polished helm with its strong-tasting pearl of pre-ejaculate at the summit. Drawing herself further up and propping herself on her elbows she was able to angle her head downwards and opening her mouth wide could slide down onto him. She heard his growl of pleasure as he felt the softness of her mouth engulf him and caress him. He tasted so good and it had been so long since she had a mouthful of cock, he didn't force her pace like Harry had always done. He was content to accept the worship of her tongue and lips. For Tamara, to have her mouth filled to bursting with the cock of a man who had had her whipped so recently but who had caressed her throughout the ordeal, propelling her to orgasm so often she had fainted, was heaven sent. And when he finally twitched and swelled against her tongue, his hand pressing demandingly on her head, she was ready to take down every drop of his spend and fondly lick him clean afterwards.

During the night he woke her on several occasions and after drinking huge drafts of wine, took her. The final time, he used her cunt juice to lubricate her backside and buggered her. At least the cock house had widened her enough to allow her to enjoy the penetration and she sank into the nearest she had come to a peaceful sleep since her arrest.

In the morning, she wasn't surprised that Pepito had her sent below to join the slaves. It was a working ship and every mouth had to earn its food. He did at least give her one of the kilts the men wore so only her breasts were naked.

She joined the rest of the slaves as they were fed dry bread and salted meat washed down with water. They were allowed to lower buckets over the side to haul up washing water and once they were all sluiced down as best they could manage, they were chained together by their ankles, Tamara having sat while a heavy leather cuff was stitched closed around her left ankle. In a long coffle, shepherded by curses and whips, they were marched below decks. Tamara had never ventured below decks before and had been imagining a stinking, dark pit of pain and terror. But as she and her sisters made their way carefully down the steep steps to the rowing deck, their chains clinking and slithering, she found a low ceilinged but nevertheless airy enough space. A cool sea breeze blew across the deck from the portholes on either side. A central aisle stretched nearly the length of the ship and on each side were benches. They alternated in height depending on whether they formed part of the upper or lower bank of oars. Tamara found herself placed on a bench near the bows and nearest the porthole of an upper rank oar. Beside her a black haired, dark skinned woman was placed and the long coffle chain was replaced with one that locked onto a ring in the central aisle. In a combination of gestures and bellowed, unintelligible instructions they were told to bend forwards and pick up the oar. Tamara was dismayed, between them they could only just lift the thing and heave it through the rowlock in the porthole. They braced their feet on the bench in front of and just below them and tried to grip the thick wood of the oar as they watched the rest of the women allocated to their stations and chained there. Any women lucky enough to have retained some vestige of clothing that covered their upper bodies were now resignedly shrugging out of them under the lecherous smiles of the guards who were taking every opportunity to squeeze and grope the ranks of breasts displayed for them. They were chatting cheerfully amongst themselves and Tamara could guess that they were speculating on which ones would be the most fun to whip. Increasingly the deck reverberated to the rumbling of oars as they were run out and the ship prepared for the day's sailing. Above her head she could hear running feet and more shouting as the sail was unfurled and peering out of the porthole she could see the ship begin to move, at least the oars wouldn't have the whole weight of the ship against them on this day at least. From the stern came the sound she was dreading, however. The drum master was hammering out a few warm up rhythms and the twenty or so men detailed off for slave duty were hefting and swinging the heavy straps they would be using to flog with. All the oars were now unshipped and one of the men yelled again and made a gesture with his arm. Tamara got the message and with her fellow galley slave giving her a nervous smile of encouragement they bent forwards and let the oar dip into the water.

For a moment there was silence with everyone tensed and ready. Tamara made sure her feet were firmly planted on the back of the slave bench ahead of her, she tried to concentrate on the huge effort she knew she would have to make shortly and also tried to put out of her mind the fact that her back was still stiff and sore from the beating of the day before. The straps the guards wielded looked heavy and seriously punishing, a stock whip was too long for use below decks but the straps looked as though they were long enough to reach every slave quite easily. The bent backs ahead of her already sported fading flares from the previous night's rowing.

Suddenly a shout came from up above the drum master and he began to beat out a slow rhythm with one hammer. The guards all shouted together and Tamara knew she had to pull with all her strength.

Gritting her teeth she almost threw herself backwards, pushing with her feet as she pulled with her arms. Slowly the oar swept through the water until the she and her partner were almost lying on their backs. Tamara could feel the hair of the slave in front of her brush her legs. From all around came the slap and thud of the whips falling on the exposed breasts of the slaves and the answering squeals. She pushed down, guided by the slave beside her who had been trained the day before and sat back up, bringing the huge oar back through the air for another sweep as she bent forwards as far as she could. Now the whips fell on their backs, encouraging them to pull for their lives.

Tamara pulled till she was groaning with the effort but the guard who walked up and down by their benches made no allowances and beat all of them in turn. The strap was weighted at its end, to fly fast and true without a long backlift being needed. Across the breasts it was a real trial. Every slave cried out under that particular stroke. It flattened the breasts and left a throbbing belt of pain across them. On some occasions it would strike across the nipples and it was all Tamara could do, when it happened, to keep her grip on the oar instead of instinctively cradling her injured flesh.

Slowly the speed of the strokes increased under the rain of whiplashes until it matched that of the drum. But steadily that rhythm increased until the helmsman up on deck was satisfied and let the drum master maintain his speed. By that time, sweat was running from every pore of Tamara's skin.

She could hardly see through the curtain of sweat-soaked hair that stuck to her forehead, and sweat stung her eyes and trickled down maddeningly between her breasts. She knew she was slavering and dribbling onto her breasts. Every muscle was screaming in protest and still the whip found her and urged her on. The deck became the place of nightmare she had imagined. It was filled with the groans of the slaves, the reek of sweat and the smack of the whips. The drum ruled her very breathing and she was about to faint when it all ceased.

Every slave collapsed over her oar and moaned as she recovered her breath. But at least they were watered; a barrel was brought down the aisle and the men filled metal cups and passed them out, counting them carefully back in, Tamara noted. It was the most divine drink she had ever taken but she could have taken on three or four times the amount. They were given some more rest time before the drum started again and they descended back into hell. Eventually they were fed and had a longer rest before they were flogged through an endless afternoon; although Tamara thought the rate of flogging was beginning to slow down towards the end. Maybe they were becoming better at keeping up with the drum. She could only hope so.

At last they were taken back up on deck and allowed to wash and eat. To her amazement, even as Tamara stretched her aching muscles and whip scorched back, she found herself casting appreciative glances at the men around her, the devastating straps hanging from their belts.

Perhaps it was the sheer amount of half-naked females around her coupled with the whip play and the arrogant maleness. Or maybe it was the fact that she was truly a slave now. Whatever the reason, she felt herself begin to moisten as she watched strong male hands rest on hips and their fingers idly toy with the leather straps they had whipped the women with. She sighed as she made her way to the cabin below decks where the slaves were kept. It was below the rowing deck and jammed into the stern. They had simple wooden pallets to sleep on and their coffle chain was fixed at either end of the cabin. Both rowing teams shared the cramped, smelly accommodation. The other team had enjoyed a rare day's rest while Tamara's team had been put through their paces.

Over the next few days the ship's routine settled down. The slaves rowed for roughly half a day at a time, changing shifts at mid-day and Tamara was amazed at how fast her body acclimatised to the work. The resting crew were allowed to stay on deck where their coffle chain was still carefully locked to rings in the deck.

After the evening meal, if Pepito didn't want to row all night and thankfully he had only required that once, when a sail had appeared briefly over the horizon behind them, the women were fair game for any man not required on the night watches. Their libidos were fired up from the long day's whipping and were further stoked by the almost inevitable discovery that one of the girls had been lazy. It was a rare evening when one or other of the slaves wasn't led – either cringing or proud, depending on her nature – to the mainmast and was hung up by wrists or ankles in the rigging for punishing. The main punishment of slow breast constriction was reserved for daylight when the sunshine could do its work and the other slaves could watch the breasts darken into shiny, tight balls of agony which were then whipped. Tamara couldn't help admiring the way the naked figure of the condemned slave would writhe and spin at the mast – if she was standing on the deck – or spin and wriggle like a hooked fish if she was suspended. It was no worse than she had done on many occasions and she now found that the fact that she was in real danger of suffering it herself, lent the spectacle an extra erotic charge. Especially as the punished slavc was immediately used by at least half the crew one after the other once she was released.

Tamara also found that her constant state of semi nakedness, the ever-present whip and the way the crewmen would just select a woman from the coffle and possess her there and then, either lying on the deck of standing against the gunwales, highly exciting. There were so few men to go around and so many half naked females. On one evening, several of the crew lifted their short kilts and as the women watched, ran their looped fingers up and down the shafts of their cocks, hardening them until they reared up above the spellbound women and then they tightened their grips and forcefully wanked themselves until spray after spray of thick sperm, plopped into the slaves' drinking water. Tamara could remember watching a similar scene unfold at Southaven and also she could remember laughing with William as the slaves had fought for a taste of the water. She continued to remember it even as she clawed and scratched her way to a bowl and drank the water with strings of divinely tasty sperm decorating it.

Inevitably, or so it seemed to Tamara, she was selected as having been lazy on a day when the air was hot below decks and the men were irritable. A slave was brought down from the other shift to replace her and resignedly she allowed herself to be led up on deck. Pepito was at the helm and saw her being led towards the mainmast.

"Hey Bad Girl!" he bellowed. "You give us good fun and Pepito might take you tonight!"

She turned and her stomach flipped over. It had been so long since he had taken her to his bed on that first night. She had just had a few quick fucks to sustain her in the interim. She smiled back up at him and steeled herself proudly, her back against the mast, her arms raised and shackled over head, her breasts thrusting forwards, provocative and so deliciously vulnerable. It was how she had always loved seeing a slave presented and as she spread her legs to have her ankles chained down, she felt a real erotic charge flow through her at the thought of Pepito's cock hardening as he watched her. In front of her a crewman laid out two hide straps and poured water on them. Then grinning evilly he laced them tightly around each breast, constricting the root immediately but not overly much. She admired his skill and judgement.

He spent a few minutes with his hand between her legs, feeling into her deeply and fetching delighted sighs from her as his fingers swirled, clenched and stretched inside her; and deliberately making her nipples harden and her breasts swell with lust even as the leather began to dry and with a casual pat on her hip the man left her.

Tamara held out for as long as she could while the ship's routine went on around her. Occasionally one or other of the men would risk Pepito's wrath by stopping what he was doing and feeling her cunt or playing with her tightening breasts and nipples. But eventually she had to give way to cries as the pain built and built inside her. She could look down and see how the breasts Sir William had loved to caress and stroke while they played with their slaves, now almost shone they were so tightly constrained. The skin had darkened to a near purple and even though her nipples throbbed they could hardly stand proud of the swollen areolas. The pain was immense and the fact that her suffering was causing quite a lot of tented kilts amongst the crew, made her cries almost orgasmic as she shamelessly thrust her pelvis out towards anyone who might play with her for a few seconds. Her torment only ended when eventually Pepito came to see her.

"You scream good! I think we do this tomorrow as well, eh?" he said, smiling broadly and putting his hand on her hip as she writhed against the mast, unable now to stand still.

"N….n….no please!" she stuttered. "Please! Please!"

Suddenly serious, Pepito grabbed her chin and forced her pain bleared eyes to focus on him.

"Please what, little bad girl?"

Tamara was so far gone the answer slipped out before she could think.

"Whip. The whip!"

"Hah!" Pepito laughed and stepped back, holding out his hand.

A short tailed whip was placed in it and Tamara recognised it as being similar to one she used on her slaves' breasts. It hurt even without constriction. There was to be no mercy and she would be watched as she suffered. She smiled at Pepito as he raised the lash.

The stiff lashes cut swathes across the blood-congested orbs and she answered each lash with a cry until she was hoarse. And when, without warning Pepito altered his target and swung the whip upwards between her legs, all she could manage was a shocked gulp but for the next ten lashes she rocked her pelvis forwards to meet each cut; offering her sex to her master like any slave should.

She never remembered being taken down but much later, when the men lying on her and fucking her had at last become fewer and farther between, she remembered the orgasms. Again and again she had come, revelling in the cruelty she now endured as regularly as she had ever handed it out. Loving every second of rough, imperious male usage.

And at last she found herself dizzily picked up and slung onto Pepito's shoulder, taken back to his cabin and gloriously fucked on real sheets again. She was amazed that she still had the energy to slam her hips up against him as his body pressed her down. But in the end he was cheering her on as she took him for ride after ride. When at last she had drained him of his strength he licked at the roots of her breasts where the leather had left bitterly deep trenches.

It was the night that saved both her life and that of most of her fellow slaves.

From then on Pepito seemed to develop a special liking for his 'bad girl' as he always called her and frequently took her to his cabin, especially on nights when a slave was suspended and whipped on deck. Eventually he noticed what Tamara was herself becoming more aware of. She had completely turned into the mirror image of her old self.

"You like the sound of the whip, yes?" Pepito said to her one evening as she knelt before him, her mouth full of his cock and her hands busy between her legs. Without thought she nodded and continued to suck him, while from outside there came the regular thwacks and smacks of a good flogging being administered to a sighing and groaning slave.

Pepito laughed and allowed her to continue until he splashed his thick sperm into her open throat, spray after spray making Tamara give muffled cries of delight at her master's virility.

When he was clean again, the flogging outside had stopped and he went to the door and called out to his men.

"Put another one up there and beat her! My bad girl likes it!" Then he came back to her, grinning broadly and took her to the bed again as another slave began to take a whipping and Tamara's cunt melted and poured her juices over her master's fingers.

With the near continual use and the hard labour at the oar, Tamara had had no opportunity to think about where they might be heading or what her future might hold. Day followed day down below decks where the slaves strained and the whips cracked. Evening followed evening, where there was more whip play and some lucky slaves were used by the men. The dreamless sleep of exhaustion claimed them all each night until one afternoon the rhythm of the drum altered and one side of the ship was ordered to stop rowing while the other continued. Up on deck the crew were furling the sail and soon Tamara could see they were heading for land. She peered at the hills she saw, trying to guess whether they were still in Alban waters or whether they had rowed across the channel into Frankland territory.

She could gather no clues and that evening after they had been fed, they were chained onto their sleeping pallets with no use having made of them at all. The men seemed tense and watchful. Tamara had to hope that that meant they were still in Alba.

The slaves listened as the boats were lowered and rowed away and heard a skeleton crew pace the decks above them. Tamara could only speculate that another raid for provisions or more slaves was underway. She fell into her usual deep sleep and only woke when there were cries and curses from above and the sounds of men running.

In the dark the door burst open and men tumbled in holding lamps, to unlock the chains and harry the sleep-befuddled women to their posts, chain them and then lash them to working as the grey dawn broke, the drum beat an impossible rhythm, the lashing was hysterical in its ferocity and Tamara realised the men were scared. Gradually however, they managed to get the ship underway and the men calmed a bit. Tamara could hear Pepito shouting on deck, he seemed to be urging the men on, there was some cheering and men carried barrels and bales through the deck and down into the hold.

"Hah! We see them off!" was all Pepito said when he came down to stroll along the ranks of his sweating slaves. Tamara could only assume that someone had put up some resistance to this raid.

But as daylight broke, panic seemed to reign again. The drum master was ordered to a frenzied rate, the men on duty below decks lashed out again in desperate haste at the slaves and then suddenly dropped their whips and ran up on deck freeing their knives and swords from their belts as they ran. The slaves looked anxiously at each other as they kept rowing from force of habit. But then Tamara saw the drum master glance out of one porthole, cast aside his hammers and run for the upper deck as well. Tamara followed the direction of his look and joined her scream to those suddenly ringing out around her. The prow of another ship was bearing down on them from a few yards away, foam curling and breaking about the lethal ramming spar that all ships carried just below the waterline. Her sail was swollen taut, full of wind and her oars were disciplined and fast. She had had sea room to get up speed and was intent on her prey.

It didn't matter whether it was an Alban ship or a Frankish one, the slaves aboard Pepito's ship were as good as dead, chained to their places as the ship sank.

Hysterical with fear she and her fellow slaves wrenched in vain at steel chains locked firmly around sturdy iron, screaming and crying in terror and frustration. With awful slowness and a deafening, grinding roar the timbers behind Tamara splintered and began to buckle as the other ship careered into theirs. She and several other slaves were flung towards the stern of their ship as the deafening noise of collision seemed to go on and on and even the planking of the deck began to buckle beneath them as the ramming spar, drove into the heart of the ship, delivering a death wound. Partly stopped from falling further by her chain, Tamara sprawled over the bench in front of hers and looked back. The timbers of their ship had split so badly that even the vertical post of the other ship's prow was protruding into their deck. There was daylight around it and she could hear men yelling and screaming. The slaves behind Tamara were pulling to the last extreme of their chain, screaming dementedly and barely inches from the invading ship, already up to their ankles in water.

Suddenly Pepito was there. Enough of the narrow stairs had survived for him to get down. His sword and face were bloodied and he was ashen pale.

He reached into a pouch at his belt and flashed one last grin at Tamara as their eyes met.

"Here bad girl! Get away!" He threw something and instinctively she caught it as he charged back up the stairs. It was a key.

With fumbling haste and watched by anxious eyes, Tamara fitted the key into the lock that held her and her partner in place. There was a sigh of relief as the key turned and Tamara was able to rattle the chain through the loops on their cuffs and then pass the key on. There were screams of frustration and fear now as hope replaced despair but the waters continued to rise. Tamara splashed her way to the stairs and climbed up the buckled but still sound steps. Already other slaves were beginning to follow, the frantic rattling of chains continued from below as she cautiously stuck her head up out of the hatch. A furious battle was taking place between what looked like hundreds of men.

Quickly she hoisted herself out and onto the deck then ducked behind some upturned bales of cloth as two blood stained men toppled past her, grappling to the death for possession of a knife that one held. She had no idea whether the slavers had been surprised by another group of pirates or whether Alban or Frankland forces had ambushed them. To a half naked slave, it was immaterial, any man could and would claim her. Her only real hope of improving her situation lay in escape. She looked around and saw that the ship which had rammed them was indeed a trireme flying the Alban rose at her masthead. Beyond it she could see the pirates' trireme desperately making for the open sea with two Alban biremes in hot pursuit. Tamara felt for the slaves on all the ships who would now be driven mercilessly. From the hatchway she had emerged from she could see a rapid scrum of escaping slaves developing and decided that they were her best chance of escape. Just as the thought had entered her head she heard a male voice yell out that the slaves were escaping.

Tamara turned, vaulted over the gunwales and took her chances with the sea.

CHAPTER TEN
Interlude; Cambria.

The lightweight wickerwork chariot shook and bucked a little as it was trotted over the tussocky grass along the lines of soldiery. Owen Daibron braced his feet wider apart and rode the shaking with practised ease. The two ponies pulling the vehicle were athletic and graceful creatures; a perfect pair of identical twins. Their dark hair flowed down their backs and gold circlets gleamed about the crowns of their heads. Beads of dampness bejewelled their hair as moisture from the misty air condensed out onto it. Their sleek skins shone too. A Pictish king had sent them, his daughters, in tribute and in a matter of months they had gone from haughty, uncontrollable brats to pliant, subservient pony slaves who fed from his hand and – as now – took his whip as he kept them up to a buttock rippling trot. They were just another product of the Slavemaker's art.

The ranks he was surveying were worryingly young. Once a boy attained the age of majority in Alba he was sent – unless his family could make out a case for extenuating circumstances – to the military academies in Cambria and it was these untried troops who now stood between Alba and civil war. They would have to do. Owen and his fellow guardians could help, but ultimately they would have to go into battle.

He reached the end of the line, reined in the slaves and stood for a moment in deep thought. He and the council of guardians had argued long into the night and now the time for decision had arrived. It could no longer be delayed. He stared back at the rank he had passed in front of and noted the look of fierce eagerness on the youths' faces. Then he sighed and whipped up the ponies once more. There was only one thing left to try and then the decision would have to be taken. Did they declare for the king, or transfer their allegiance to the queen? It was a simple matter of expedience, the brethren of the guardians had survived and prospered by always making sure they were on the winning side. Owen was charged with continuing that tradition.

From among the other ranks his fellows emerged, each riding the traditional chariot pulled by the cream of the slave girls offered in tribute to the guardians and in thanks for good harvests or freedom from pestilence. The grey robed figures looked ghostly in the mist as they formed into a line behind Owen and headed into the woods, making for the great stone circle that lay at the heart of their order.

The ancient trees loomed out of the mist and the air was filled with dripping water from their leaves. The slaves' booted feet padded softly on the moss and grass and Owen only occasionally flicked at their backs with his driving whip. They knew their business well enough and trotted prettily in step, the wickerwork of the chariot's body creaking slightly every now and then.

After only a few minutes the sinister shapes of the standing stones appeared and Owen drew his chariot to one side by a tree that stood at the edge of the clearing around the stones and hobbled his ponies before knotting the reins around a wheel rim for good measure. His fellows did the same and a silent line of twenty robed figures made their way into the circle.

The grass was level and cut short inside the circle, and in the centre was a stone staircase descending straight into the earth and down this the line of figures made their way.

The stairs led them into an earthen floored chamber that stretched away beyond the ability of the torches, hung on the great stone pillars in the centre, to illuminate. There were twenty pillars illuminated and each one had a naked slave girl tied to it. She stood with her arms stretched back and around the enormous girth of the pillars to the point of real discomfort and the chamber was filled with soft, gag-muffled groans. But it wasn't just the stringent bondage that was causing the girls' discomfort. Each one sported massive breasts, swollen with milk. They were strapped at the roots to increase the pressure and the nipples were covered by silver cones that squeezed the engorged flesh cruelly. At each girl's clitoris was a ring and each labium had been pierced with three rings. A thin strip of silver wire was crimped around each ring, criss crossing the slit of the sex. These slaves were off limits to all. By continual manipulation and dosing with some of the guardians' carefully gathered roots and plants, they were kept in constant lactation and were solely for the use of the ruling council of the guardians, whose members were now present. The wire guarding the vulva could quite easily be removed but it would be a foolhardy man who trespassed on the guardians' private property.

The slaves were well overdue their milking and that was the principal cause of their distress. At the sight of their lords and masters they strained at their bonds, pushing their breasts forward, begging for release. But there was one final detail to attend to before that could take place. The guardians well knew the elemental energy that could be released by a female enduring erotic pain and in the ritual they now intended to carry out, it was a vital ingredient. Each robed man approached a girl and took from a hook above her shoulder, a short, stiff tailed whip. It looked quite innocuous with lashes only about six inches long, but the reaction from the slaves was instant. Above their gag straps their eyes opened wide and the begging note to the grunts and moans was unmistakable.

Owen took his whip and stood in front of his designated slave – a blonde Eirean girl gifted to him by a warlord from there for help with a potion that produced a son and heir. Her blue eyes were wide open as she contemplated what the next few minutes would bring her at his hands. Like his brothers beside him, he reached out and unscrewed the nipple cones. The girl's eyes rolled and closed as she absorbed this new pain and then there was silence as he contemplated the difficulty of the ritual ahead and assessed how much pain would help them achieve success.

The men turned to look at him as they waited for the sentence to be passed.

"Twenty, brothers," he said eventually. "On each breast."

Immediately they went to work and the background noise in the chamber became considerably louder. The stiff lashes of the whips punished the tight skin and the lead pellets embedded in the ends of the lashes added a spiteful bite. The slaves' neck and shoulder sinews stood out as they strained to escape the lash but all they could do was achieve an attractive swing to their swollen breasts and encourage further cruelty. Unlike the triple crown slaves, the milk slaves experienced pain as purely that. And it was that pain that gave their secretions such power.

For several minutes the whips whispered down and stung their dancing and squirming prey and then that part was over and twenty slaves hung in their bonds, panting and gasping as their masters took small metal cups and began to compress and massage the purple striped breasts, collecting the milk as it spurted and sprayed. The slaves sighed in contented relief as they were emptied for the time being.

When his slave's breasts had run dry, Owen went to stand in the very centre of the chamber where there was a low stone altar. In the centre of that was an enormous copper bowl, already half full with a thick brown liquid which exuded a pungent, vegetable aroma. Above the bowl, her feet only inches away hung another slave girl. She was suspended by her wrists from a chain which itself hung from an iron ring set into the ceiling. She had been there for some time and her hooded head hung forwards. She had been subjected to a full body whipping and the criss crossing marks on her body bore testimony to it. Her sweat and cries had helped the initial brew attain some potency, which the milk slaves were now about to bring to a peak. Owen carefully sluiced his cup of milk in the bowl so as not to waste a drop, then he stood aside and let his brothers do the same. When all had added their libations and the hanging slave was stirring and moaning softly, Owen spoke.

"Let us put forth our thoughts now and consider the future. What is given to us to see in the scrying bowl may not be what must come to pass, yet it may guide us. Now!"

All the men held their arms out and advanced a step until they touched the rim of the bowl and then for a long time they stayed quite still and silent. All an observer might have noticed was a faint mist rising from the bowl and winding around the figures grouped about it. Then in response to some invisible signal they all stepped back as one.

Owen knew that as leader of the order he was privy to some of the visions his brothers had had. He himself had seen Isabella Dulac; she had been creeping through the dark, seeking him. He had seen another woman he didn't recognise also running and being silhouetted against flames. He had seen a battle and heard the shouts and screams, but it seemed to him that the screams were shriller than male screams. He had seen the face of the king, smiling, and he had seen soldiers he did not recognise marching through Tamesbury. He knew that at least one of his brothers had seen a sea battle and a ship being sunk, another had seen a great battle being fought in front of a Frankish castle. Another had seen a long coffle of women being brought to the guardians for slavemaking. Two, he knew, had seen Queen Anneka looking in relaxed good humour but the bowl never gave clues as to whether the visions were in the present or lay in a possible future.

One by one they all repeated what they had seen and Owen nodded when he had shared their visions. Then at last there was silence. He knew that the council itself was split on where their allegiance should lie in the coming weeks and it was waiting for him to make the decisive move as leader of the order. Sometimes the bowl vouchsafed almost identical visions to all the brethren and then their path was clear. Fragmented visions, however, such as they had experienced bespoke a future that was fraught with uncertainty and danger. And as leader of the order, if he brought harm on it through his decision, tradition demanded his life would be forfeit.

He drew himself up and pronounced his judgement.

Interlude: Tamesbury

Queen Anneka lay back in her chair a little more and twitched her robe further apart at the front. The brunette kneeling between her spread thighs, buried her head a little deeper and forced her tongue a few vital inches further up into her mistress' vagina. Captain Berghaus stood in front of her in her audience chamber, a few yards away. He fidgeted his feet on the marble floor uncomfortably and the queen smiled as she noted how he kept his eyes downcast. She twitched her robe open further still to bare her breasts and beckoned to another slave standing beside the opulently upholstered chair. The slave approached and bent over her mistress, immediately starting a passionate suckling at the royal nipple.

The queen sighed in pleasure and addressed the girl kneeling between her thighs, still tonguing assiduously in the hopes of avoiding a whipping.

"You, work my back passage – gently!" she told her.

The queen held her breath and then let it out in another sigh as she felt the greased steel phallus begin to move in her rectum. "And keep licking me, you idiot!" she chided sharply as the slave failed to maintain the required stimulation. The chamber echoed the sounds of a desperately slurping tongue for a few moments.

"Now Captain. What was your question again?"

"How much longer, your majesty?" The captain strove to keep the irritation out of his voice.

"As long as it takes. No longer. You have my word on it," the queen replied.

She waved a hand and a few feet behind the slave who was attending to her breast, the beating which the captain's arrival had interrupted, resumed. The recipient was one of the royal household's own triple crown slaves, a robust specimen with big breasts and meaty thighs who could withstand hours of punishment and still have the queen writhing and moaning on her day bed for an afternoon. The two men wielding the whips went back to work with a will. Delivering a good flogging for the queen might result in an extra slave being gifted to a man's house.

The queen glanced across to where the slave was chained with raised wrists, she stood quietly under the twin assaults on her back, legs spread and braced. Her breasts shaking and rippling prettily in the wake of the impacts on her back, her eyes were heavy lidded with lust. It was widely rumoured that the Slavemaker and his brethren could use triple crown slaves' eyes to see through. She didn't know whether it was true or not but the girl made a pretty picture and she smiled at the thought of the pleasure that lay in store. The slave's eyes flicked up momentarily and met hers, then they resumed their customary docile, downwards gaze while the men continued to work steadily on her. The queen reflected that if anyone had been using the slave's eyes to see through at that point they would have seen her looking very relaxed and happy. That thought made her happier still.

"But majesty, how long is that?" the captain persisted, breaking into her thoughts.

"It will be very soon. I want two more raids to raise the anger of the South Downs nobles and they will take place shortly."

"But the renegades' numbers grow by the day. I have still the same number of troopers I arrived with."

The queen was becoming irritated and summoned another man to start beating the slave who was kneeling between her legs. He stepped forwards and nervously judged his target, aiming for the slave's back and avoiding, at all costs, the pale flesh of the royal inner thighs. He swung the whip vertically down the slave's back and the queen arched in delight as the tongue and the prong in her rectum both jolted in response to the well aimed lash.

"Captain!" shc gasped. "I must wait until the people are desperate!"

With a final attempt to concentrate on something other than her growing pleasure, she fixed her eyes on his frowning face. "Send for reinforcements if you fcel you must," she growled, clamping her hands on the head of the slave now slavering between her legs as she was whipped. The captain's face clouded at the studied insult.

"No. We wait. But do not wait too long!"

Rocking her pelvis against the slave's face, the queen began to come. "Do not presume to order me! Now go!"

The captain turned on his heel and stalked away from the debauched scene.

CHAPTER ELEVEN
The South Downs.

Tamara's time with Black Harry on the journey to Southaven had taught her the rudiments of survival and four days after her escape from the wreck of Pepito's ship, she was sitting in relative comfort before a small fire, gnawing on spit-roasted rabbit.

Once she had made landfall, she had found cover under a pile of the previous autumn's leaves in the woods behind the beach she found herself washed up on and had made herself a bed. Exhaustion had allowed her to sleep until the following dawn, and when she had awoken she found the beach was a scene of wreckage and flotsam from the battle. Of Pepito's ship, only the top of the mainmast was above water and it looked incongruous as it leaned drunkenly above the waves at the mouth of the bay. On the beach she found some small barrels of provisions and although they were too heavy to carry, she at least made a decent meal before she carefully searched the tide line for any items of clothing that might have washed up. She kept her eyes averted from the saturated and ragged forms that she knew were bodies and eventually found a ragged shirt that wasn't bloodstained and wrung it out as best she could before putting it on over Pepito's kilt. She still had no idea of whether she was in Alba or Frankland so the only sensible course was to avoid every habitation until she could orientate herself properly and try to form some sort of plan.

She had walked inland and on the second day, hiding from hunters returning from emptying their traps, she had heard them speak Alban. From that she judged that Pepito had gone east as far as the South Downs and indeed the land was becoming more rolling and open as she went, making it more difficult to stay under cover of the trees. No plan had come to her mind and so she had simply kept walking for two more days and now, as the dark closed in again she carefully arranged turfs around the heart of the fire to keep the light from the burning twigs from straying too far. But as she sat back and wiped her mouth, she saw she wasn't alone.

The woman who had silently emerged from the trees was long legged and dressed in a short tunic of hide, roughly cured and ragged. At her waist she had leather straps which held a long knife at one hip and a short, stabbing sword at the other. In one hand she held another knife; pointing at Tamara. Her hair was blonde, falling in thick and greasy tangles over her finely boned face, her breasts strained the hide to contain them and her cleavage was very obvious even from where Tamara sat.

"Who are you?" the woman asked in strongly accented Alban.

"I could ask you the same," Tamara replied, standing up slowly and wondering who was going to enslave her this time.

The woman nodded at something behind Tamara. "You could, but then these two could ask you again."

Tamara whirled round and realised that two more women had appeared from behind but she barely had time to register their presence before something caught her a stunning blow to the back of the head and she knew no more.

She came to feeling sick and weak, tied out on grass, on her back, before several large fires burning brightly in a wide clearing in amongst tall trees. She tried to move but by craning her head could see her ankles and wrists were roped to pegs driven deep into the turf. As her mind cleared she again craned her head up and was able to see others pegged out as she was and yet more hung by their ankles from roughly constructed wooden frames. All were naked but the women who strolled amongst the prisoners, occasionally pushing one or other of the hanging ones to make them swing, were clothed as the blonde woman had been. All were armed and seemed to move with more swagger and self confidence than any women Tamara had ever seen.

Suddenly they all seemed to see something and crowded into a large circle around the naked captives. Tamara's neck muscles grew weary and she lay back for a moment. Into her range of vision stalked a tall, dark haired woman who glared down at her, arrogance radiating off every inch of her. She wore tight fitting leggings and boots of soft doe skin, her jerkin was also good quality leather and she had a shirt on underneath it. She was spectacularly built with breasts that thrust against the layers of clothing that covered them as if anxious to be bared for admiration and worship.

Beside the tall woman came a shorter one, older and with fair hair, wispy and faded, Tamara thought. Her eyes were oddly dark in one so blonde and Tamara felt afraid of her immediately. She too gazed down with arrogance but also with contempt. The two women stalked along the line of prostrate captives and then examined the hanging ones.

"No doubt they will all claim to be slaves escaping from the ship that sank over in Weyton Bay," the first woman said loudly, addressing the whole gathering.

"Of course they will," the smaller woman said, going over to one of the hanging slaves and spitefully grabbing a nipple and twisting it. The girl gave a yelp and twisted on the ends of her ropes. "But the king's spies are everywhere! We can take no chances. Let me beat their confessions of spying out of them Ladyship."

The woman scurried to another hanging slave and delivered a meaty smack square on the exposed vulva.

"We need new troopers, Jane, not whipped out drudges!"

The smaller woman looked downcast for a moment but had a thought which seemed to cheer her up. "As Ladyship wishes, but we surely can't let 'em join without doing the test. They all gotta do the test!"

That also seemed to strike a chord with the rest of the women and there was general cheering and laughter.

The tall woman came to stand in the centre of the clearing and Tamara craned up once again as she addressed the captives.

"You may all be fugitives like us. Then again maybe you aren't. You've all been freshly whipped, I'll grant, though any woman can be beaten easily enough these days. But if you can prove to us you can accept a woman's dominance rather than a man's – you'll have a chance to join us and help to free the women of this land!"

There were cheers from all sides and sudden purposeful activity. Hands untied Tamara's wrists and ankles and helped her to her feet. She looked around at the all-female helpers and saw faces alive with excitement. The woman who was being helped up next to her, Tamara vaguely recognised as coming from the ship as well. She rapidly counted ten captives and hoped that more than that had escaped from the ship, but she had no time to dwell and was hustled towards a large tent, outside of which a party of the renegades, as Tamara now knew them to be, placed a large couch on the grass. It must have been looted in one of their raids as it was beautifully carved and upholstered. It was low and had just one raised end, covered with scarlet silk. The one they seemed to just call Ladyship, stood beside it and to much encouragement from the crowd, she began to strip.

The blonde woman helped her, obsequious and somehow sinister, almost fawning over her as she helped untie the leggings and ease them off the long and shapely legs. Tamara had to admit she cut a spectacular figure, carrying her nudity with complete confidence. Her large breasts with their darkly tawny areola, swung and shifted weightily as she moved and Tamara found herself wishing she could sample the taste of the thick, rubbery nipples that protruded from their centres. At her groin a dense thatch of pubic hair beckoned to further exploration between her long thighs. She sauntered along the line of tightly held prisoners, smiling a cold, humourless little smile.

Then she turned and they could all see that branded deep into the flesh on the back of her left shoulder was a crudely fashioned letter; 'r' for renegade.

"If you can pass the test, you will be able to bear the brand of our sisterhood. If not.....well, we can't just let you go now you've seen us. Can we?"

Over to the right of the clearing someone slung a rope over a high branch of a tree. One of the women began to work the end into a noose and Tamara swallowed nervously.

Ladyship turned back to her couch and lay back on it, planting her legs on either side of the bench, running her hand up and down the slit of her cunt.

More women brought a brazier that glowed with white hot coals and in their midst was an iron rod. Tamara knew its end was shaped into the 'r' she had seen on Ladyship's shoulder. Once she herself bore that brand, it would be more than even William could do to rescue her. But if she failed, the rope awaited. She felt like bursting into tears at the bitter unfairness of it all. She had survived everything and endured. But now she was to be branded as one who was outside the law; lower even than a galley slave or a cock house whore. And forever she would bear the shame even if she ever did reclaim her status and property. William would always know that just beneath her robe – however opulent it might be – she bore a mark that lowered her beneath the lowliest farm slave. How could he ever take her back? But at least, she told herself sternly, if she survived, the possibility was there that he might. If she failed the test, there was nothing.

"You! Get over here and pleasure Ladyship. The best you can hope for is the iron, mind! But the rope's waitin' if you can't do her properly!" the blonde woman cackled at Tamara.

Her vision blurred by tears, Tamara advanced unsteadily and knelt at the end of the couch. Before her the spread legs and thighs framed the luxuriant bush and the peeping lips of her cunt.

She glanced over at the rope – a noose had been fashioned fully now – and began to slide her torso forward.

As her face approached Ladyship's groin she could catch the sharp, animal aroma of the woman. It was a scent she had become accustomed to over recent months. The days when she could relish the perfumed scent of a freshly prepared slave lay in her dimly remembered past.

Now she took her pleasure where she could. But that wasn't the issue here, it was Ladyship's pleasure that counted.

The soft pubic hairs at the join of the woman's thighs brushed her nose and with a whimper of despair Tamara stuck her tongue out and buried her face in the pungent hollow. Her tongue sought for and found the slick nub of the clitoris still nestling behind its convoluted hood. It responded almost immediately to the rasp of her tongue and once she had started, Tamara herself responded to the tangy taste and the feel of a vulva against her lips. It had been a long time since she had tasted woman. With her hands she caressed the insides of the spread thighs and tilting her head she quested deeper, lapping at the vaginal opening, bathing her face in the musk of Ladyship's sex. The woman groaned and pushed herself farther down the couch to help Tamara's explorations. Immediately she was able to penetrate with her tongue and relish the rich juice flowing from the cunt. With heat growing between her own legs, Tamara settled eagerly to her task and jumped when she suddenly felt fingers stroking her own vulva and entering her with lubricated ease.

"She's a wet one, Ladyship!" Jane's voice called and Tamara felt herself burn with shame even as she continued to burrow her way between Ladyship's legs, her tongue now passionately questing along the perineum and towards the anus, her forehead rubbing itself in the juices pouring from her. Suddenly she felt the woman's hands reach down and grasp her own, hauling them up to fasten them around her breasts. Now Tamara was able to rub, twist and twirl the thick nipples, pulling them just a little and fetching appreciative moans from her. Then, greatly daring she gathered her knees under her on the bench, careless of the fact that it meant her bottom was waving in the air, and lifted her face away from the cunt, replacing it with one hand and kissing her way up the body, across the soft, yielding stomach and eventually reaching the hills of the breasts, trembling and swollen with lust. Her fingers sank into the woman's cunt and were immersed in her moist warmth even as her mouth engulfed the resilient flesh of the nipple and her teeth began to nip and bite teasingly. Ladyship arched underneath her and her thigh raised between Tamara's own, Jane's fingers went from inside her, permitting her to rub herself brazenly on it.

"Shall I cane her Ladyship?"

Tamara's head jerked up but Ladyship's hand came down hard on it and forced it back to her breast.

"Yes! Cane her! Hard!" she hissed as Tamara tried to whimper around her mouthful. Ladyship took a fistful of Tamara's hair and raised her own head.

"Stay down for every stroke till I come, you whore!" she whispered fiercely.

Tamara screamed around her mouthful of nipple as a blazing line of pain carved across her buttocks. Another line followed it and she screamed again. Beneath her, Ladyship arched and thrust against her fingers as they clawed and twisted in pain inside her. Tamara took another lash and this time clenched her teeth on the nipple. Ladyship screamed in her turn and arched even more, clutching Tamara's head to her breast.

"Yes! Beat the whore! Thrash her!" she shouted. The cane sliced in again and again, too fast for Tamara to register individual blasts of pain, the taste and feel of the woman beneath her merging with the agony and the growing heat at her own belly. There was a flurry of cane slashes, both women screamed and began to climax, throwing their bodies at each other, mashing their breasts against each other, Tamara's hand frantically fucking the writhing Ladyship.

Then after a seeming eternity of spasming and jerking, the two collapsed, undone.

"Brand her," Ladyship gasped at last.

Hands seized Tamara and dragged her closer to the tent. There was a short stake hammered into the turf with rope fed through a hole near its top. She was pushed face first down onto the grass and her hands were tied to the stake, stretched out in front of her. Someone knelt on her back, almost winding her and pinning her helplessly. She heard the rasp of the branding iron being withdrawn and the tapping of it on the edge of the brazier to rid it of clinker and then there was a second's silence. An appalling pain burst through Tamara's brain, blinding and choking her and sending her back down into merciful darkness.

Interlude. Frankland Coast

From the terrace of the inn, Leopold Dunbar could look down on the harbour and see the king's ships huddling behind the breakwater as the seas broke in thundering foam over the stone. The onshore wind was too strong for the oars to pull against and there was nothing for it but to wait until it abated. In the meantime the king fretted helplessly, the galley slaves were chained in the cells beneath the castle that towered over the harbour and were getting restive and the soldiery was getting bored. Meanwhile the last news that had got through from home was all of a rapidly worsening situation. The queen grew bolder by the day. The people were weary of the king's absence and the high taxes brought about by the war and the army of renegade women was laying waste to estates just a few miles from the capital.

Dunbar and Sir William had caught up with the king's army just after it had won a decisive battle and taken the castle of Roncevais. The Franks would now be easily contained by the Count of Burghund until the following spring, leaving Edward free to return home. The news of the queen's blatant manoeuvring in regard to the Courcey estate only lent urgency to the march to the coast but then the winds had turned and the storms had not slackened off for a week.

Dunbar drew his cloak closer about him and returned inside. Sir William was leaning on the railings of the low gallery that surrounded the main room of the tavern. All the furniture had been cleared except for two tables. Two naked women lay on these, each on her back, her legs raised and spread at one edge and her head dangling off the other edge. Each table was at the head of a queue of laughing, drinking soldiers. At the far end of the room sat more soldiers, lounging at their ease and shouting ribald comments to their colleagues. As each queue approached each table it split into two. One moved to each woman's head, the other moved to between her opened legs. A simple animal rutting took place, each man spilling himself as quickly as he could, leaving the woman to cope as best she could. Once a man had finished he joined the crowd at the tables.

"How're they doing?" Dunbar asked as he took his place beside Sir William.

"They're still matching each other, man for man. I might call a halt for a few minutes, let them take a break. It'll prolong the contest and keep the men happy for a while longer."

"Good idea. I'll be interested to see how Jocelyn's holding up. I'm minded to take her to wife, William, she's a willing ride in bed and as resilient to the whip as any man could want."

Sir William smiled at his friend. "I'm only glad she has repaid part of my debt to you. Do with her as you will, of course. But I would suggest that she is kept strictly under the whip, wife or no!"

He turned and held up a hand calling for a break to be taken. There was good natured banter among the men as the queues broke up and they headed for the drinking tables.

"She's entirely a product of my dear Tamara's expertise with slaveflesh," Sir William said as they strolled down to the tables. "She always said that the key to getting the best out of her was to use her to the extreme. Tamara was a superb judge of slaves." His eyes took on a distant look for a moment, but he seemed to pull himself together as they arrived at the tables. The two tied- down women were panting for breath and were gleaming with sweat and sperm. Their faces were plastered with fresh and with crusted sperm, their mouths hung open slackly as they gulped in air. Their heaving breasts and stomachs were streaked with sweat that ran off the sides of their heaving ribs, tracing watercourses around the landscape of dried sperm. Beside Jocelyn lay Seven, her various rings shivering and trembling as she panted.

Both women had been used at both ends for over two hours now with only two short breaks. Bets had been taken on which one would pass out first. The odds had favoured Jocelyn but Seven was giving her supporters a good run. It had done the men's standing with the soldiers a world of good, although there were camp followers and slaves aplenty, the chance to enjoy a gentleman's slave was not one to be passed up.

Dunbar lifted his slave's head and looked down into her bleary eyes. He clicked his fingers and she obediently stuck out her tongue – which had been the star of the show, even eclipsing Seven's rings. Since Jocelyn had been his, Dunbar liked to think he had improved on what Tamara had started. The girl did have the most remarkably prehensile tongue and he had had some of the studs at the front of it removed and replaced by small rings. She now sported four of those and gave great pleasure when called on to fellate. He had also added four more studs farther back. When she had been strapped into position for piercing, kneeling beside the low table and with her tongue stretched out and clamped, he had told her that she should be grateful to her ex owner for making her such an outstanding slave. He had been greatly amused by the venomous look she had given him. But after the struggling and cries had died down, she had seemed to settle back into being a thoroughly enjoyable slave. After this contest was over, he was planning on telling her that he had got the marriage paperwork prepared. Meanwhile, Sir William was holding Seven's head up and giving her some water. Dunbar did the same and then the owners stood back and waved the men forward again.

They made sure that both queues were of equal length and then they left the men to it, took some wine and retreated to the gallery once more.

Dunbar glanced out at the terrace and noted that the western horizon was looking brighter as the evening light faded. He turned and was about to impart the good news to Sir William when there was a roar from the inn's floor and cheers and laughter.

"It would appear that Seven has passed out," Sir William said. "You are the winner and the contest is at an end." He raised his glass in salute and Dunbar waved at his triumphant supporters.

"But while you're there lads, you may as well finish her off!" he called down. There was the start of a groan of female protest which was quickly stifled and the queues shuffled round to form one longer one, to see how much more Jocelyn could take.

CHAPTER TWELVE
Southern Alba

In the days that followed her capture by the renegades, Tamara learned that all the galley slaves had passed the test by pleasuring the women put before them and had earned their brands. The brands themselves slowly settled in and faded to merely painful rather than agonising. The woman who had initially appeared at Tamara's camp fire claimed her as 'sister' and undertook her induction into the ranks of the renegades. It transpired that the watchfulness of the 'sister' was the real deterrent against agents, the display of the noose was just an initiation rite. The blonde, who introduced herself as Isabella, took Tamara into her tent and her bed.

To her surprise, the woman she had only heard referred to as Ladyship on that first night and who she found out was named Margaret, was an effective leader. Labour was strictly organised and tasks doled out on a rota basis. There was a clear hierarchy of sergeants and captains, designated by yellow and orange strips of material bound round the upper arms. They kept an eagle eye on everything that took place in the camp. Each day she was assigned tasks varying from sewing and tailoring to cleaning and cooking. Any spare time that Tamara and any of her erstwhile companions had was spent in weapons practice. And here, Isabella took charge of her. She taught Tamara the arts of knife throwing, archery - whenever a scarce bow could be found, and basic sword craft. Again to her surprise, Tamara found she took to it well and even began to enjoy herself, sometimes forgetting the shame of her brand for hours at a time. When all the women bathed in the mornings down by the river, she could see that they all bore the same mark; but some bore two and a couple even bore the brand on their buttocks as well as on both shoulders.

She asked Isabella about them.

"Sometimes you get petty thieves and mutinous bitches. Ladyship has one very simple penalty but sometimes they are very slow learners," Isabella told her.

Discipline was indeed harsh. Every evening after the meal had been taken, the women crowded around Ladyship's tent and Jane called out the names of those who had been reported by the officers for laziness, cheek or sloppy work. Ladyship never heard a defence plea, the accused stepped forward and was immediately grabbed by two captains who stripped her and twisted her wrists while holding her arms out straight, causing her to bend forwards. Ladyship then fondled the naked prisoner, running her hands over the quivering flanks, the hanging breasts and groping between the legs. Then, while she frequently had Jane lick her out, the victim was flogged. There was no rhyme or reason that Tamara could see to the punishments, but that in itself kept everyone on their toes; simply sewing a crooked seam could result in fifty or a hundred lashes, depending on Ladyship's mood.

As there were usually seven or eight punishments each evening, the sight of females enduring punishment was almost as common as it would be anywhere else in Alba, Tamara thought. Inevitably she responded as she always did to women being whipped and to her delight, most of the others did as well. The result was a nightly orgy. Couples paired off randomly as the whips rose and fell and the victims wailed. Tamara, however, usually fell into Isabella's arms. The two had found that they had a lot in common, being both fallen nobles. And, quite apart from the punishments, they slept together in their tent. Tamara found for the first time since her arrest that she slept well after an hour or so with her face buried between the Frankland woman's thighs, tonguing and fingering the deliciously flooding cunt, while Isabella returned the compliment.

The sisterhood of oppressed femininity had overcome Isabella's Frankish origins when she had first joined the renegades, and although she told Tamara in great detail about her capture and the man who had spotted her trying to pass herself off as one of her own slaves, she was curiously vague about how she had escaped and found her way to Alba. Isabella's description of her captor made Tamara think of her own dear William, but she dismissed the idea as being too much of a coincidence. She couldn't help but notice, however, how Isabella's eyes would cloud as she approached the subject of her escape and arrival in Alba and she would withdraw from sex for the night, turning over and wrapping herself in her blanket if Tamara pressed her. Then there were some nights when Tamara would wake and find the bed empty. At first she had fretted but Isabella always turned up quite soon and would slide in beside her bringing the scent and chill of the night with her and dive headfirst between Tamara's legs, the subsequent orgasm being sweet enough to allay any fears or questions.

After some weeks had passed, Ladyship suddenly announced after an evening's punishment session that Jane had received good intelligence concerning a rich estate just a few miles south. An ox-drawn cart was due to deliver substantial amounts of weapons in two days' time. The weapons were intended to better prepare the garrison against attack from the renegades and that made it all the sweeter.

"Jane is very clever at getting this type of news," Isabella told Tamara that night, her voice muffled by the amount of Tamara's breast she was kissing at the time. "If she says it will be good pickings, it will be."

A large party left the next day, each woman taking a pack with enough rations for three days.

In the late afternoon of the day after that, Tamara found herself hidden in bushes beside a road as it wound through a small copse. She had her knife and was becoming sickeningly aware that she was expected to use it. She shook with fear and disgust as she looked at the wicked point and considered what she was supposed to do with it, her mouth was dry and she toyed with the idea of making a run for it but she glanced at Isabella and realised she was being watched by the Frankland woman. That settled her down and made her determined to do whatever it took to continue to survive.

But when it came the fight was over almost before it had begun. The cart rumbled slowly around a bend in the road accompanied by a small group of men who didn't seem at all bothered about keeping a lookout or deploying into a defensive formation. And when the renegades broke cover, they made no attempt to form a shield wall and simply ran instead, leaving the women to gasp at the size of their haul. Ladyship led the charge and was the first to break cover, as she was the first to start throwing down the loot from the back of the cart. There were enough bows and quivers full of arrows to equip every woman in the army and enough money to buy anything they couldn't steal.

It did occur to Tamara that for so rich a cargo it had been a poor guard party and a strangely cowardly one at that.

Back at the camp, Ladyship announced that it was time they started to plan for a full scale revolution. The fires burned bright late into the night and the ranks of the renegades sat and stood around as their commander marched up and down, drunk on success and ambition.

"We have the arms now and we have the numbers! No more roadside ambushes and sacking villas. Now we go for towns! We will take Eastingdale and hold it while our downtrodden sisters flock to our flag! And from there we will set a flame to the corrupt heart of Alba and burn Tamesbury itself!"

Beside Tamara, Isabella went very quiet while the rest of the army cheered and yelled. For her part, Tamara couldn't shake off the feeling that something was wrong. From William she had learned a few basics of military tactics and the behaviour of the men guarding the wagon bothered her. Before they had run she had seen that they were veterans and not pressed gutter sweepings. Again, from William she knew that a veteran would never run from a bunch of women. They had too much pride, garnered from having survived battles all across Frankland. But these had –and they had left a valuable horde behind. It bothered her.

She listened to Ladyship and Jane exhorting them to storm the nearby town and establish a base for the rebellion and when they were dismissed she found that Isabella had gone. At first she thought nothing of it but then it occurred to her that if she had been seen, she would have been reported for disloyalty and that was known to be a misdemeanour with, usually, a very high punishment tariff.

Isabella wasn't at the tent either and Tamara felt a tight little knot of disquiet form in her stomach. She set off around the camp looking for her and eventually reached the perimeter and there she found her.

She was standing with her back to a tree, her legs spread wide and it was the graceful line of the leg just palely visible in the gloom that alerted Tamara.

She crept across, not sure why she felt the need for stealth but certain that she did. As she approached she could hear Isabella taking deep, rasping breaths, the ones that Tamara knew so well presaged orgasm. She rounded the tree and faced the woman.

Isabella's tunic was raised and her right hand was sawing at her clitoris with brutal harshness but her face was more ecstatic than the face of any woman Tamara had ever seen. Her eyes shone even in the dark, her teeth were bared, and she showed no alarm at Tamara's appearance but simply put her head back and succumbed to the orgasm she had been working towards. Tamara watched her lock rigid and then shudder as the spasms ran through her before she relaxed and smiled at her.

"My lord is here!" she whispered.

A chaotic rain of thoughts sleeted through Tamara's brain. If Isabella had a lord then she was betraying the renegades. With the renegades, she realised with a shock, she had found a sort of peace right at the bottom of society. Whatever else she was, here at least she wasn't a slave.

She turned to run back and warn everyone. But then the men appeared.

They didn't emerge from the pitch dark under the trees, they were simply in front of her eyes where they hadn't been a second before. They had bows with burning, pitch-soaked arrows already aflame and these they loosed towards the centre of the camp. There were more who overpowered the sentries and then from under the trees the main force emerged, swords drawn they ran silently, grimly determined as Isabella clapped a hand over Tamara's mouth and bore her down onto the grass.

"It is too late! You must let my lord do his work and trust to his mercy!" she whispered in her ear.

Tamara nodded, already she knew the renegades' fate was sealed. The soldiers she had seen were businesslike and disciplined. There would be no victory for the renegades this time.

Slowly the two women stood up as fires blossomed behind them in the camp, the flames leaping high among the tree tops and casting jumping shadows across them as they heard the shouts and screams. Isabella caught her breath suddenly and dropped to her knees. Tamara turned and saw a grey robed figure standing before them.

The robes marked him as being one of the guardians and Tamara's heart quailed as she saw his pale face and piercing blue eyes lit by the flames of the burning camp. His hood was thrown back and he was smiling down at Isabella.

"Well done, Isabella!" he said in an unmistakable Cambrian lilt as he bent to give her his hand and pull her up. Tamara thought that Isabella now looked as though she were a woman in heaven itself.

Her eyes were wide and adoring and her whole body seemed poised to obey any command he cared to give her. Behind him several other robed figures were emerging and striding towards the sounds of fighting. They bowed slightly as they passed him and Tamara realised with a sick lurch of her stomach that she was in the presence of the Slavemaker himself, the head of the guardians' council.

"It took just a small casting of illusion to allow our lads to get close enough to fire the tents and soon all will be ours. It was your reports that guided us and I will see that you are rewarded with all that your heart desires."

Isabella bent to kiss his hand.

"I beg to wear your mark, lord," Tamara heard her whisper.

"You shall," he replied then turned to the soldiers who were trussing the stunned sentries. "Gather them all in and bring them to the centre of the camp!"

Tamara suddenly realised the danger she was in.

"No! Wait, please! I'm no renegade, I'm Lady Tamara Courcey. I have been falsely arrested and enslaved. I demand……." Her voice trailed off as she caught the Slavemaker's eye. He was regarding her with amused contempt and there was something about him that made her knees tremble in sheer terror. He didn't have the overwhelming physical presence of Pepito – or even Black Harry – but he had an invisible cloak of menace and authority that seemed to reach out and envelope her.

"Lady Tamara Courcey? I think not. You are a branded renegade, while Lady Tamara resides in honour at her villa far from here."

"N-no! Please!"

The Slavemaker clicked his fingers and turned back to Isabella whose gaze never left her lord's face. Tamara had ceased to exist for her and there was no help there. Soldiers darted over and trussed Tamara's hands behind her, jamming some kind of rag into her mouth when she tried to scream and protest.

The morning brought a scene of dejection for the renegades and triumph for the youthful troops. Almost every renegade had been captured alive. The only exceptions were a group who had formed around Ladyship and who had fought hard. Tamara never found out how many perished but Ladyship herself was in chains and Jane was missing.

The robed figures of the guardians moved in and out of the seated ranks of ragged and defeated women. It seemed as though some kind of selection process was taking place. Some women were moved by soldiers to stand in a long coffle, others were moved to the other side of the clearing and made to sit back to back with their hands tied behind them. There were far fewer of these. At last one of the grey robed men came to squat in front of Tamara, his hood was thrown back and she could see he was in his mid-thirties with a hard, stern face and dark eyes. He reached out and took hold of her chin, tilting it up so she had to meet his eyes.

"I am not a renegade!" she began. "I am….."

"You are what?" the man asked softly, a cold smile momentarily lighting his harsh features. "Shall we see?"

Suddenly Tamara felt she was falling backwards, as if down a deep well and the man's face grew distant and faint, but his voice still sounded clearly in her brain. "You are what?"

Recent memories bubbled to the surface of her mind, her orgasm in the face of imminent branding as she finger fucked Ladyship and was caned. Kneeling before Pepito and sucking his cock as other slaves were put to the whip outside and she feverishly worked her own fingers inside herself, loving the taste of man and the subjugation of women. Fighting for a taste of sperm in the drinking water on the ship, orgasming under punishment at the cock house, impaled on the infernal strap-ons, beaten by ever-present whips. Being possessed in the street while Black Harry bartered her away. After the humiliation of the stocks, she felt again the hot confusion of pain and ecstasy as Dunbar flogged her and had her fucked on the scaffold. In ruthless, harsh detail the memories played themselves out and then there was…..nothing.

A scream of despair welled up in her throat and she rejoined the real world, lying flat on her face, where she must have thrown herself as she screamed. She knew now that she was lost. She was no longer Lady

Tamara Courcey, she had no name now. Just a nature. She was a slave.

Above her, as she sobbed brokenly, she heard the man's voice.

"She's a definite," he said and moved on.

By late morning whatever process had been going on was complete. The majority of the women were harnessed to the ox carts that had transported the army's equipment from Cambria, the oxen themselves allowed to amble along behind on the return journey. There were far too many women for them all to be employed in this way and some of the wagons were hastily converted into prisons by having wooden cages built on them.

The Slavemaker, with some of his brethren came to give the captain of the departing units of soldiers their orders.

"Take your time, there is no rush now and we will rejoin you in Cambria when all our business here is finished. These women will make good serviceable slaves and their conditioning will start as soon as they are safely back at Conwy. Make sure you pass through as many towns as you can. Let no one be left in any doubt who these wretches are, nor what their crime is. I have prepared documents that will allow you, in the king's name, to commandeer any and all stocks and gibbets for the display of the prisoners. Do not miss an opportunity to show them to the people. And it goes without saying that they are to earn their keep, should anyone want their bodies," there was general laughter among the troops as they looked forward to pimping their way back to their barracks and dividing up the spoils. The Slavemaker raised his voice. "As for you, lads! I expect you to remind these slaves of the duty they owe to their lords and masters…..you may remind them as often as you wish – and as often as you can!"

There was more laughter and cheers as he waved the train on its way and the whips began to crack over the straining backs of the renegades, once more under their masters' yokes, and the carts started to rumble on the long journey home. A journey which would spread the news that the king had stretched out his hand and order was restored.

When all was quiet, Tamara looked around. There were about thirty or forty women left with about twice that number of men left to guard them and about ten of the guardians. The Slavemaker paced slowly along the line of restrained and fearful females.

"Now we will begin," he said quietly at last and flicked his hood up to cover his head. Instantly his face disappeared completely in impenetrable darkness. Tamara sucked in her breath in shock and she shivered at the thought of what her future might hold. There could be no doubt that the guardian who had examined her had seen what she had become. Had seen how the months of slavery had slowly revealed her true nature which had blotted out whatever had gone before. They would surely work on that and make certain that Lady Courcey was buried forever.

As her thoughts ran on she heard a ripple of dismayed murmurs spread from her left along the ranks of the prisoners and she turned to look.

Isabella, her face still a mask of ecstasy was being led by a leash buckled to a thick leather collar around her neck towards the Slavemaker. She was naked and they could all see that branded high on the inside of her left thigh were three crowns.

Once she had reached her lord she knelt down beside him and he took her leash in his hand.

"Witness your futures!" he told them simply. "A woman can aspire to no greater height than to serve her master utterly, with every breath, with every part of her being, as Isabella serves me and has done these past months. By the time the king arrives, he will be presented with the cream of the renegades prostrating themselves before him and only too eager to proclaim to the country at large their complete and utter submission."

Tamara gazed up into the total blackness of the Slavemaker's hood and realised that finally - this time - she really was completely lost.

Interlude. Tamesbury.

Captain Berghaus strode purposefully towards the palace. Behind him came a hundred hand picked men from his troop of battle-hardened mercenaries. The populace took one look at his face and the drawn weapons in his men's hands and stood back, allowing him free passage along the crowded streets until finally he entered the market square before the palace. His pace did not slacken as he approached the gates and the two guards on duty were flung aside and pinned back by the surge of armed men who then spread out to challenge and disarm any who might think of stopping their commander before he could confront the queen.

Early in the morning the man he had paid to keep an eye on the comings and goings at the south gate of the city had reported that a wild-eyed blonde had ridden a horse to the gate and demanded audience with the queen. Quite apart from the fact that he said the woman was in a clearly distressed state, she had ridden the horse cruelly hard and it was foaming with sweat and was lame. No one would have treated a horse like that unless their need was desperate.

That on its own boded ill. But just as he was setting out to find out what the news was, a rider had galloped in from the east to report that the king's fleet had been sighted off the mouth of the Tame. All of a sudden it became clear that the queen had delayed too long and the chance of taking Alba was gone.

Unless he acted decisively Otto Berghaus was as much at risk from his own men as he was from King Edward.

He kicked open the doors to the audience chamber and strode in, taking in the scene that confronted him. The queen, still wearing her nightdress, her hair in an unravelling plait down her back was caught in the act of slapping the face of a kneeling and weeping blonde woman, crouching at her feet.

She whirled at the sound of the doors crashing open.

"How dare you!" she shouted, before taking in who it was and then blanching as she realised her predicament.

The blonde woman seized her chance of escape and scurried over to seek the captain's shelter.

"Save me please, Sire!" she wheedled. "I spied for her and done everything she told me! And then when the guardians come and took us by surprise, she says it were my fault! Help me kind sir! She'll kill me given half a chance!"

Captain Berghaus stared at the queen and took a fistful of the blonde's hair.

"Let's hear what this one has to say," he told his men without looking away from the queen. "Make sure her majesty there doesn't try to step outside."

"You cannot – you dare not - imprison me!" the queen screeched as the men closed in and made it clear that while she might bear the title of queen; here and now, they were in command.

"Talk!" Berghaus commanded the blonde woman.

In a halting, sobbing voice the woman told them how the queen had sent her to infiltrate the ranks of the renegades and how she had used her position within the army to steer it where the queen had wanted it to go. Whenever the queen had wanted the renegades to seize weapons, it had been to her, Jane, that she had sent messages and Jane had seen that it was done.

"But then the soldiers come, Sire!" she sobbed at the end. "From just out of the dark, out of nowhere, with burning arrows! There was nothing we could do........"

Berghaus pushed her away and let her escape. "Sounds like the guardians' sorcery. And if they've got the renegades it's all over."

"No, listen, I can still pay and you can still overtake them if you ride now!" the queen's voice trembled as she pleaded.

"I do not think so. We are not enough to take on a trained body of men supported by wizardry. And in any case, the pretence that the renegades are any sort of threat is gone. No, Madam, we must make our money by different means!" He turned to his men. "Search the palace from top to bottom. Take anything of value that can be carried!"

As the men ran out gleefully to be about their business, Berghaus approached the queen. "I warned you not to wait too long. Now I am afraid I must bargain for my life and for my men's lives with the only card I have in my hand."

He reached out with a mailed glove and took the queen's face between his fingers and thumb and smiled at her as her lower lip began to quiver. "You see, the king's fleet is on its way, Madam. And I rather think that I can gain some favour with him and save him some inconvenience. All I need do is anticipate the order I am perfectly certain he will want to give."

With his other hand he reached out and tore the queen's nightdress from her. She whimpered as she was presented to him, vulnerable now and no longer untouchable. His eyes feasted on her proudly jutting breasts, quivering as she took panicky breaths, and on the shaven crotch with its deeply cleft sex.

"I've never fucked and whipped a queen," he said, thrusting her back against her desk, making her overbalance backwards onto it. Her legs opened involuntarily and he stepped between them, shedding a glove and fumbling his fingers into her dry entrance, before beginning to stir her up. "Neither have my men….." he added with a smile.

"No, please! I can tell you where the treasure is hidden," she quavered as she helplessly registered the imperious hand inside her.

Captain Berghaus laughed. "You mean there is more than I have a handful of now? Of course there is, and you will tell me! Eventually I will allow you to tell me everything!" He stepped closer to pin her down and reached into his tunic to produce a pair of heavy iron, screw clamps. The queen flung her head back and screamed as he settled first one and then the other over her nipples and began to tighten the screws.

From above came the noise of furniture being overturned and from below came the sound of more women screaming.

Late that afternoon the king's fleet disembarked and the portion of the army he had thought it prudent to bring home, formed up to escort him to the palace but they had not gone more than half a mile through cheering crowds before they were met by Berghaus's mercenaries.

They were flying a large white flag of truce as a standard, the ten foot pole on which it was mounted was held aloft by two burly soldiers. Captain Berghaus bowed and went onto one knee before the king who dismounted and stepped forwards.

"Your Majesty," Berghaus began. "We came to your country in the pay of the queen. We would depart it in peace having been paid and we would give you a gift in recognition of your generosity in allowing us safe passage."

"What is to stop me having you massacred where you stand?" the king asked coldly.

"Nothing, Sire. Except the spilling of more blood. Desperate men make formidable fighters."

"True. But while I decide, you will tell me, please, every detail of your agreement with the queen."

When the captain had finished speaking there was silence for a moment before the king made his response. The crowd stood mute, caught between fleeing and staying to see what would happen. The two groups of soldiers kept their hands on their weapons, their eyes watchful and nervous. A slight breeze ruffled the white flag.

At last King Edward spoke. "You may keep what you have taken in lieu of payment from the queen, and you may depart. There is nothing to be gained by bloodshed. So now," he added as a sigh went up and there was a faint rattle as swords were fully returned to the bottoms of sheaths, "I would see the gift you intend for me."

The captain rose to his feet, smiling. "Nothing will give me greater pleasure, Sire!" he said and waved at the men behind him.

Two of them released ropes and the white flag collapsed to reveal a T shaped cross on which hung the naked body of Queen Anneka. Her elbows had been bent back over the crossbar and her wrists chained together in front of her stomach. Her head was stretched back and held in place by a gagging strap which had been nailed to the crossbar. She had been thoroughly whipped and there were some whistles of appreciation from some of the men in the crowd. Dusky red welts laced her breasts, stomach and thighs, even emerging from between them, suggesting that she had not been spared a cunt whipping. Closer inspection revealed a crusting of sperm on her thighs, breasts and face.

The king stared up at his wife and grinned broadly.

"Captain, you are an astute man and I accept your gift gladly!" he moved closer to the mercenary and added quietly, "It would have been a little tricky for me to have sentenced her to what she so richly deserved, but now that your men have saved me the difficulty, I shall have no problem in casting her off for having shamed me in front of my subjects. She shall be sent to the Slavemaker and I have no doubt that once he has finished with her she will fetch a price that will outweigh whatever she has cost me!"

The two men shook hands and the queen was passed to the king's men who bore her back to the palace, while Berghaus and his men passed unmolested towards the docks.

Sir William Courcey turned to his friend Dunbar as they re-commenced the royal progress, following the bizarre standard of the naked queen, now conscious and struggling weakly against her utter humiliation.

"I think every schoolboy in Alba, for hundreds of years to come, will learn about what has taken place here today."

Leopold Dunbar smiled at his new wife, riding in a palanquin beside him. Her eyes were wide with excitement as she drank in the sight of so spectacularly punished a woman, so blatantly displayed.

"And probably not just the boys, William!" he said.

CHAPTER THIRTEEN.

The cages were crudely made of stout timbers with wide enough gaps between the bars for limbs to pass through but not bodies; and Tamara had tried on the first night she had been put in hers. But then inexplicably the urge to escape had faded until finally, and far too late, she realised that thc guardians had been adding something to the food and water rations. The cages hung about four feet off the ground, slung on ropes from tree boughs and like all the other women now, whenever a soldier or a guardian approached, she would back up against the bars on all fours, which was all the height of the cage allowed, and shamelessly expose herself, rubbing her buttocks against the bars, trying to get them to see how open and desperate she was.

At first, she, like most of the rest had fought and protested when they had been taken from the cages and staked out on the grass for use. In fact it had taken quite prolonged use of the whip on her back and buttocks before the young man who was beating her could slide his fingers into her with relative ease, but from there on she had responded enthusiastically to repeated use with her ankles freed and her knees drawn up under so that her bottom was raised. But as the women had eagerly emptied the bowls that their rations arrived in and drunk the fresh water shoved through the bars in wooden cups, somehow, eagerness for the next meal had been accompanied by an eagerness for the next orgasm. By about the third day as far as Tamara could recall, when the men came to take away the bowls and begin to let them out one by one to use the latrines in the morning, she had found herself inviting use by the tall young soldier who had her on a collar and leash. She crawled close beside him, rubbing her side against his leg.

"You're coming along well, just like the Slavemaker said you would," the young man had mocked her, before he had stopped her, made her lie on her back and play with herself, legs splayed wide in broad daylight. All it had taken to make her abase herself was a chance to get a mouthful of his cock afterwards. But when she had ground herself to a climax, rubbing and penetrating herself with both hands, he had reneged on the deal.

"Very nice, you whore! But it took too long. You're due back in your cage in a minute, so if you're lucky I'll maybe let you have a suck later," he had said and then hauled her after him. She had scurried to keep up, ignoring his treachery, concerned only not to annoy him in case he did let her suck him later on. As it turned out another soldier presented himself at the front of her cage in the afternoon and she had crawled forwards to where he was holding his flaccid member and pushed her face against the bars. He had tantalised her by moving back a fraction and she had found to her horror that she was prepared to hang her tongue out to try and lick him, just like a bitch on heat – as he reminded her.

He had laughed derisively once she had humiliated herself and then he had moved back in to let her tongue him properly. He tasted acrid and bitter from not having washed but also pungent and musky from other women's bodies. Tamara registered these facts only hazily, her main concern was to see him harden and erect so that maybe he would let her fill her mouth with him and grant her some good swallows of hot, fresh sperm. To her delight he responded to her licks and in a few moments the veined, hard member reared in front of her face and he held it down for her to feed into her mouth, sliding her lips sensuously over the swollen helm, ensuring her teeth were kept from scraping it as it slid into her, filling her mouth completely. He reached between the bars of the cage and held her head steady so he wouldn't make her swing as he began to slowly thrust in and withdraw.

Suddenly a hand had reached in from the side and grasped her right breast. As she had become used to, it didn't caress, it squeezed cruelly and the fingers clawed into the soft flesh, raking and scoring. But she couldn't bring herself to cry out which would mean releasing the firm grip her lips had on the shaft of the cock, feeling the soft skin slide back and forth on the steel hardness beneath.

"Make sure you spend as deep in her throat as you can and report any lack of enthusiasm in her swallowing to me." The voice was soft and yet masterful, she knew it was the Slavemaker himself.

The hand withdrew and Tamara found that, far from inspiring terror in her as he always had before, now she just wanted to feel his hand mauling and enjoying her breast while this anonymous young man spurted his jism deep into her throat.

But in the end she had had to make do with just the soldier's hand jamming her head down onto him while he fucked her mouth forcefully enough to make her choke when he came.

He must have reported her because the next morning, after she had squatted over the latrine ditch in front of another youthful soldier who had flicked her nipples repeatedly with the handle of her leash as she tried to relieve herself, she had been tied to a tree at the edge of the clearing where their cages hung, it was the same clearing where Ladyship's tent had once stood and she understood that the Slavemaker was not missing one opportunity to drive his lesson home. Her arms were simply tied around the trunk of the tree as if she was hugging it and she found she had to try and hollow her chest to stop the bark rasping her nipples painfully. The soldier who had tied her left her for a minute and she was able to look around. The cages hung from nearly every tree and the naked women they contained were all crouched at the fronts of them, all staring hard at her. But their looks weren't of fear or anger, they were of eager anticipation. Even Margaret herself was squatting with her legs apart and one hand was beginning to idly rub between them. Tamara glanced over her shoulder and saw a burly, older man approaching her with a wicked length of hide in his hand and a jolt of fear-laden excitement hit her belly as she realised it was going to be as serious a flogging as any she had undergone. The man stopped a few paces behind her, threw down the whip and took off his shirt. His broad chest was covered in a thick pelt of black hair and a line of it crossed his belly and went down the front of his britches. Tamara heard a sigh from the other women and realised that not only were they eager to see her lashed, they were actually envious of the male attention. Strangely enough Tamara knew exactly how they felt and she hollowed her back and spread her legs as the man retrieved the whip and shook it out. He smiled when he saw how she had ensured he had a good view of her cunt.

"Slavemaker said you're the pick of the bunch!" he told her with a toothy grin and then he drew his arm back.

For all the time that Tamara had been enslaved, she had endured and then finally begun to enjoy her beatings but it had been a dark and reluctant pleasure. Now she watched over her shoulder in open and easy delight as the muscles moved under his skin, his powerful chest bunched as he began to swing the lash forwards and the whip blurred as it sped towards her. The noise of the impact echoed around the clearing and Tamara followed it with a cry of release as her back exploded into hot pain and her loins immediately burned with lust. The second lash was accompanied by shrieks of excitement from the cages. After the fourth lash, Tamara looked around and saw every caged woman frantically working her hands between her thighs. Three more thunderous lashes snapped across her back, scouring her ribs where the tip dug into her. Tamara rocked under the impacts but always looked back over her shoulder, making eye contact with her flagellator, urging him on, begging with her helplessly juicing cunt.

For the first time pain seemed to directly moisten her and drown her in unreasoning lust. There was no thought involved. He whipped her; she wanted him to take her. It was that easy and she revelled in the newfound simplicity of her life. Again and again the whip sliced across her, sometimes wrapping her breasts and causing her to groan in delighted agony. In the end he moved in on her so quickly that she was still expecting the lash when what she got was a hard, thick shaft slipping into her so easily it was fully embedded by the time she realised it was there. But once it was in she worked herself hard on it, swivelling, bucking, humping shamelessly. The man smacked her scorched flanks from time to time to goad her onwards and she eventually broke and screamed her release, ramming herself desperately backwards onto his cock.

He slid from her almost before she had stopped coming and it was only when he freed her and she fell to her knees that she saw he was still erect, his gleaming shaft sticking out from his loosed laces. He clicked his fingers and she crawled beside him into the centre of the clearing where he planted his feet well apart, grabbed her hair and guided her face to his cock as she knelt before him. Gratefully Tamara slid her lips over his massive helm and began to caress its underside with her tongue. She deliberately kept her licks gentle and slow so as not to encourage him too quickly towards his climax.

"That's good!" she heard him say. "The bitch learns fast!" Her heart swelled with joyful pride and then she heard another voice.

"They have all done well! No batch of slaves has ever taken such heavy doses in such a short time. It will be entertaining to see how they turn out, and with the 'r' brand as well as the crowns, I think they will be real collectors' items!" Tamara heard the Slavemaker's voice but his words seemed not to have anything to do with her. All that existed for her was the stinging at her back, the heat in her loins and the taste and the hardness of the cock in her mouth, which then began to swell and pump. Carefully relaxing her throat muscles as she had flogged her own slaves into doing, she accepted his sperm as it splashed out into her, with complete ease. Even earning a pat on the head from her flagellator as he led to her cage again.

For the rest of the day, one by one the women had been taken out and had fellated man after man in the centre of the clearing, even Margaret had pulled at her leash in her eagerness to take a mouthful of cock. It didn't matter to them that they had all heard the Slavemaker confirm that not only were they being drugged, they were being drugged more than any women before them; the very size of the doses made it irrelevant.

And now on the fifth day they had been fed and taken to the latrines but none of them had been used in any way and they waited in silence for the Masters' next move. Men moved to and fro about their business but it seemed that today, the women were to be left to wallow in bitter frustration. Around her Tamara could see the others reacting in various ways to the sudden lack of sexual use. Some were staring around, hopefully, looking for men; some were rocking to and fro in their cages, their hands joined in between clamped-together thighs. Some, like Margaret herself, had given up any patience or pretence and were vigorously masturbating with both hands. Still no one came. By mid morning Tamara had given in and had joined in with the masturbation that was now going on in virtually every cage. The only ones who weren't frigging themselves were the ones who had collapsed after they had climaxed all they could. By late afternoon, the groans and cries of female orgasm had faded into whimperings as rubbed raw clitorises were goaded into one more orgasm, stinging vaginas were savagely plundered by demanding fingers one last time. And as dark fell, when the Slavemaker allowed himself to be seen, having been watching for most of the day, strode into the clearing, he was well pleased.

The best batch of triple crown slaves in history was nearly ready.

They were fed and then taken out on leashes on all fours and led to where the soldiers' tents were. Tamara crawled patiently beside the young man who held her leash, glad of the cool air playing on her overheated crotch. He took her into his tent and to her delight stripped off and then lay on his bed, which was no more than a blanket roll on top of piled bracken but which to Tamara, when she was allowed onto it, felt like paradise after the hard wooden bars of her cage. There were two men sharing the tent and they both used her.

At the sight of the first young man stripping off, Tamara felt herself melt and moisten all over again, all her previous discomfort forgotten. He lay on his back and lazily beckoned her across. She crawled over and he pulled her across him, making her straddle him with her thighs wide apart. On the other side of the tent his companion was shrugging off his clothes as the man beneath her held his rigid member upright and guided her down onto it. It was the most deliciously deep penetration she had experienced for a very long time and she sighed happily, even though she was vaguely aware of the stinging at her clitoris. The second man approached as she started lifting and lowering herself, his hand was working at his own cock and it was already hard and thick. Tamara didn't need telling and immediately turned her head so that she could suck him in as she rode his colleague. The hands placed on her head told her that she was expected to once again swallow whatever he pumped down her. The man she was riding reached up and grasped her breasts, gripping and rolling his hands, squeezing them back against her chest. The man who was in her mouth started to run his fingernails down her back, scoring and irritating her welts. Tamara felt as though she had never been so complete and so happy. She was being used carelessly and painfully by two men who would spend into her and throw her out probably, but with no doubt at all in her mind, it was how she wanted to be – no needed to be - treated.

The cock in her mouth was almost choking her it was so thick, but she sucked as hard as she could and worked her pelvis back and forth as she rose and fell on the one in her cunt. She evidently did a good job as both cocks emptied themselves into her before she had had a chance to climax herself. She was unceremoniously pushed off the bed once the cock in her mouth had slipped free from her lips and made to lick both men clean, kneeling in front of them.

Then they threw her out.

She landed sprawling on the grass between the rows of tents and shelters. Without even thinking about it she got back onto all fours rather than standing up, and looked about her. From several of the tents came the sounds of female orgasms being approached, accompanied by the sounds of males propelling them there with all their strength. From others came female cries as heavy smacking sounds announced that some of the soldiery was administering discipline prior to taking its pleasure. Tamara immediately felt herself melt once more, the ache between her legs was almost physical. She desperately needed to come.

Flicking her leash over one shoulder to stop it tangling as she crawled, she began to go in search of a man who would use her in whatever way he liked. Never for one second did it occur to her that she was unrestrained and unguarded. She could simply have stood up and walked away. But instead she found a shelter at the front of which sat a young man, idly polishing his armour. He was dressed only in his breeches and as Tamara watched his strong arms work, she was consumed once more with a fierce desire that almost took her breath away. She crawled closer but he ignored her, and as she came near she could see why. He had just finished with none other than Margaret. The tall, black haired woman was lying spread legged on the bed, her chest still rising and falling deeply, her breasts trembling in the aftermath of orgasm. Tamara hated her. She scurried forwards and with no hesitation began to lick and kiss the young man's bare feet, ramming her tongue between his toes and caressing his legs with her hands.

He made no move to either take her in or to kick her away and so she persisted until a voice spoke from behind her. It was the Slavemaker again.

"Does she not please you?" he asked.

"Begging your pardon, Sire, but I like more tit on mine. And I was about to take a belt to that one in there, when this 'un turned up!"

"Then please do so. And make it a thorough beating." Tamara felt her leash taken hold of and a sharp tug on it indicated that she should sit up.

Tamara burned with shame and frustration and sat back on her haunches, pleading with the man with her eyes. He didn't even look at her, just put his armour down and took up a belt, before standing up and going inside to deal further with Margaret.

The Slavemaker strode off, making no allowances for Tamara being on her hands and knees. She had to scuttle desperately after him with the delicious noises of a heavy strap being plied on Margaret ringing in her ears. Once she had caught him up properly she kept close beside him and felt utterly privileged to be so close to the man who was more her master than any she had yet encountered. If she had been capable of further thought, she would have included William. But he was gone from her mind entirely. All that mattered was that the Slavemaker had found her a tent with two soldiers lounging on their beds.

They sat up respectfully as the tall, robed figure appeared at the entrance. Tamara got another jerk on her leash and realised she was to stand up. Feeling quite uncomfortable in the pose so close to the Slavemaker himself, she obeyed and a powerful hand grasped her hair and propelled her inside.

"Is this one to your liking?" he enquired.

"Yes, Sire," the older of the men replied. "She's fair enough to be sure. May we do with her like we did with the last?"

The Slavemaker let go of Tamara and went to join the men who were staring hard at her body, assessing it for pleasure. She stood up straighter, aware that the need at her crotch was growing by the minute.

"And what did you do with the last one?" he asked.

The older man came forward and boldly grasped her right breast, making her catch her breath at the sharpness of the excitement it caused her.

He explained how they had tied the previous slave's breasts tightly about the roots and hung her by them from a tree branch and then tied two pairs of straight green twigs together to form pincers for the nipples. They had whipped her simultaneously from front and behind before taking her down and then having her as a sandwich, penetrated vaginally and anally.

Tamara listened spellbound; consumed with envy for the lucky girl.

"And did she render satisfactory service?" the Slavemaker asked.

"Very, Sire!" the man agreed happily.

"Then please feel free to repeat the process with this one – or indeed to refine it further. I do not want any limits on their usage! Nothing must come between the master of one of these and his pleasure."

Tamara's pulse raced as the two men eyed her now with openly predatory glee.

"Would it be agreeable, Sire, if we hung her up by her ankles this time? Only we noticed there's lots of nettles around here, and it seems a shame to let 'em go to waste. They scream a treat with those and the whip as well!"

"That sounds very suitable! Do not spare her anything you wish to subject her to, just make sure she is returned by dark."

The Slavemaker strode out but just as he passed Tamara, he paused long enough to push his hood back and expose his face to her for the first time since her capture. She drank in the sight of his fair features and pale skin, adoring him with every fibre of her being, longing to be allowed to serve him in any way he chose. He must have read something of that longing as he smiled and nodded before going out and leaving her to her fate.

After dark the women were all rounded up and delivered to the centre of the camp where a circle of roughly woven hurdles had been hastily put together. They were all shoved in together on all fours while the men leaned over the fence and discussed how they had performed during the day. Tamara stung and hurt from her lower belly right through to her anus and from her knees to her crotch, while the whip had burned her from her buttocks to her neck and her nipples throbbed from having been squashed by the improvised clamps. But at least she had climaxed on several occasions and one had been under the whip alone.

Now she needed to come again and fortunately she was not alone in that predicament.

As her leash guided her into the makeshift corral on all fours, her nostrils registered the unmistakable scent of female arousal. All around her, sitting, kneeling, crawling – but none standing – were women who now shared her need for continual stimulation. No sooner had the gate swung shut behind her than she felt soft lips brush against the still-engorged lips of her cunt. Immediately she backed onto them and felt the tongue search for her clitoris, she rolled over onto her back to facilitate the penetration and immediately another woman lay alongside her and encouraged her to start nibbling and tweaking at nipples that had clearly been whipped very recently. In the confined space of the corral, the women could at last give vent to the orgiastic natures the Slavemaker's concoctions had created in them. Tamara rolled amongst bodies slicked with sweat and sperm, she delved deep into them with her tongue to taste the residues and the fresh secretions, sharp teeth nipped at her breasts and nipples, sending sharp little daggers of exciting pain down to her groin. Her nails clawed and raked welted female skin as others raked hers and fetched sighs of pleasure from her. She spread her legs as wide apart as they would go even if there was no one licking her, it was almost as sweet to hear the men discuss her opened body. Every now and then a leash would be plucked up by one of the men leaning over the hurdles and the woman would be dragged out, only to be returned a few minutes later, dripping fresh sperm from one or other of her orifices and would be climbed on by others eager for another taste of the masters. Sometimes they were just lashed at random as they squirmed and writhed on the ground and Tamara cupped her breasts proudly, lying on her back with two women eating at her cunt, while a grinning soldier leaned over her and struck with his belt. She came even as the heavy leather fell, smacking meatily across her quivering mounds.

From the shadows, the brethren watched, well pleased.

"They will take the elixir tomorrow, I shall not waste time with explanations, they are beyond any such things now," Owen said. "And then we may proceed to meet his majesty."

His companions moved off to make preparations and left the Slavemaker to listen to the sounds of the orgy that he had created in progress. The women had turned out well and it was fitting that renegades had now been turned into the most passionate sex slaves ever to have existed. He had looked into one or two of their minds and seen only the hunger for more pain and more pleasure with no divide between them.

And there was no memory there. Their lives before their treatment had been wiped completely, making them voracious for anything that would please their masters with no shadow of a suspicion that they had ever been anything other than sex slaves. He looked down at Isabella, kneeling patiently beside him. Part of the pleasure of beating her and using her was to know that somewhere deep inside Isabella the slave, Isabella Dulac, was screaming in protest at what she was taking such pleasure in having done to her. This new batch provided quite a different pleasure, absolute devotion and submission so complete that it surpassed anything any man could ever have experienced.

And it all came from a low-growing, unregarded, purple-leafed plant he had found growing beside the roads in Frankland. In quite modest quantities, its dried and powered leaves added to what the guardians already used, provided spectacular results.

He had briefly thought about giving it to Isabella but had decided that she gave better sport as she was. For the renegades, however, it was poetic justice and would earn high praise – and more – from the king.

One final benefit made the Slavemaker smile as he clicked his fingers and walked towards his tent with Isabella crawling obediently beside him; when these lads joined the main army in Frankland, the tales they would tell about the advantages of following the Slavemaker would spread in no time at all.

The following morning Tamara watched in simple delight as one of the guardians unfolded the front of his robe and disclosed a divinely thick and hard cock which he then brought off himself, spilling his jism into a clear liquid in a cup. She was given it to drink and drained it greedily and with no second thought.

On the day after that, dressed in simple linen shifts and with no thought except how and where they could next serve any man the Slavemaker wanted them to, they were harnessed to carts that carried their bedding and food and joined the column as it moved off to meet the king. Those not required for pulling walked behind the carts, their leashes tethered to the backboards.

The meeting that finally laid the ghost of the attempted rebellion of 1251, took place on a hill overlooking the small town of Gatesham. The royal camp was pitched at a crossroads on a hill and it was there, on a fine October day that Owen Daibron and King Edward toasted their success amid scenes of great feasting and joy that peace had once again come to Alba and order was restored.

The queen, who had been kept naked and bound in a wooden cage on the back of a cart, and who had provided many villages along the way with hours of fun as they baited her, was handed over to the guardians.

"Make her worth some money, Owen!" the king said as he handed across the bedraggled woman who had once held sway over hundreds of slaves herself.

"I shall, your majesty. And I would like to present to you, as a token of my brethren's loyalty to yourself, the new class of pleasure slave that we are now able to create. I have not branded them yet as I would like you, your majesty, to decide on a fitting brand for such exquisite submissions as these slaves are now capable of."

The king inclined his head to acknowledge the compliment and the Slavemaker clicked his fingers. Several of the new slaves stepped forwards, and amongst those selected was Tamara.

At once there was a disturbance from the ranks of the king's closest companions and Sir William Courcey stepped forwards.

"My Lord! There has been some terrible error. That is Lady Tamara – my wife who was so wronged by the queen!"

The whole crowd looked at the dark haired woman that Sir William was pointing at. She was tanned and undoubtedly handsome under the thick tangles of hair, with long, shapely legs and high prominent breasts.

But when Sir William came close to her and asked if she was alright, she regarded him blankly. He urged her with increasing desperation to tell him what had befallen her, how had she come to be with the renegades; but while remaining quite docile she regarded him as she might a complete stranger and looked around for the Slavemaker to tell her whether this man needed pleasuring.

If Leopold Dunbar had not backed Sir William up, his claim might not have been registered but as it was, Owen Daibron had no choice but to offer his humble apologies.

"She did indeed make such a claim at the renegades' camp but I am much afraid I paid it no heed. I had heard nothing of her arrest and escape. And how did she come to be there at all?"

"We will probably never know. But do not distress yourself," Sir William sighed at last, patting his dispassionate wife on her haunch as he turned away. "Such things happen in time of war. And in any case

I'm sure she will make as good a slave as she made a mistress. "

"William, you have been wronged," the king said. "But it is hard to see how you can be compensated."

"All that I can do, I will of course," Owen said. "A brace of this new class of slave will at least fill your bed!"

Sir William laughed. "That is the main thing after all, Master Slavemaker! A handsome offer and one I shall be pleased to accept."

"But we must not forget the lady herself," the king reminded them. "I take it there is no way she can be restored."

"None, my lord. I am sorry," the Slavemaker admitted.

"Then we must see what can be done for her as she is. Does anyone have any suggestions?"

Leopold Dunbar stood up after a few moments of thoughtful silence. "My lord, surely the worst punishment that can befall a slave of such quality as the Slavemaker has described, is to find herself masterless and thus purposeless and bereft of the pleasure of serving."

Owen Daibron nodded and Dunbar smiled. "Then I think I have a suggestion that might produce the best outcome that can be expected from such an unfortunate circumstance."

The journey had been quite enjoyable. The cart she had been harnessed to every other day had not been too heavy and the men had been very cruel about harnessing the women tightly, making the crupper straps dig deep between their lips and the breast straps had also been cruelly tightened. Added to the steady whipping, it had resulted in minor ripples of orgasm almost constantly. And each night of course the men needed to be kept entertained. She had wrestled for the possession of a leather covered phallus in mud pools beside streams, and used it standing foursquare in front of any man who wanted her to when she won. She had made love with any woman she had been told to. She had been constantly whipped for no other reason than that it gave someone pleasure and she had been taken by any man who wanted her, whenever he wanted her. But best of all, on several occasions she had been allowed to fellate one or other of the brethren themselves.

Their column had passed through villages and small towns on the way and there the 'r' brand had meant they had served time in the stocks – it had felt strangely familiar to her but she couldn't fathom why. It had been very exciting however, to see how much the men had enjoyed beating her and pelting her and then – once she was released – taking her. On one occasion the Slavemaker had decreed a day's rest and had had her and another slave put up, face to face, hung from the chain at the end of a gibbet arm. A long queue of men had paid handsomely to whip them and they had stayed there all day before being taken down and allowed to watch the Slavemaker take his personal slave, Isabella, from behind. She had nearly fainted with joy when they had been allowed to lick the spend from the Frankland woman's anus and thighs.

He had patted their heads and allowed them to sleep together.

She was perfectly happy.

And then they had come to this place where there were crowds who, strangely, didn't seem to want to use them, but then the Slavemaker had picked her and a few others to accompany him and they found themselves before the king. Then a man who seemed strangely familiar had come to talk to her. He seemed sad about something but it wasn't anything to do with her. She had spotted a soldier carrying a stock whip on the far edge of the crowd and was trying to catch his eye. The man kept talking to her and she looked around for her master to see if she should kneel and offer him pleasure.

There was more talking and she wished someone would use her or let her go back to where the other women were and where she might be able to have fun.

Then they left her alone and did some more talking.

At last a heavily built man approached her. Again he seemed familiar but this time it was because he was connected to a whipping somewhere a long time ago. It had been a very good beating she thought. She took a bit more interest in him and looked at his robes wondering how big his cock was under them. He wanted her to do something but it didn't involve pain or pleasure so she dismissed it and waited patiently for the next opportunity to serve and suffer.

Then her master, the Slavemaker himself, came to stand in front of her and the world came back into focus as he spoke to her.

"You must choose your owner. Of course whoever you choose you will always, ultimately, serve me. Even when you are sold or given away, you will always serve me in the guise of whoever's collar you wear. Remember you exist only to give and experience pleasure through suffering."

The fact that her master was ordering her to make a choice robbed that task of the terror she knew it would otherwise inspire. It would never be for her to choose anything. Ever again.

With renewed interest she looked around at the people now watching her carefully. The man who had first talked to her a lot was handsome enough but she couldn't see the harsh cruelty she was really looking for in the way he stared at her. The king was also handsome but again, didn't seem to have the dedication to wringing out of a slave's body every ounce of pleasure for himself that she was looking for. She looked further and found the heavily built man who for some reason she associated with a good beating. He was watching her intently and beside him stood a palanquin to which were harnessed four beautifully turned out slaves. Their complex head harnesses sported swan feather plumes and their cruppers were pulled very tightly between ringed labia. Their areolas, nipples and navels were jewel encrusted and this drew her attention. She approached them and saw that the stones were set at the heads of steel pins that had been driven into the flesh, and into the nipple vents themselves. Her belly immediately melted and began to run with juice as she saw how well prepared the slaves were.

"Do you like them? They're from Frankland so I can do what I want with them." A woman's voice sounded from behind her and she turned. "I won some money for my lord and they were a gift from him."

The woman who stood behind her was dressed in a beautiful flowing dress of deep red. She was quite young, very pretty – and seemed vaguely familiar, although her voice and speech, thick and rather slow, were strange.

As the woman came closer she could see why. She smiled and let the tip of her tongue protrude, it bore four rings through it and as she playfully stuck it further out, studs were revealed, more than she had ever seen. Her breasts felt tight and swollen with lust as she considered what such a tongue could do for a clitoris or for a master's cock and how much pleasure the affixing of such things would have given whoever had ordered it. And then she took in the woman's eyes. They were dark and regarding her with such predatory malice that her choice was made on the spot. For whatever reason, this woman would let nothing stand in the way of extracting every bit of pleasure she could from her helpless body.

She stepped forwards and knelt down before her mistress.

The woman's hand stroked her hair as men said things around her which no longer concerned her.

"You must have a name," the woman said in her slow, thick speech as she bent down and whispered in her ear. "I shall call you……Tamara. Yes, that will do nicely. I shall enjoy myself so much with you, Tamara!"

She ran the name through her mind and found it sounded good somehow; fitting. She was a slave called Tamara and she belonged to this beautiful and cruel mistress.

POSTSCRIPT.

History records that on the following day, the cream of the renegades received a brand that the king himself had devised. It was a simple filigree design of iron in the shape of the rose of Alba. It was seared into the lower bellies of the women and a single crown was also seared high up on the insides of their right thighs. It is also recorded that a slave by the name of Tamara also had three rings set in each labium at the same time.

Sir Leopold Dunbar was granted the Delacourt estates and the friendship between him and Sir William Courcey persisted, Sir William frequently being asked to stay and make free use of the slave who had once been his wife.

Fuller descriptions of the licentious feasts that both men gave may be found in Holinsworth's *'Chronicle of Western Alba'*, a contemporary account which still makes intensely erotic reading to this day. It contains a detailed description of the many modifications and piercings Lady Jocelyn Dunbar lavished on her favourite slave.

Owen Daibron – as everyone knows – treated the remaining thousands of the renegades to double crown standard and in order to prevent the market being flooded and the stock devalued, he shipped them south and east to the Persian city of Tyre and journeyed far overland to meet the Emperor himself. There, using the slaves, he negotiated the treaties that saw Persian ships trading freely with Alba and which helped to build the Golden Age as Alba's influence inexorably spread south into Eropia as the Franks crumbled and the Deutsche Federation was forced back into the east.

His classic record of his travels, *'The Journeys'* has been both a rich source of historical information and a literary classic ever since.

'The King's Rose' as the design worn by the honoured slaves came to be called, was reserved to the crown and only exceptionally gifted slaves were permitted to wear it. Gradually, however, its use died out over the centuries and it was only brought back after the Act of Restoration was passed in 1746.